SWEET LEGACY

TERA LYNN CHILDS

templar

A TEMPLAR BOOK

First published in 2013 by Katherine Tegen Books,
an imprint of HarperCollins Children's Books, a division of
HarperCollins Publishers, New York, New York USA.

First published in the UK in 2013 by Templar Publishing,
an imprint of The Templar Company Limited,
Deepdene Lodge, Deepdene Avenue, Dorking, Surrey, RH5 4AT, UK
www.templarco.co.uk

Cover design by James Fraser
Cover photograph © 2013 by Aleksandar Nakic

First UK edition

Mixed Sources
Product group from well-managed
forests and other controlled sources
www.fsc.org Cert no. SA-COC-1565
© 1996 Forest Stewardship Council

ISBN 978-1-84877-942-6

Printed and bound by
CPI Group (UK) Ltd, Croydon, CR0 4YY

For the ladies of Blue Willow Bookshop,
especially Cathy, Becky and Valerie,
for more reasons than I could ever list

CHAPTER 1

Grace

The monsters are waiting.

As Gretchen, Greer and I tumble out of the swirling crazy of the portal we created to bring us here, we are immediately surrounded by mythological beasts. There must be two dozen, at least. All sizes, all shapes, all… textures. Many I recognise from Gretchen's lost monster ring binders: a furry Calydonian boar with tusks three feet long, a pair of massive birds whose feathers look like arrowheads and a double-headed serpent monster that I think is called an amphisbaena. Others I've never even imagined, like the giant white worm or the hyena-like one with no mouth that I can see. They are all standing in a semicircle around the open space where the portal dumped us into the bleak, black abyss that the monsters call home: Abyssos.

When Gretchen described this place, I thought she was exaggerating. I couldn't believe it was as horrible as the picture she painted.

I was wrong.

Between the slick-looking black stone and the nauseating

combination of smells, sounds and faint green light, I almost wish I could autoport back home and forget I ever saw any of this.

But I can't. We're here for a purpose, and I won't abandon my sisters or our duty.

Tugging on my backpack straps to anchor it tighter against my body, I force myself to control the fear as we face down the waiting monsters.

Waiting… like they knew we were coming.

For half a second I think – I hope – that these are friendly monsters, the ones Gretchen told us she met when she came in here after Nick. The ones who want to help us.

But one glance at her – stance braced wide, a dagger in each fist, fangs on display and a look of pure menace on her face – tells me to forget that idea. These monsters aren't here to assist. They're here to either capture us or kill us.

Neither option leads to a good ending for us or the world we're trying to protect. I knew this was going to be dangerous; I just didn't expect the danger to find us so quickly.

My already racing heart speeds up in my chest.

"Fangs down." Gretchen inches forward, putting herself between me and Greer and the monsters. "They're mortal here. They won't want to tangle with our venom."

I glance at Greer. Her fair skin and highlights shine

like a beacon against the gloom. It's her face, though, that stands out the most. Her expression is haunting, her cheeks are ghostly pale, silver eyes wide and staring straight ahead. She usually holds it together on the outside, even when she's falling apart on the inside. Seeing the signs of her panic on prominent display sends my heart rate up another notch.

I curl my lips and let my fangs drop, hoping the gesture will make me appear stronger and more dangerous.

The boys fly out of the portal right behind us. Nick bumps into Greer, knocking her off balance, but Thane manages to land sure-footed at my side. He reaches out to steady Greer before she hits the shiny black ground.

My brother's reflexes are lightning fast.

"What in Hades?" Nick asks, already swinging his backpack around to the front and unzipping the main compartment.

"They were waiting," I say, my voice weak.

Greer adds in a tense whisper, "They knew we were coming."

She says it like it's more than a guess. With her power of second sight, it probably is.

Gretchen flicks a glance over her shoulder, exchanging a look with Nick – a silent question, *Did you do this?* Does she still doubt his allegiance? Does she still think he's spying on us for the enemy – well, for *one* of our enemies? We have so many it's hard to keep track.

There are the ones who want us dead before we can open the door to the monster realm, the ones who want to wait until *after* and the ones who want us for the bounty on our heads – freedom from this awful place. We're lucky anyone is on our side. Nick is supposed to be.

Does Gretchen think *he* might be the reason the monsters are expecting us?

His mouth tightens and he gives her a quick shake of his head.

She stares at him – studying him, evaluating him. Gretchen doesn't trust easily, and I know she still has doubts about Nick. I don't blame her. When he first showed up in her life, she had no idea he was anything more than a normal boy. Then she learned he was sent by the goddess of justice to protect us. And just when she started to believe him, she found out he was also working as an agent for the monster side. He insists he was a mole, and she believes him. *We* believe him. But still, there's always room for doubt.

Finally, she nods in response before returning her attention to the monsters, who have started grunting and shuffling in anticipation of the fight. I guess that was answer enough for her.

"Circle up," Gretchen instructs.

Adrenaline pours into my bloodstream and my hands start to shake.

I try to calm my fear and draw on my courage.

I've trained for this. Between Gretchen and Greer's lessons, I feel like I've earned a monster-fighting black belt in a few short weeks. But this isn't a training exercise. I've never been this frightened in my life, not even when the two warring factions clashed in the gym at Greer's school and we were caught in the middle. Then I didn't have time to be scared.

"Get behind us," Nick says calmly as he steps around me, taking position at Gretchen's side.

Thane follows around to the other side, flanking Gretchen and setting me and Greer firmly behind their wall of defence. He's only here to watch over me, to look out for his little sister. He's not actually part of this war. He's not equipped for what we're about to face. He's just a boy.

"Thane, no." I tug at his shoulder. "We're not helpless."

When he glances back at me, I bare my teeth to display my fangs.

His eyes narrow slightly, as if he's deciding whether my venom-spewing fangs are up to the task, and then he nods. It's crazy how proud that makes me feel. For once, *I'm* the one who can protect *him*.

"Grace is right," Gretchen says. "We've got the deadly weapons. Girls in front, boys as backup. Everyone, arm yourselves."

As Greer and I step into position, Gretchen hands us each one of her daggers before reaching behind her back and pulling another pair from the waistband of her cargo trousers. She's like a walking armoury. I wonder what she has hidden away in her pockets.

Beside her, Nick holds what looks like a razor-sharp Frisbee in one hand, his fingers curled through a set of holes in the centre. The object is part bowling ball, part discus, with a deadly blade-like edge. And from the way Nick is manoeuvring it with simple wrist movements, it looks like he knows how to use it.

In a flash, Thane reaches behind his head and pulls out a sword I didn't even realise he had. It must have been hidden behind his backpack. He grips the hilt in both hands, slashing it in front of him and looking more like a medieval warrior than my big brother. The blade makes a *whoosh-whoosh* as it cuts through the air.

I'm suddenly very glad he came with us.

Gretchen catches my eye. "Get ready."

She nods, and that tiny bit of reassurance centres me. I shove my heart back down where it belongs and turn to the monsters, focusing my full attention on the enemy.

When I do, one of the monsters – a horrible-looking man with blue-black skin and glistening stains around his mouth – raises one arm and shouts.

"Epitithentai!"

As one, the monster horde roars and charges forward.

Everything happens in a blur. The monsters descend on us,

and before I can blink we're fighting for our lives – or our freedom. It's not like they're clarifying which side of the war they're on as they're trying to bite and claw at us.

A golden sheep runs at me, maybe sensing that I'm the weakest opponent here. I'm not so proud that I won't agree with that assessment – I'm much better with a keyboard and mouse than a dagger.

The sheep seems harmless. I grab a handful of fleece and hold it away from my body, hesitant to hurt the little thing.

With my opponent under control, I try to keep track of everyone else.

Gretchen is taking on two of the biggest monsters, ripping a dagger through the chest of one and giving the other a side kick straight to the… groin, I think. It's hard to tell under all that fur.

Greer does one of her crazy Tae Kwon Do jump-kicks at the head of a creature that looks like the opposite of a griffin – the head of a lion and the body of bird. She knocks it to the ground and pins one wing to the ground with a dagger. I'm in awe. She acts so elegant and proper, but she can kick monster butt.

Nick sends his metal disc flying through the air; it slices through the arm of one creature and the shoulder of another, lodging itself in the chest of a third.

Thane is amazing. Like music in motion, he swings his blade in a rhythmic movement of figure eights. Infinity.

He looks lethal, and completely comfortable, like he was born to wield this weapon. Clearly my brother is keeping more secrets than I ever imagined. The monsters around him keep their distance, as if they can sense his deadly skill with the sword. My brother, the warrior.

"Grace!" Gretchen shouts. "Those sheep are *poisonous*."

"Oh." I turn back to the creature before me to find it trying to reach around and bite my wrist. "Shoot."

Still reluctant to hurt the fuzzball – poisonous or not – I'm deciding what to do when Nick appears at my side. He grabs the fleece with both hands and flings the beast into the black.

"Thanks," I say.

He gives me a quick smile before turning back to the fight.

Then I'm under attack.

A beast tackles me from behind, knocking the dagger out of my grip as I hit the ground. *Stupid, Grace.* I should have stayed focused on my own fight, instead of worrying about watching everyone else. I feel hot breath on my neck, saliva dripping onto the back of my T-shirt– at least I think it's saliva. If it were poison it would probably be burning my skin already – I hope. I try to push up to my hands and knees, but the monster is too heavy. I spot my dagger glinting in the faint green glow about six feet away, out of reach.

Desperate, I scramble. My fingertips slip against the

black stone of the ground. The beast's weight is slowly squeezing the air out of my lungs. I'm trapped.

The monster makes noises against my ear.

He's not speaking any language I've ever heard, but I don't need an interpreter to know what it boils down to. He's hungry, and I'm tasty.

With a roar of my own, desperate to not be a monster meal or a disappointment to my sisters, I shove up against the weight bearing down on me. My effort dislodges the creature just enough to give me some wiggle room. I quickly flip over.

It jerks back, like it's stunned to meet me face to face.

That makes two of us.

Hovering just above me is a giant rooster head. Its body, the heavy part holding me down and keeping me in the cage of its legs, is that of a horse. An image from Gretchen's monster ring binders flashes through my memory – a hippalectryon.

The thing outweighs and outpowers me by at least a factor of ten. I'm assuming its tiny bird brain isn't terribly clever, though, so outwitting the beast is my only chance. I just need to keep my wits about me long enough to make that happen.

While it blinks black, beady eyes at me, I stretch my lips in a wide grin, faking way more confidence than I feel and making sure to flash my fangs as I say, "Hey there."

At first it doesn't move, so I twist to the side, stretching my neck to reach my fangs towards its nearest leg.

That jars the creature into motion, and the whole thing rises up on its hind legs, kicking its front ones up like a wild stallion. Before it can stomp back down – and crush me with its massive hooves – I roll to the side, out of the way.

The beast lands with a heavy thud, letting out an ear-splitting crow.

For a second, it looks around, realising it's lost me. I do a quick scan for my lost dagger, but I don't see it anywhere. I don't have time to look. I'll have to use my built-in weapons instead.

I scramble to my feet, ready to get my bite in before it finds me again.

"Grace, no!"

Gretchen rushes past me and dives onto the hippalectryon's back. Before I can react, she sinks her fangs into the feathered neck.

Instead of disappearing out from under her, the thing simply sinks to the ground. It collapses into an unmoving heap, eyes open and unblinking.

Wow. It's dead. *Really* dead.

I meet Gretchen's gaze over the beast's back.

"You don't need to be a killer," she says. Her eyes shadow – with pain or maybe memory. "Try to wound them or knock them out."

She jerks her head towards the sea of monster bodies

left in her wake. When I look closer, I can see most of them are still breathing. I know it really affected Gretchen when she realised she had killed her first monster. I'm sure she doesn't want me or Greer to experience that.

I smile sadly. "You can't protect us forever."

She studies me for a moment before turning away. "I know."

Then, she's off, back into the fight, as another creature steps in front of me.

This one looks mostly human – a sickly pale woman with a mouthful of gnashing teeth. A pair of broad, dark wings rise up behind her, almost fading into the green-black of the world around us. But what catch my attention are the long claws extending from each finger, like a set of kitchen knives.

My gaze freezes on her hands. The rest of the battle fades away into the periphery until the only thing left is the dull grunt and clank of other fights and the glinting of green light on blade-like claws.

My dagger is lost to the dark. I have nothing but my fangs and my novice fighting skills to protect me – and what little courage hasn't fled at the menacing look in her eerie orange eyes.

The winged woman moves towards me, and I have to fight the instinct to back away. Self-preservation is hard to overcome, and I'm on the verge of running. Fleeing.

I feel a hand at my back.

From the corner of my eye I see Greer standing at my side.

"I've got you," she says.

I nod. "Thanks."

Together, we step forward. Some of my courage returns. With my sister at my side, I know I'm safe. And I'll do whatever I have to do to keep her safe too.

CHAPTER 2

Greer

My heart stutters. This is the creature from my vision. Every detail is the same, like a memory come to life. Earlier today, sitting at Grace's dining table, I saw this monster nearly slice my sister into shreds. My head throbs and my hands shake as Grace and I go after the hideous woman with blades for claws.

Seeing a vision and believing it's true are two completely different things.

I didn't *want* to believe it was true.

"You go right," Grace mutters. "I'll go left. Maybe we'll confuse her."

Sucking in a sharp breath, I start right.

The picture of my vision fills my mind: Grace, with this creature's claws at her throat. I feel the same terror now as I did when I first saw this moment. Memory and reality blur until I can't tell which is which. I only hope the rest of the vision comes true as well.

I glance around and realise Thane is nowhere in sight. The other fights have spread out beyond my range of visibility in the faint light of the abyss.

In the vision, Thane saved her life.

Panic sets in. How can he save her if he's not near enough?

My stomach heaves.

"Greer!" Grace shouts, tugging me out of memory and into reality.

And the reality is that I'm the only one who can help her now.

The clawed woman has turned to face Grace, leaving her back vulnerable to me. I watch, stunned, as the creature reaches out and wraps one hand around my sister's throat. I stop thinking – stop remembering – and lunge forward. I grab a wing with each hand, ripping apart with all my might. My fear makes me strong – not as supernaturally strong as Gretchen, but strong enough. Beneath my palms, I feel the crack of bones snapping.

The beast turns on me with a howl. Without releasing Grace, it swings one arm wide, knocking across my temple and sending me stumbling back.

The world around me blurs and I squeeze my eyes open and shut in an attempt to clear the picture. I can't save Grace if I can't see.

Desperation drives me. I push to my feet, fighting dizziness and nausea as twin sets of Grace and the clawed woman – bladed hand still around my sister's neck – move in and out of focus. When the two images finally converge, I gasp as I see the claws of the other hand moving towards Grace's throat.

I try to shout for help, but the nausea overpowers me and I bend over, clutching my stomach.

I look up, my vision spinning, expecting – fearing – that I'll see Grace eviscerated by the woman's claws. Instead, I see Thane running. Sword held high, he swings it in a sideways arc, connecting the flat edge with the woman's head.

Her hand goes slack and Grace falls from her grip as the clawed woman crumples to the ground in an unconscious heap.

I want to cry with relief. Every lesson Mother ever taught me about maintaining my composure in the face of crisis evaporates, and I'm overcome by emotion. I let it overtake me.

"Are you okay?" Thane demands of his sister.

Tears tickle at the corners of my eyes and I blink them away, trying to regain control. Grace is alive. Everything is going to be all right.

"Yes, I'm—" She shakes her head. "Greer," she says. "Help Greer."

Help me? I don't need help. I try to tell them I'm fine now that my vision has come true, but it sounds muffled and weak.

My tongue feels like a sponge, growing and expanding in my mouth until I feel like it's going to choke me from within. I frown, trying to comprehend this strange sensation.

Thane is at my side instantly, pulling his backpack off and digging around inside. He's frowning. He's worried about me. No one ever worries about me. *Greer can take of herself, Mother always says. If she cannot, she will not learn how by being coddled.*

I can't take my eyes off Thane's face, the serious and concerned look wrinkling his forehead. It's a good forehead. Strong, solid. Loyal.

What an odd thought.

The boy is loyal, a faint, foreign voice echoes in my mind.

"She's been scratched," Thane says to Grace.

She asks, "Is that bad?"

He doesn't answer.

I don't even care.

He saved her. He saved Grace and my vision came true. I have to let him know, have to tell him about the vision. He should know that he's supposed to be here, that I knew what would happen. I have to at least smile. My mouth refuses to cooperate.

"Damn it," he curses as he pulls a bottle out of small zippered bag. "Forgot cotton balls."

"Here," Grace says, followed by the sound of fabric ripping. "Use this."

Thane takes the piece of shirt Grace offers him. He twists the cap off the bottle, pours some of its contents onto the cloth and then reaches for my face.

Stormy grey eyes meet mine, and I'm transfixed.

"You're going to be fine," he says. "But this is going to sting."

The instant he dabs the cloth on my cheek I see stars. Bright, bold streaks of light flash across my vision even though my eyes are open, like fireworks inside my head. Like when I held the pendant of Apollo in my palm to seek out how to get Gretchen back from this awful place.

The pain is so sharp I feel my consciousness fading.

"What happened?" I hear Gretchen ask.

Thane replies, "Keres venom."

"Hell," Nick utters.

"She'll be fine," Thane says, like he won't allow anything less.

Grace insists, "Of course she will."

I can hear the fear in her voice, but I refuse to be frightened. I refuse to drag my attention away from Thane's eyes, sure and steady and focused on me. He keeps dabbing the wet cloth on my face – on my forehead, my chin, my lips – but his gaze doesn't shift. Something in his eyes pulls at me. I need him. I know nothing about him except that he's Grace's adopted brother, but I feel myself getting drawn in, deeper and deeper, into the dark grey of his eyes.

As the liquid sears my face, his eyes anchor me, keeping me strong.

Soon, though, even that is not enough.

Finally the pain gets to be too much, and I succumb to the lure of the unconscious. As I close my eyes, I whisper, "You saved her."

He whispers back, "You knew I would."

I open my eyes, but nothing changes. I saw black, and I still see black. Blinking several times does nothing to change my vision. Natasha must have drawn the blackout shades. I have asked her countless times not to do that without alerting me. Waking up to sunlight is far preferable to encountering utter darkness.

Perhaps I will have Mother speak with her this time.

No, I will handle it myself. No need to bother Mother.

I draw in a deep breath – and practically choke on the stench. Why does my room smell like decaying garbage?

When I try to move, pain pulses through my body.

Oh, yes. Now I remember. Not my room. Not my house or even my realm. Memories wash through my brain like a vision, but these things have already happened. The monsters. The battles. The creature that almost killed Grace and knocked me off my feet.

"Ugh," I groan. That explains the throbbing pain.

"Greer?" a male voice asks in the dark.

I smile.

"Thane?" I realise I'm lying down and attempt to sit up. "Where are you?"

"Shhhh," Grace says.

An instant later the world around me lights up with a warm yellow glow. Grace, flashlight in hand, appears in front of me. Strands of hair hang loose from her ponytail, but she is smiling and unhurt.

We're in a tiny space, barely tall enough for her to sit up without brushing her head on the ceiling.

"What's going—"

She pushes a hand over my mouth before I can finish the question. "We're in a cave," she whispers, "waiting for Gretchen and Nick to get back."

Thane appears in the glow next to her, bent over in the cramped quarters. He fills the space with his body and the energy of his presence – strong and certain, not afraid like before I blacked out. He looks relieved.

"Stay still," he warns. "The poison is still in your system."

"Poison?" At Grace's warning look I lower my volume. "What poison?"

He leans closer. "The antidote to the Keres venom," he whispers right next to my ear. "It's a poison, one your system can process, but it takes time."

Grace moves to my side. "Thane saved you. He knew exactly what to do."

I don't miss the look she gives her brother, but his eyes don't leave my face. She's asking a question he isn't ready to answer yet. I have the same question – and then some.

He reaches out and gently touches my face. I wince at the slight sting.

"The wounds are healing," he says. "Shouldn't be much longer."

He drops his hand, but he doesn't pull it away; I feel the heat of it right next to mine, like he wants me to know he's right there if I need him.

"How did I get here?" I ask. "What happened to all those monsters?"

There were so many of them. I know we were holding our own, but Grace and Thane had to stop to take care of me.

Grace shrugs. "They're gone. A few of them are dead. Some ran away. Gretchen and Nick are dragging the unconscious ones into another cave and tying them up so they can't bring back reinforcements."

She says it casually – a few of them are dead – but I can tell the deaths bother her. She's too kindhearted for them not to. They don't bother me. After seeing one of those horrible creatures nearly slice Grace's throat open, I'd be happy to see every last one of them drawn and quartered.

"After they finish, Gretchen and Nick are going to scout around," she continues, "to make sure there aren't any more lying in wait" She nods at her brother. "We brought you here so you could recover somewhere safe."

"The antidote is almost as bad as the venom," Thane says. His thumb brushes against my palm, and a shiver races up my arm. "But it was the only way."

I hear his unspoken meaning: it might hurt like hell, but it's worth the pain. Better the unpleasant side effects of the poison than the alternative – death. He didn't just save Grace's life, I know. He saved mine.

And he barely knows me.

I have to thank him. I have to *tell* him – about the vision and our strange connection and my gratitude. But not in front of my sister – *his* sister. My head aches. I hope that's not as complicated as it seems. He's not *my* brother.

I glance at Grace and find her watching me. She flicks her gaze at Thane and then back at me, raising her brows in silent question. I don't know how to answer. I don't understand what's going on between me and her brother any more than she does.

She flashes me a quick smile and then twists her head towards the cave entrance.

"Hey, did you guys hear something?"

Thane shakes his head, and I say, "No."

"I'm sure I did," she says, turning back to me with a wink. "I'd better go check. I'll be right back."

She hands the flashlight to Thane and then turns to crawl to the front of the cave. She's giving us some privacy.

The moment she's out of the light, I say, "Thank y—"

His mouth brushes over mine before I can finish, strong but soft. It's gone just as quickly, but he stays close, his face hovering inches above mine.

"Don't thank me."

I shake my head. It makes no sense – he saved our lives and we *should* be thanking him – but if he doesn't want my gratitude, then I won't force it on him. He's earned that consideration.

I won't keep the rest of it inside, though. I won't keep my vision – and his fulfillment of it – a secret. I have to share it with him, so he understands. So he knows why I needed him to come with us, why he's supposed to be here.

Why I know he's supposed to be part of this story.

"I saw it." My voice is barely a whisper. I don't want Grace to overhear, but I need to say it out loud to Thane.

Even if he already knows.

I can't stop the tears stinging my eyes. "I saw you save her. Back in the apartment, when you said you wanted to come with us. I saw precisely what just happened. I knew you were going to save Grace." I blink away the moisture. "I didn't know you were going to save me."

"I know."

That is the craziest part. He *does* know.

"But *how*?" I ask.

I have no idea how or why I see what I see. The entire process is a mystery that feels more like chance than skill. I know I inherited Medusa's power of second sight, while Gretchen got Sthenno's super strength and Grace got Euryale's autoporting ability. I know that I have visions of things and that those visions are coming true. I have

26

no control over it, not yet. And I have no idea how Thane fits into the picture.

"How?" I repeat.

"Greer, I—" His grey eyes shadow over. "It's complicated."

"I have an IQ of 154. Try me."

He takes a deep breath and looks me in the eye. "I… don't know how to."

"There was nothing there." Grace's cheerful whisper cuts through the darkness, but not the tension. "Guess I was hearing things."

If she was trying to leave us alone to talk, she didn't give it enough time.

Thane pulls away to a less intimate distance. The space between us feels like miles.

Grace crawls back to my side.

"Here," she says, pressing a water bottle into my hand. "You should probably stay hydrated."

I cast one more look at Thane, who is staring towards the cave entrance, lost in thought. We will finish this conversation later.

"Thanks," I tell Grace. I twist the cap off and take a drink.

The water is cool and crisp and I feel it hit my stomach, spreading out in an icy wave. If my stomach is this empty, hours must have passed since I forced down a protein bar before we opened the portal. This is time wasted.

We didn't venture into the abyss to sit around in a cave recuperating.

"We need to get moving." I shift, testing the pain. It's a little better. My body isn't one hundred percent, but my mind knows we should be doing something.

"*You* need to rest for a little longer," Grace replies.

"I'm fine," I insist.

"*Besides*," she says, giving me a scolding look, "Gretchen and Nick are coming back here when they're done scouting. We have to stay put."

I am not a particularly patient person. Sitting around waiting goes against my nature. But a small part of me is relieved – I am nowhere near full strength yet. Besides, we can't do this alone. We need to remain where Gretchen and Nick left us until they return. Which means that, for now, we wait.

My questions for Thane wait, too. In the dim glow of the flashlight, I watch him while he pretends not to watch me.

CHAPTER 3
Gretchen

Even with my eyes fully adjusted to the practically nonexistent light of the abyss, I can barely make out our surroundings. Black, black and more black, with a greenish tint, just in case it wasn't revolting enough. Good to see nothing's changed since last time.

The beastie ambush was a surprise. I'd like to know how they knew we were coming and where we'd come out – especially since we didn't even know we were coming until a few hours ago.

Luckily, my sisters held their own, and the boys turned out to be more useful than I expected. Not that I'd admit it to them, but I'm glad they came.

"Looks like the coast is clear," I say when I'm pretty sure none of the monsters have stuck around for a second try. The last thing we need is a repeat performance now that Greer is injured and we're down by one while she recovers.

If Thane hadn't acted quickly with the antidote, we'd be down by one permanently.

I turn to head back to where we left him and my sisters

– I don't like the idea of them being out of my sight in this place – and run smack into Nick.

His hands wrap around my arms and he holds me in place.

"Gretchen…" His dark blue eyes narrow in pain. "I had nothing to do with that attack. I was just as surprised as you were."

I watch him for a moment, checking for some reaction in his face and for some flicker of doubt in my gut. His face remains completely steady, and my gut is more worried about getting back to my sisters than the boy in front of me.

Question answered.

Finally, I nod. "Yeah, I know."

He flashes me a cocky grin, like he knew I'd believe him. I see the relief below the surface, though. He's worried that I'm still not convinced he's on our side. To be honest, I'm worried too, a little – worried that maybe I'm putting my feelings first. In any case, I've decided to trust him, and my gut agrees. Decision made.

Without another word, we turn and start back for the cave where we left the rest of our group. We haven't gone five steps when I hear something. I raise a hand, wordlessly telling Nick to stop. He freezes behind me, and I tune my ears to listen. Vast silence, punctuated by moans and groans from the depths of the abyss, nothing more. Maybe I only imagined—

Then I hear it: a soft shuffle. Quiet footsteps on the cave floor; more than one set — at least five that I can count. The swish of something dragging across the ground.

Whatever it is, it's coming towards us from the other side of the rock formation just ahead.

I place my hand around Nick's wrist and — without waiting for him to respond — pull him after me. Seeking a better strategic position, I move up, over onto the nearest boulder. He follows right behind, and I release my grip so I can move stealthily.

Belly-crawling across the smooth surface, I inch towards the edge of the rock, towards the sound that could be a million things. A million dark and nasties.

Whatever it is, I have to draw it away from my sisters.

As I lean forward out over the edge to get a better view, I hold my breath. Surprise is a crucial advantage. Whatever is coming doesn't know we're here yet, and I don't want to give away our position until I'm ready.

I peer down, but I can't see anything in the inky space below. The shufflings stop — all but one. Then I hear a loud *"Oof!"* followed by a vehement *"Shh!"*

"Sorry," a small voice says. "Not know we stopping."

"Shhhh!" Louder, and more irritated.

"If you no want Sillus—"

A loud smack, followed by an angry "Shut. *Up*."

Then a muffled "Sorry" that sounds more like "Rawry."

I smile. Leaning out as far over the edge as possible,

31

I can barely make out several shapes below in the faint glow. One gleams in the green light, golden, metallic.

The golden maiden.

I hadn't realised how tense I was at the prospect of another battle this soon after the first until now, when the relief washes over me. The creatures below are no threat. For now, the fighting can wait.

I turn to grin at Nick, throwing a playful punch at his shoulder. Pushing to my feet, I scramble back down the way we came, leaving him to catch up.

Back on ground level, I have to smother a laugh when I see one of the onyx guards struggling to hold a palm over Sillus's little furry mouth – or, I should say, his *big* furry mouth. The group of seven creatures is trying so hard to be quiet – and they're failing miserably. As I step out in front of them, I say, "You guys suck at stealth."

"Aaaack!"

"Shhhhh! For the love of Zeus, Sillus," the golden maiden blurts. "Do you want the entire Nychtian Army to hear you?"

The little monkey monster peers out from under one of the pegasus's silver-grey wings. "Sorry. Sillus say sorry. How many times?"

The golden maiden rolls her shiny metal eyes at him. Huffing out a tight breath, she turns to face me as Nick steps to my side. "Gretchen, we—" She blinks. "Wait – *are* you Gretchen?"

"The one and only."

She smiles. "And this must be your friend." She looks at Nick, cool and appraising. "The one you came here to rescue last time."

"Hi," he says, stepping forward and offering her his hand. "I'm Nick."

She takes his hand between hers and gives him a squeeze. Then, turning to me, she says, "But you are not alone. We had heard—"

"Three huntress come through," Sillus interrupts. "All three, in Abyssos!"

This time everyone in the party – including me and Nick – shushes him. His eyes widen. We all glare at him. Then he seems to finally get the message and draws his fingers across his mouth like a zip.

"We were hoping to find you," the golden maiden says. "We heard you and your sisters had come through a portal. There is news you need to know."

That sounds ominous.

"Fine," I say. "But it's not safe out here. You're not the only ones who know we're here. Let's get my sisters to your cave; then we can talk."

"I'm afraid that is impossible." She shakes her golden head. "The cave is no longer safe."

"Army find," Sillus says, his voice quiet for once. "Break everything."

One look at the golden maiden and I don't have to

ask why. The sad look in her eyes says it all. The monster bosses down here must have found out she and her friends helped me rescue Nick. They got punished. Anger rolls through me. If I ever see that dog-headed freak they call the boss again, he'll wish I'd never been born.

I don't like it when people get hurt for helping me.

"I'm sorry," I say. "I should never have—"

"You are not at fault," she insists. "You did not wield the axe."

The cave had been an oasis of light in the dark abyss, a home for creatures who never hurt anyone, for the beasts who taught me that not all monsters are bad and that the abyss is worth saving. The image of the Nychtian Army taking an axe to the makeshift shelters and furniture makes my blood boil. I'll make them pay, for that and so many other things.

"We have another place," the golden maiden says. "It is not so… commodious. But it will serve."

"Sounds fine." I give her a grateful smile. "Let's get my sisters safely there. Then you can tell us your news."

"Yes," the golden maiden says, "and you can tell us of yours."

I study her. She always seems to know everything – or at least more than me. Maybe she already knows about our plans to travel to Olympus to rescue the gorgons. Maybe she knows, but maybe she wants me to tell her just the same.

She's a cryptic one.

"So, Sillus," I say as we start walking, draping an arm over the little guy's shoulder, "how did you get back here? Last I knew you were running wild in San Francisco."

He shakes his furry head. "Is long story, huntress. *Long* story."

I laugh but then quickly bite my lips as the golden maiden turns to scowl at my outburst.

"I'm sure it is," I whisper to the little monkey. "You'll have to tell me when we have time to talk freely."

My smile fades. As we head back to the cave where Grace, Greer and Thane are hiding, I wonder what this news is. I hope it's either good or useful, because we could use some of that.

The golden maiden hadn't exaggerated about their new location. Smaller, colder and with only a small magical fire in the corner to chase away the shadows, the new cave smells like mildew and dirty gym socks. There must have been a phoenix living here before they moved in.

But my sisters are here and it's safe, and right now that's my top priority.

Greer looks much better than when I left her – she'd been pale and passed out in Thane's arms – and Grace seems very relieved that our sister is recovering. I'm sure we're both wondering just how Thane knew to use hellebore to cure the scratch of a Keres demon.

Right now he's standing sentry over Greer, and I want her rest undisturbed, so I'll save my questions for later.

I cross the cave to a bench – really just a long, flat rock – where the golden maiden sits, staring into the fire. They're pretty much without amenities here, and what passes for furniture is whatever pieces of stone suit the job. And it's all my fault.

There's no time for guilt. Greer is almost well enough to move on, and we have a big mission ahead of us. And first, we need to hear what news our Abyssian friends have to share.

I sit down next to the golden maiden on the bench. "Is it anything I want to hear?"

She inclines her head as she lays a golden hand on my thigh.

That's what I was afraid of.

"One of our spies" – she glances pointedly at Sillus – "overheard the boss talking about a mission to Panogia."

I should have known it was something about the pet-store mash-up who runs things down here. First he kidnaps my guy, and then he busts up my friends' stuff, not to mention the big battle back home that finally convinced Greer that some things are more important than a snooty tea.

"We already know about that. We faced his army earlier today," I reply, remembering the crazy scene in Greer's school gym. It feels like days, not hours, since we got caught between the Nychtian Army from the abyss and the Arms of Olympus. "We took care of them."

Between the three of us opening a giant sucking portal and Grace autoporting us the hell out of Dodge, we'd come away from the skirmish unhurt. And all the beasties had been sent straight home.

"Not the army," she explains. "He has sent assassins."

"No. After us? Why didn't he just kill me when he had the chance? When I was in his office."

Zeus's bounty and the reward of freedom from the monster realm must have become too great a temptation for boss man. My muscles tense. I should have taken care of that flipper-fisted moron the last time I was here. I might not have made it out of the abyss alive, but he'd be off our backs.

"You are correct." The golden maiden shakes her head with a quiet squeak. "He did not send assassins after you."

"Boss no kill huntress," Sillus adds. "Need huntress. Three."

Oh, yeah; can't forget that.

Sillus is right. Killing us doesn't make sense for the beastie side of the war. The boss is on the side that wants us to open the door so monsterkind can run free in the streets of the human world. Killing us first would definitely prevent that from happening. They want to wait to kill us after.

My eyes narrow. "Who?"

She hesitates just briefly. "We cannot be certain," she says, "but he seeks the woman who produced the Key Generation."

"What does that mean?"

"We believe," she says, her voice soft, "he means to kill your mother."

Grace gasps.

I turn my head and find her standing right behind me. I hadn't even realised she was listening.

"How did they find her?" she asks.

"That I do not know," the golden maiden replies. "I know only that they have sent several teams to your realm. They believe she holds the key to finding you, to controlling your powers."

"Why send assassins?" I ask.

"The boss believes that if she is dead" – the golden maiden swallows hard – "your powers will die with her."

"No," Grace whispers.

I grab her hand.

"Is that even possible?" I ask.

The golden maiden shrugs. "We do not know. The lore concerning your line, your legacy, has been hidden for so long. I suppose it is conceivable, but we do not have enough information."

"It doesn't matter if it will or not," Grace says, her voice tight with emotion. "If the boss believes it, then our mother is in danger. We can't let them kill her. Not now that we know for certain she's still alive. Not now that we can find her."

I can see the pain in her silver eyes, and it hurts me to see her hurt.

"We won't," I promise, even though I don't know how.

We have to go after the gorgons – they're being held prisoner, in constant immediate danger – but we have to protect our mother, not just because they might be able to use her to kill our powers, and not just because she's our mother and a link in the chain leading all the way back to Medusa, but also because I know what this means to Grace. She is so proud to have found the clues to our mother's location – that her name is Cassandra Gregory and what her phone number was four years ago – and I know Grace desperately wants to meet her.

And I find myself desperately wanting to make my sisters happy, no matter what.

"We have to protect her," Grace insists. "*I* have to. I have to go back."

I'm surprised by the certainty I see in her determined gaze. The Grace I first met a few weeks ago would be frightened and full of doubts. She was too afraid to stand up to a mean girl at school or ask out the cute boy she liked. The Grace in front of me sits strong and sure of what she has to do. I'm impressed. As the multi-hued glow of the fire flickers in her eyes, I smile at the transformation.

No doubt our mother will be proud.

We will just have to rescue the gorgons and save our mother at the same time.

"Right," I say, the plan forming in my mind as I speak. "We can handle things here. You go home and find our mother."

Grace lights up with a hopeful smile.

Nick steps forward. "I'll go with her."

I swing my gaze his way.

His midnight blue eyes confront me, like this is a test. He's offering to help, but will I let him? Do I trust him? Am I willing to put my sister's safety in his hands?

I've already made my decision.

Without hesitation, I say, "Good idea."

He gives me a tight nod.

That's a lot of trust I just gave him. He knows how big that is, especially when my sisters are involved. They are more important to me than anything.

"No, I'll go," Thane says. He scowls at Nick. "Gretchen might need you here."

Clearly he's not ready to trust Nick quite that much.

"I should be the one to go." Greer pushes unsteadily to her feet. "The boys will be far more useful down here than I am. Besides, you might need my… special skills to find her."

"Sillus stay," the little monkey freak says, moving closer to my side. "Help here."

"Nick and I will be fine," Grace insists, ignoring

Thane's scowl. "Gretchen will need your muscle," she tells her brother. "And give me ten minutes online and I'll be able to find our mother."

Good, because Thane is keeping secrets. I don't really want to interrogate him in front of Grace – she loves him and might not like what he has to say – so his staying behind is a double win. It will separate them for a while, and it will keep him in my sights.

I meet Grace's gaze. "You're sure? I'm not alone down here, you know." I nod at the friends filling the cave around us. They might not be able to take on the entire Nychtian Army, but they're more than adequate backup.

"I know," Grace says, laying a hand on my shoulder. "I think you need at least one of us down here with you. And I'll feel better knowing Thane is at your side."

"Fine," I say. "If you're sure."

"More than ever." She smiles, and I can't help but smile in return.

My little sister, all grown up – although maybe she just *feels* like my littler sister.

"Hey, which one of us is oldest, anyway?" I ask.

She frowns, probably wondering why I'm asking now of all times. "Greer," she says, "and then me."

I nearly choke. "I'm the baby?"

"I knew I had to be oldest," Greer says. "I'm the most responsible."

I roll my eyes.

"Then make yourself useful by being *responsible* for divvying up the supplies," I say, pushing to my feet and getting to work. "We won't need to keep rations for five. And you two will need some of the weapons back in our world. As soon as Greer is strong enough to continue, we'll move."

"I'm strong enough now," she insists, and proves the truth of her words by hefting two heavy backpacks off the ground and carrying them to a nearby table.

Our super healing powers must be taking care of the poison quickly.

My gut clenches at the thought of my sisters and me splitting up. Both missions are important, though, and I know how Grace feels about finding our mother, so of course she wants to go after her. It's the best option. Doesn't mean I like it.

I quickly join Greer at the table of backpacks and start digging through to separate out the things we won't need any more. If our initial encounter down here taught me anything, it's that we need to move light and fast if we're going to get though the abyss, get into Olympus, and get the gorgons without launching into all-out war. We don't have the numbers for that right now. We'll save the war for later.

As I start pulling things out, Nick steps up next to me at the table and helps.

"I'll protect her," he says quietly, "with everything I am."

I don't pause in my work. "I know."

"You're so sure of me now?" he asks with a smile. "What changed?"

I shrug. "Nothing. Everything." I flick him a glance. "It just changed."

He nods and reaches for the six-pack of water bottles in my hand.

"Promise me one thing," he says.

I keep my eyes on the backpack. "What's that?"

"That you'll protect yourself" – he rests his hand over mine – "until I'm back at your side to do it myself."

I snort – partly because the request is ridiculous, but also because the undertone of feeling in his request is too much. I don't deal well with emotion. I don't like the idea of separating from him, either. "In case you hadn't noticed," I reply, "I'm pretty good at taking care of myself."

"I noticed," he says, without moving his hand. "Promise?"

Something in his tone makes me look up. His midnight blue eyes are steady and intense. I want to make light, but I think we're long past making jokes about serious situations. In the end, I nod. "Promise."

CHAPTER 4
Grace

The creatures around me are beautiful – not like supermodel beautiful or even bouquet-of-flowers beautiful. I try not to gawk at them slack-jawed like a total idiot. I mean, in the past few weeks I've seen a lot of weird things I'd never seen before. But these creatures, Gretchen's friends, are in a class by themselves.

They are unique.

Some of them are beasts I've studied in mythology, like the pegasus with its breathtaking wings and the centaur guy with the body of a horse. Others are completely new and surprising. The golden maiden and the twin guards – shiny black stone, like they were carved from the world around us – are especially intriguing.

I don't want to stare, but I can't help it.

I force my attention back to Greer.

"Do you need anything before we go?" I ask. "More water? Some food? An emergency blanket?"

She seems so much better now after a few hours of rest, but I can't get the image of what she looked like immediately after the attack – eyes glazed over and skin inflamed and an angry shade of red – out of my mind. She would have died if Thane hadn't given her the antidote. That moment terrified me. I was frozen and I didn't know what to do. Thank goodness Thane was there, that Greer encouraged me to let him come.

We came too close to losing her.

My hands shake a little as I fumble with the zip on the backpack.

"I'm perfectly all right, Grace," she insists. "Truly."

I watch her, study her, checking for – I don't know, signs of pain or a bad reaction to the poison or something. She pats me on the arm before grabbing one of the reorganised backpacks and carrying it over to where Gretchen has piled the ones staying here. Except for the dishevelled hair and slightly pale skin, she looks fine, though. I hope that means she really *is* fine.

"She's stronger than she looks," Thane says.

He's watching her intently, just like I was doing a second ago.

He's right. She may not have Gretchen's physical strength, but inside she's tough. Bugging her and making her reassure me over and over isn't very helpful or healing.

"I know," I reply, turning to lean back against the table.

Thane doesn't move. He just stands there, staring blankly across the cave. He's not quite looking at her any more, like he's trying to act casual.

After more than half a lifetime together, I can read him too well. I can see beneath the surface. Greer drops a bottle of water, and his eyes are immediately on her as she bends to pick it up. Though he's trying to hide it, his attention is fully focused on Greer. Something more is going on here than he wants me to know, and considering everything that's happening, it's past time he told me. Secrets lead to problems.

I clear my throat. "Can we talk for a sec?"

He looks at me, questioning. I lift my brows in return – I'm serious about this – and he shrugs. I nod my head towards the cave entrance, away from the ears of everyone gathered inside. He throws one last glance at Greer, as if he has to reassure himself one more time, and then follows me towards the cave entrance.

Total privacy isn't really an option in this tiny space, but we're as far from the others as we can get while still being safely inside.

I stop in front of the narrow tunnel that leads back out into the main cavern of the abyss, turn to face him and cross my arms over my chest. Thane stands perfectly still, unblinking and tense. I don't need Greer's power to know he knows exactly what I'm going to ask.

"Tell me," I say.

He hesitates and then shakes his head.

"What's going on?" I demand. "You clearly know more about all of this" – I wave my hands at the general circumstances of my life – "than you should. That sword. The hellebore. Tell me."

"No."

No? I jerk back, shocked. "Why not?"

He shakes his head again, his stormy eyes darkening to almost black.

"You know everything I know," I insist. "I have no secrets."

He cocks one brow at me.

A flash of heat burns my cheeks.

Okay, I have *almost* no secrets. I haven't been completely open and forthright about how I'm sorta, kinda, maybe dating his friend Milo. Maybe when I know for sure if we're together, I'll talk to Thane about it. For now I'm too afraid to mess things up. Besides, that's hardly relevant to our situation here.

I correct my statement. "I have no secrets *about this.*"

He softens, just barely – there's a slight drop in the rigid stance of his shoulders – but I can tell he's battling this on the inside.

"Grace-face, I—" He cuts himself off, frowning like he's thought better of answering. "I can't."

What a cop-out.

"You can," I throw back, "but you *won't.*"

He shrugs as if there's no difference.

I study him intently, trying to think of some reason that he wouldn't want to tell me the truth. He's not the kind to be embarrassed, so I'm sure that's not it. He also wouldn't keep something from me unless he felt he had to. The only other thing he's ever been this secretive about is his past – the time before Mom and Dad adopted him into our family.

He'd only been seven. What could that have to do with this?

"If this is about your past," I say, "it doesn't matter. I don't care about anything that happened before we even met. I love you. Besides," I continue, "I know you. I know it can't be anything bad."

He stares at me, unblinking.

I whisper, "It can't be *that* bad."

His cheeks flush with colour, and I'm stunned by his reaction. He's scared, of what he's done and of me finding out. I don't know what to say. Thane doesn't have a bad bone in his body. Sure, he and Dad fight about his plans for the future, and he barely gets by in school, but he's kind and loyal and good. He loves his family above anything. The idea that he ever did something so bad that he's afraid to tell me… I don't believe it.

As I shake my head, he drops his gaze away. "Leave it, Grace," he says. "Please."

That shocks me even more than his refusal to answer. Thane doesn't beg – ever – which only makes whatever he's hiding scarier. He's my brother in every way that matters. I won't push him to tell the secret that causes him so much pain as long as it's not dangerous.

I stiffen my spine. "Will it endanger my sisters or our mission?"

He flinches, as if the very idea hurts him. "No. Never."

Thane and I exchange a look, and I know he understands.

"Will it endanger *you*?"

He shrugs again and drops his gaze.

"Oh, Thane." I step forward and pull him into a hug, relieved when he hugs me back tighter than ever. I'm scared for him, but I'm also amazed at his strength, at his willingness to shoulder all of this on his own. He's incredible.

"Excuse me," a male voice says behind me. "Can't a monoceratus get through here?"

"Oh, sorry," I say, moving out of the way of the entrance.

Turning to see exactly what a monoceratus is, I'm smiling as I look up into the glowing face of a unicorn.

"Holy goalie," I mutter.

"Yeah, yeah," the single-horned horse says, walking past me into the cave. "Gretchen and I already went through this once. I'm a unicorn. Woo-hoo."

I turn to see if Thane is as awed as I am, but he has already disappeared back to Greer's side. The unicorn walks past me, heading for the golden maiden. Something tickles at the back of my memory. Why do I feel like I've thought about unicorns recently? I can't imagine why.

It's not as if they're a part of everyday conversation like when I was eight. Maybe there was one in the monster ring binders I scanned before Gretchen's loft blew up. That must be it.

I return to the group at the heart of the tiny cave. Greer has almost recovered. Nick and I need to leave soon. We can't afford to waste any time. We have to go save my biological mother from monster-realm assassins. I only hope we can get to her before it's too late.

"The line is heavily guarded," the unicorn tells the group. "Not a chance of getting through without drawing their attention."

Gretchen swears. "There goes that plan."

"Isn't there another way to get to our realm?" I ask. "A back door or something?"

"Back door," Gretchen's monkey friend says with a giggle.

The creatures around me exchange mocking laughs and skeptical glances.

"Not one that you would survive," the golden maiden answers diplomatically. "The only ways of exiting Abyssos are through the door or through the godly realms."

"Godly realms?" Gretchen asks.

The golden maiden explains, "Hades and Olympus."

"What's wrong with them?" I ask. "Can't we use one of those entrances?"

She shakes her head. "The path from Olympus to Panogia is more heavily guarded than even the door. With an army at your side you could not succeed."

She doesn't have to voice the implied, *You would not survive.*

"That's why we're going through the abyss to get there," Gretchen says. "It's the only way to bypass the tough security."

"Hades then?" We can't just let the assassins find and kill our mother; I can't, I won't – not when I haven't even met her yet. Not when we're so close. I have so many questions.

"The underworld is worse," the unicorn says. "Airtight security to keep the dead from returning to life."

"And the journey through Hades itself would be no easy task," the golden maiden adds. "Most likely you would not even make it to the Panogian path."

"Where does that leave us?" Greer asks. "There is no way home?"

She doesn't sound as freaked out as I am. "We're trapped here?" I gasp. "Forever? We just give up?"

"Of course not," Gretchen says, but without her usually infallible certainty.

The group falls silent, and I scan the crowd for any signs of an idea. Anything. There has to be some hope, some way we haven't thought of.

Greer clears her throat. "What about autoporting?"

We all turn to face her.

"What?" I ask.

"Autoporting," she repeats, checking her fingernails. Yep, almost back to normal now. "Maybe you can use your power to get home."

Why didn't I think of that? I have this power – for just this kind of situation, I hope.

Hopeful, I turn to Gretchen.

"Maybe," she says, considering.

"It *must* be possible," I say. "Euryale autoported to me that night on the pier."

"Not her body," Gretchen argues. "You said she wasn't really there."

"She wasn't, but…"

"If her powers are tethered," the golden maiden suggests, "that might explain her incomplete autoportation. It is likely her captors took precautionary measures."

"That she could still project even her image at such a distance," Nick says, sounding impressed, "is a sign of her tremendous power."

"Let's do it," I say, clapping my hands together. "It can't hurt to try. If I can autoport me and Nick back to our realm, then once you rescue Euryale she'll be able to get everyone else home."

"Your power must be well honed," the golden maiden warns. "Travel between realms is not easy."

What about this life *is* easy? Fighting monsters out to

kill or capture me, watching my sister almost die, being trapped in this dark smelly place? Everything is hard compared to my life before meeting Gretchen, when I spent most of my time in front of a computer screen. It's *all* hard. I bite back the sarcasm and focus my energy on positive thinking.

"I can do it," I insist. I have no choice. *We* have no choice.

Gretchen hesitates, studying me. Well, she won't find any doubts. I'm confident – or at least confident enough to try.

Finally, she says, "Get your bags."

Minutes later, Nick and I are standing at the centre of the group, each of us carrying a backpack of extra supplies. He doesn't have to go with me – his allegiance is to Gretchen – so I appreciate his coming to help, especially since he already knows the boss and his prized assassins. That information might come in really handy.

Gretchen stands before me, Sillus sitting at her feet, her hands on my shoulders. "You take care of yourself. Find our mother, get to the safe house and stay put. We'll meet you there when we get out."

"I will," I promise. "You stay safe too. Find the gorgons and get Euryale to autoport you all out of here."

She smiles, like she's a little amused by my concern for her safety. Or maybe she's uncomfortable having someone worrying about her for a change. Well, she'd better get used to that. I'm brilliant at worrying.

I see her glance at Nick, who gives her a look full of longing. I'm glad she doesn't doubt his loyalty any more, because that one exchange tells me how he feels about her. She's his sun, moon and stars. As soon as we get through this mess – this war – I'll make sure she does something about that.

For now, we each have our missions.

Taking Nick's hand in mine, I suck in a deep breath.

"See you soon," I say.

Gretchen backs away.

I close my eyes and focus. The times I've autoported before have always been in really dangerous situations, when I was fuelled by fear. I try to channel those feelings of desperation. Every ounce of my energy, my concentration, *my very being* is funnelled into autoporting us home. Home. Home, home, *home*.

Bright light penetrates my eyelids, and I sense the world around us shifting. We're moving, travelling through the portal. It's working! I'm sending us—

Nick's arm is around my throat before I can breathe.

"Move an inch and I'll snap it like a twig."

The menace in his voice is unmistakable.

"What?" I gasp. How could I have been so wrong about him? Gretchen will never forgive him. She'll never forgive herself.

CHAPTER 5

Greer

"Ready to go?"

Gretchen moves the instant Grace and Nick disappear, slinging a backpack over her shoulder and heading across the cave. All right by me. The less time spent in this wretched place, the better. If I hadn't truly needed to rest, I would have insisted we proceed sooner. Besides, any longer and I'm sure Gretchen would toss me over her shoulder and push on. Good thing I recover quickly.

"Right as rain," I say with an ambitiously cheerful smile.

Mother always says if you project the image you wish the world to see, eventually it will become reality. I don't wish to be miserable and in pain, so I will pretend I'm not.

As I push to my feet, my body no longer feels like it's melting from the inside out. The hellebore Thane used to counteract the venom was hard on my system, but apparently it worked. I'm not dead, in any case, and that has to be a point in favour of the antidote.

Thane hands me a backpack that feels lighter than

before. He doesn't meet my gaze as he hefts his own pack into place.

"You didn't need to carry any of my load," I say.

"I know," he says, adjusting his straps.

I'm not a wilting flower who needs a boy to carry her gear, but my legs feel like overcooked spaghetti at the moment, so I choose not to argue. "Thank you."

Gretchen stands at the cave entrance with several of the creatures who brought us here. A few plan to accompany us on our journey, to see us safely to Olympus. No, I am not ready to think about Olympus yet. I'm not ready to worry that far into the future. One step at a time. Stepping out of the cave and into the great vast cavern beyond without tripping over my tennis shoes will be an auspicious start.

I will face the future as it comes.

Gretchen nods as Thane and I approach, then turns and leads the way out through the tunnel. The portal was only the doorway here. This is the *real* first step of the journey.

The golden maiden follows in second place, along with the little furry monkey who came through the portal with Gretchen the other day and an oceanid named Petraie who looks like she's made out of water. She's fascinating. Her skin is dark grey, rippling like the sea beneath a storm. I wonder what it feels like.

As strange as these companions are, they are welcome

56

additions to our group. The idea of the five of us – let alone *three* now that Grace and Nick are gone – fighting the great monster horde had me somewhat concerned. If there weren't a vastly bigger saving-the-world picture and a millennia-old legacy at stake, I might have signed up to stay home.

But the gorgons need our help. So does the human world. It's our destiny, our responsibility, to carry on the tradition. I push the fear aside, put one foot in front of the other, and follow my sister out of the cave.

With Thane at my back, I actually feel safer than I have in weeks, since before I found out about my sisters and the previously hidden world of myths and monsters exploded around me.

Thane is strong, yes, but that's not why he makes me feel so safe. He's dedicated. Driven. No, devoted.

That's the word. He's *devoted* – to Grace, to his family, to Gretchen and me.

I get the feeling he would do anything within his power to keep us safe and make sure we succeed. Unlike Nick, who clearly is interested in Gretchen but also believes in the cause, I think Thane couldn't care less about the cause. His motivation is us – Grace, especially, and, for some reason I don't quite understand, me.

From the moment he opened the door at Grace's apartment and his dark grey eyes looked into my silver ones, our connection has been undeniable. I know

I'm safe as long as it's within his power to protect me.

We emerge from the tunnel, and the group huddles up before proceeding.

"We move in silence," Gretchen says. "Nothing above a whisper from here on out."

Now why is she looking straight at me as she says that? Grace is the one with the tendency to talk too much. I choose to ignore her implication.

"Keep close, in tight formation." She scans her gaze over the entire group. "Use the buddy system. I'll pair up with the golden maiden. Sillus and Petraie, and Greer and Thane. Keep track of each other. Whistle if there's a problem."

My eyes roll instinctively.

Gretchen scowls. "Problem, Greer?"

I want to say, *This isn't kindergarten*, but I don't think she'd appreciate the snark. Besides, the statement is all too true. This *isn't* kindergarten. This situation is serious and dire. Extra precautions are warranted.

I swallow the attitude. "No," I reply. "No problem."

"We go without pit stops," she continues. "Until it's an emergency, keep moving."

"How long?" I ask. "How far is it to Mount Olympus?"

Gretchen looks to the golden maiden for the answer.

"There is a shortcut," she says. "We can reach the entrance in perhaps a dozen hours, if we encounter no trouble."

No trouble? Only if our luck improves.

You are good to be cautious, a voice echoes in my mind. *Trouble seeks you.*

Did I just hear that? I blink and shake my head. Perhaps it is a side effect of the hellebore. Thane said it would be hard on my system.

I keep the voice in my head and my cynicism to myself as Gretchen turns and starts walking, the golden maiden at her side. The monkey and the oceanid take the middle, while Thane and I bring up the rear.

"Twelve hours," I mutter.

"Can you make it?" Thane asks. "If you're still too weak—"

Gretchen cuts him off with a glare over her shoulder. I glare back, but she's already turned around and begun marching on.

"I'm fine," I reply with a whisper. "It's just a long walk."

"It is," Thane says, not whispering, but somehow still quiet enough to avoid Gretchen's wrath. "We'll make it." He glances sideways at me. "Together."

"Together," I whisper.

I can handle that.

Our hopes of travelling without trouble evaporate in the first hour.

We're just rounding a big black rock formation that looks like any of a dozen we've passed since starting out when Gretchen pulls to a sudden stop. There, not twenty feet from our path – not that there is an actual path to see, just a general direction we're heading in – at the shore of the inky black river we've been following, is a pair of ugly beasts splashing themselves with water.

We all shuffle to a stop behind her, trying to be as quiet as possible.

Following Gretchen's motions, we tiptoe around the outcropping, pressing ourselves as close to the rock as we can, staying as deeply hidden in the shadows as possible.

I even hold my breath, as if the rasp of air from my lungs will somehow alert the creatures to our presence – although I'm not entirely certain why we are bothering with stealth, considering some monsters obviously already know we're in the abyss and these two wouldn't be much trouble to take care of.

Still, I don't voice my opinion. I think the idea that our venom actually kills the monsters in this realm really bothers Gretchen. Not that she's said anything, but I don't imagine she likes being a killer. Huntress, yes; a mythological bounty hunter, so to speak. Killing is different.

But arguing with Gretchen is like arguing with a brick wall, and just as effective. For the sake of travelling in peace, I keep my mouth shut – and my breath held – until we are well out of range of the bathing beasts.

Besides, I suppose the last thing we want is to draw any unnecessary attention. Our goal is to travel through the abyss quickly and quietly. My recovery period has already set us back several hours. We want to avoid any more delays. Our real mission lies beyond. We don't need the distraction of fighting two random monsters.

I sneak a glance at Thane, walking silently at my side. He's been stealthy as a mouse since our first steps into the abyss, whether there were monsters around to hear or not. It's unnatural how quiet he is.

After a quick check to make sure Gretchen isn't watching, I whisper, "You're like a ghost."

He scowls at me. "What?"

"You're so quiet," I explain. "How do you keep from making any noise?"

Even in my soft-soled sneakers, I can't quieten my footfalls entirely. They still scuff and squeak against the stone. He's wearing work boots but not making a sound.

He shrugs. "I just am."

"You just are?" I repeat. "That's not an answer."

He cuts me a glance. "If you had spent time on the street, you'd know how to be quiet, too."

I blink several times. He lived on the street? Grace has never said much about his background – nothing, really. Why would she? I know he was adopted, like her, but I didn't know he'd been old enough to have lived on the street. I suppose I just assumed he was adopted as a baby like my sisters and I were.

"I'm sorry," I say softly. "I didn't know."

We walk on in silence. I'm unsure what to say now, and that makes me uncomfortable. I'm not usually the sort of girl who's at a loss for words.

I keep picturing little boy Thane, his chiselled features softened by youth, stormy grey eyes wide and round, fending for himself. Homeless. Hungry and alone.

It's unconscionable.

Finally, I ask, "How long?"

"How long what?"

"Were you on the street?" I can't imagine what that's like. "How old were you?"

The muscle along the bottom of his strong jaw pulses and clenches. He doesn't like to talk about himself, especially about personal, emotional things. I understand. I keep my emotions close to my chest, too. It's precisely why I'm known as the ice queen.

I'm about to tell him to forget I asked when he says, "Six months. I was seven."

"I…" Seven years old – a little boy without the strength and self-confidence he has now. He must have been very vulnerable.

I like to think I don't take my life for granted. I understand that I'm privileged and that many kids – *most* kids – have nowhere near the advantages I've had. But in this moment, as I walk to my destiny side by side with this boy who is so very different from me, but then not so different, I feel like I've never appreciated those advantages more.

"Do you—" I begin, then realise I'm about to ask the wrong question. *Do you want to talk about it?* To which he will reply, *No.* Instead, I ask, "Have you talked about it with anyone? Do Grace or your parents know?"

That muscle in his jaw clenches again. Tick, tick, tick.

A dull ache throbs at the base of my skull. I lift my hand to rub the spot, trying to relieve the pressure.

"Some." He shifts the heavy backpack on his shoulders. "Not much. They don't need to know."

I twist my head side to side, loosening my tight neck muscles. "They might not need to," I say gently, "but maybe they want to."

When he doesn't reply, I add, "Maybe I want to."

This gets his attention – but not in a good way.

"No," he says, his voice gruff and uncompromising, "you don't."

I can practically feel his pain. He increases his pace to catch up with the pair in front of us. He says something to them, and seconds later Gretchen's monkey friend drops back to my side.

"He say switch buddy," the furry thing says. "Okay?"

Hand on my neck, I study Thane's back as we keep walking. He wants to be an enigma? All right, he can try. But there is little I can't accomplish when I set my mind to it. I do love a challenge.

"Yes," I say to the monkey. "Everything is just fine."

I march on, thinking, studying… plotting. Thane might have been able to keep secrets from his family until now, but he'll have a more difficult time trying to do the same with me.

CHAPTER 6
Gretchen

By late afternoon – what I *think* is late afternoon, for all I can tell in a world without a sun – everyone is exhausted. Greer is getting snippy – in other words, back to her usual, charming self. The oceanid is grumpy. My own feet are starting to feel heavier. Thane and the golden maiden are the only ones who seem like they could go on walking forever. Even little Sillus, with his boundless energy, is too tired to keep walking.

I lift him up onto my shoulders and give my inner whiner a kick in the butt, and we push on. No time to rest. Besides, every time we've stopped for more than a minute, monsters have shown up, just like when we came through the portal – like we're broadcasting our location.

Not that I had doubts left, but this definitely puts Nick in the clear. He's not even in this realm any more. He can't be feeding info to the enemies. Either we have epic bad luck or they're tracking us somehow. I've searched all our gear, twice. No one in the party has left my sight since we started. If something is telling the monsters where we are, I can't find it.

That just means I have to stay on guard and aware of our surroundings.

Sillus rests his chin on my head and sighs.

"So," I ask, "ready to tell me how you ended up back here?"

He shifts on my shoulders.

"Sillus minding own business," he says, his jaw bouncing against my scalp as he talks, "when portal appear. Right there in middle of Miss Greer basement."

"Greer's basement?" I echo.

"Yes," he says, with exaggerated awe. "Open up and suck Sillus in."

That's a far cry from the long story he promised, but it is troubling.

A portal opening in Greer's basement is a huge coincidence. Those things can open up anywhere, but what are the odds that it would happen in the basement of a sister of the Key Generation? What are the odds that one would open up right where my sisters opened the portal that got me out of the abyss last time?

Pretty damn low.

"What else happened?" I ask.

"Sillus get suck in," he repeats. "Said so."

"I know that," I say, my back muscles tensing. "But did you see anything else? Anyone or anything unusual about the portal or your trip back?"

"No, all normal," he says with another sigh, as if he's

66

sad to disappoint me. Then he jerks up, nearly knocking himself backwards off my shoulders. I wrap my hands around his legs to keep him on. "One thing strange."

"What's that?"

"When Sillus go through," he says, "see other door."

"Other door?"

"Not one," he explains. "Many door."

"Many doors?" My stomach flip-flops. "More entrances to our realm?"

"Yes," he says. "More."

"How many?"

I feel him shrug. "Seven, eight, ten." He shrugs again. "Twenty. More."

Twenty doors? Twenty portals between my world and the abyss. Sthenno said things are changing now that my sisters and I are reunited. This must be part of that change. I try to imagine what this means. More monsters in our realm? More cracks in the seal? More creatures out hypnotising a human army to fight us when we finally break the seal?

This is not good news. We're already vastly outnumbered. The imbalance is only going to get worse. We need to get the gorgons and get home. I don't like the idea of Grace being back in San Francisco with more and more beasts roaming the streets, even with Nick to protect her.

He's not completely useless in a fight, but they can't take on an army on their own.

We have to get back there fast.

I pick up my pace, knowing that my exhausted companions will have to struggle to keep up. There's no time to waste. We can rest when the war is over.

After a few more hours, my feet are dragging over the stone, and I'm embarrassingly relieved when we round a corner and the golden maiden tugs me to a stop.

"That is the entrance," she whispers.

Across the open space in front of us is a massive door.

Twenty feet tall and ten feet wide, it glitters gold even in the dim glow of the abyss and our weak flashlights. Every last inch of the surface is intricately carved with mythological creatures and designs from ancient Greece: gods, monsters and heroes of old. The Olympians couldn't have put out a brighter *This Way to the Home of the Gods* sign if they'd framed it in neon and painted it Day-Glo orange.

I scan the area, expecting to see a legion of guards ready to spear us to the spot. This is the entrance to Olympus. It should be heavily protected.

There isn't a sound, not a sign of another living creature within a hundred yards at least. My sense of smell is muddled by the general stench of the abyss, but I don't sniff anything out of the ordinary. The door is completely undefended.

"Impossible," I mutter. This can't be for real. "What's the catch?"

"It is not," the golden maiden explains, "as easy as it looks."

"Of course not," I grumble.

What would be the point in making anything easier for us? Half the thrill is in the challenge. Straightforward and simple is so boring; takes all the fun out of saving the world.

"Let me guess?" I venture. "We try to open the door and vats of molten lead dump onto our heads."

The golden maiden gives me a wry smile. "Not precisely."

"Then how do we get in?"

"Is there a doorbell or something?" Greer asks, stepping up to my side.

"We wouldn't use it if there were," I snap, my exhaustion getting the better of my patience. "We're not advertising our presence."

"It was a joke, Gretchen," she says, crossing her arms over her chest. "Lighten up once in a while."

Clearly *she's* feeling better.

I clench my teeth and contemplate using her head as a door knocker.

"Petraie knows the way," the golden maiden says before I can lunge for my sister. "She will guide us. Though perhaps we should rest for a short time. You will need all your strength once you reach the dungeons."

"*We* will?" I didn't miss her subtle hint. "Aren't you coming with us?"

"I am," she says, "but I do not require rest. I shall stand guard."

I'm too wiped to even feel compelled to argue.

"Wake me if anything comes up." I smile at her and then turn to the group. "We're going to take a short break before we go in. Rest up while you can."

I don't deny that I need a nap too. When life gets back to normal, I definitely need to work on my endurance. Dropping my bag on the ground, I quickly find a comfortable position and close my eyes.

Seconds later I feel a warm ball of fur cuddle up next to me. I wrap my arm around Sillus's little body and am asleep in less than a heartbeat.

"Gretchen, wake up."

I blink awake in an instant. The golden maiden is leaning over me, a concerned scowl in place.

"I hated to disturb your sleep," she says, "but a group of creatures approaches. I thought you might want to investigate."

I nod, shaking the sleep out of my brain.

"Where?"

She leads me up a rocky incline. At the top, she gestures to the canyon below, where nearly twenty monsters are heading our way.

The one in the lead – a woman with hooves for feet – holds a glowing object in one outstretched palm. At first

I think it's for light. It's dark enough in here that even a lightning bug would help.

Then the hoofed lady turns, taking the group away from our location. The red light in her palm dims. She immediately changes course, heading back towards us, and the red light flashes brighter.

It's like a compass, only this one doesn't point due north; it points to huntress.

"It's leading her right to us." That must be how they keep showing up. "We need to go. Now."

We hurry back down to our makeshift campground and get everyone up and ready to continue as quickly and quietly as possible. I can tell the short rest was worth the delay. Everyone is moving faster – with less grouching.

Petraie leads the way to the door.

The oceanid smiles shyly before moving to the rock wall next to the door. She runs her fingertips over the stone, like a blind person reading braille. I can't tell what she's looking for. It all looks the same to me: one big mass of rough black surface – granite, maybe, or some kind of volcanic rock. Probably something that doesn't exist in my world.

"What exactly is she looking for?" I ask the golden maiden.

"There is a hidden entrance," she explains. "A side door of a sort, one that bypasses the security measures in place to guard the primary door."

"Lucky for us someone thought to make this," I reply.

The golden maiden gives me a sly grin. "Lucky for us someone on Olympus wanted undetectable access to the abyss for romantic assignations."

"Someone?"

She shrugs, her shoulders squeaking quietly with the motion. "Rumour claims that Hera once had an affair with Alcyoneus."

"The king of the giants?" I sputter. "No way."

"Ahhh," Petraie says, interrupting our gossip.

She pauses in front of an unexceptional-looking patch of black. Then, after clenching her hand into a fist, she presses it to the stone and pushes.

At first, nothing happens. I think maybe she's wrong. Maybe it's a *different* unexceptional patch of black. Then – slowly, with a rough scratching sound – the surface behind her hand pushes back into the wall.

I scan over my shoulder to make sure the monster group isn't within earshot yet. Thane has his back to us, his shoulders rigid and his hands flexing in anticipation. I turn back to the door.

An instant later, a section of stone the size of my car slides silently back into the wall and then to the side, out of sight.

"This way," the oceanid says, stepping inside the hidden passageway.

We're following a water nymph into a secret entrance to Olympus. This might be the craziest thing I've done yet. I don't know where this leads or what waits for us on the other side, but I know that bad things are coming from this side of the passage. As I follow Petraie inside, I reach down and pull out my daggers.

I feel better with a blade in each hand.

"There they are!"

I turn at the sound of the shout. The compass-wielding woman leading the monsters has just rounded the nearest rock formation and is pointing at us across the clearing.

"Run," I scream, moving back to the entrance and bracing myself in a fighting stance. "Petraie, can we close the door?"

Thane takes a matching position at my side.

Something cold and wet touches my shoulder as the oceanid moves past me, brushing me in her hurry. As the monsters race towards the tunnel, Petraie frantically moves her hands over the rock on this side of the door.

"I cannot—" She shakes her head.

The first monster reaches us: a Teumessian fox that is quick as lightning. I spin left and focus all my strength in a powerful side kick to the chest. The fox flies backward, taking out the next fastest beast with the momentum.

Thane rushes out of the tunnel, pulling his sword off his back as he goes after the next wave of attackers.

"Any time now would be good," I call out.

"I am hurrying," Petraie insists.

I hold position at the door as Thane takes on a pair of

ursa hybrids. A man with waist-length hair and a row of razor-like teeth gets past Thane. I'm about to give him a taste of my dagger when Greer spins out next to me, landing a solid kick to the side of the head. The man collapses, unconscious, on the ground.

"Nice," I say.

Greer gives me a tight smile. "Thanks."

"Yes!" the oceanid finally shouts. "Here."

The door starts its slow, grinding slide back into place.

"Thane!" I shout. "Retreat!"

I stay in ready position, prepared to take on the rest of the monsters that are closing in, as Grace's brother runs back inside. Then, with a puff of wind that sucks most of the air out of the tunnel, the door seals us in – and seals the monsters out.

There is a faint clicking sound before the glow from Thane's flashlight illuminates the enclosed space; it looks like a tunnel carved into a mountain of the shiny black stone.

"Whew," Greer says. "That was close."

"Tell me about it." I pull out my own flashlight and flick it on. "Let's get through here before they figure out how to open that door."

We wind our way through an unending black tunnel, our path illuminated by nothing more than our flashlights. Every so often I hear a high-pitched sound and I tell myself it's Greer's sneakers on the stone. She's been squeaking

74

every few steps since we started out yesterday. I just hope it's not rats.

Petraie stops in front of me.

"The tunnel ends here," she says.

"Please turn off your lights," the golden maiden instructs, "and maintain absolute silence until I indicate the coast is clear."

Thane and I shut down our flashlights, plunging us into even deeper black.

We wait, silent, in the dark tunnel as the golden maiden walks to the door at this end of the secret passage. The sound of a knock – faint and eerie in the darkness – echoes around us.

I sense Greer moving to my side.

"This is insane, right?" she whispers. "I can't believe we're about to step into the home of the gods. My parents would die if I ever told them about this."

As much as I want to make some snide comment, to make her feel silly for being so freaked out, I can't – because I feel exactly the same way.

This experience is getting a little surreal, even for me. Sure, I've been hunting monsters straight out of mythology since before I had boobs, but the idea that the residence of the Greek gods – the *gods* – is on the other side of this door is mind-blowing.

"My ex-parents," I reply, "would have probably beat the hell out of me for making it all up."

I hear her sharp intake of breath. That's when I realise I might have gone overboard on our bonding moment. I don't talk about my childhood. These circumstances are making me more reckless than usual. Greer did not sign up to listen to me complain about my sucky former life. That's all best left in the past.

"I—"

Her arms are around me before I can take it back.

"I'm sorry," she whispers against my hair. "I'm so sorry."

I don't know if it's the darkness or the emotion in her voice or the absolute craziness of the situation, but I find myself blinking back tears. I didn't feel sorry for myself when I lived with Phil and Barb; I'm certainly not going to feel sorry for myself now that I've escaped them and made a bigger life for myself.

Still, I can't help lifting my arms to hug Greer back.

I give her a quick squeeze that says *Thank you* and also *Mention this ever again and I'll glue your mouth shut while you sleep*. She must get the message, because she takes a step back just as the door reopens and the golden maiden sticks her head into the passageway.

"All clear," she calls out.

"Let's go." I step out of the tunnel. "Olympus awaits."

CHAPTER 7

Greer

I have been a guest in the most expensive, designer-created homes in San Francisco and in cities around the world. I have attended operas in ornate, gilded theatres, walked the halls of the world's greatest museums and shopped in the most exclusive boutiques in New York, London, Paris and Tokyo. But I have never, in all my travels, seen anything as breathtaking as the halls of Mount Olympus.

At first, I'm blinded by the brightness; everything is sparkling white in brilliant light. It takes my eyes a full minute to adjust after the darkness of the passage and the abyss beyond.

When I can finally look my fill without squinting, I attempt to take it all in.

Every surface is marble: the floor, the walls, the delicate columns that sweep up to the marble ceiling. It's the purest white stone I've ever seen, purer even than the coveted Makrana white Mother insisted on for her bathroom. There isn't a fleck of colour or a shadow of a vein in sight.

Capping the columns are intricately carved capitols formed from graceful acanthus leaves. Set in the spaces between the leaves are fat, round gems in every colour of the rainbow: bright red rubies, rich green emeralds and deep blue sapphires trail down the fluted length of the columns, sparkle like multi-hued stars in the ceiling and paint the inlaid floor with a priceless mosaic of precious stones.

To say I am in awe would be the understatement of the century.

"Greer," Gretchen hisses, gesturing at me from an alcove halfway down the hall where she is waiting with Sillus, the golden maiden and her human-looking twin.

Almost as shocking as the gleaming halls of Olympus was stepping out of the tunnel and finding myself face-to-face with a flesh-and-blood version of our golden maiden. With the exception of their… material, they are identical – exact copies right down to the waves in their hair.

Apparently Hephaestus crafted more maidens in his forge than the four known golden ones. When the door between realms was sealed and the golden maidens were deemed more monster than human or god, he created more human-like maidens to replace those locked into the abyss.

The more human maiden calls herself Alaia, which makes me wonder if the golden maiden has another name.

I push aside my questions and my appreciation of the surroundings. I cannot forget why we're here and why getting caught would be a very bad thing. Some of the gods are the ones who want us dead to prevent us from opening the door; they would rather let the monster realm be permanently sealed away, killing every last creature that lives inside. They believe that is the only way to protect the human world. They are unlikely to offer us ambrosia and scones if we're found on godly grounds.

Maybe, if things go well, I can come back for a leisurely visit in the future. Another time, when so many lives and the balance of justice in every realm are not at stake.

I hurry to catch up with the rest of the group.

I'm still two alcoves away from Gretchen when I hear footsteps.

I freeze, right there in the middle of the halls of Olympus, standing out against the gems and pristine marble like a moth on a Michelangelo. With the sound distorted by echo, I can't tell where they're coming from. I don't know which way to run. My brain stops working and panic sets in.

I drag in a breath to shout for Gretchen, who is watching me with an irritated look on her face – she can't hear the footsteps yet – when a strong hand claps over my mouth. Thane drags me across the hall and behind a statue of Aphrodite in the nearest alcove.

As the footsteps get louder, he presses me against the goddess of love's flowing marble skirts. His entire body holds me in place, keeps me from slipping into view. His eyes – fierce and swirling, like the roiling clouds of a spring thunderstorm – are unfocused as he listens intently.

I know it's wrong, I know this is the worst timing ever, but I take a moment to study him. From this close, I can see the faint remains of several scars – around his eye, below his right cheek and along the jawline in front of his left ear. They are pale and flat and must be from old wounds, unlike the ones in my vision of him dabbing green liquid on a trio of jagged lines scratched into his chest. That is recent, although I still don't know if it's past, present, or future.

He's strong, yes, but vulnerable, too.

Thane looks down at me and catches me studying him. His eyes soften, and my breath catches. Something sparks between us, an energy in the air – invisible, but no less powerful.

As he dips his head, the dizziness hits. My brain swirls and my knees buckle under me. Thane's strong hands wrap around my arms; otherwise I would collapse to the floor. Then I don't feel anything. I only see.

The place is grey, dark and dripping. Smoke fills the space, casting everything in a hazy blur.

There are two women – strong, beautiful and in danger.

One is tall, blonde, statuesque. I recognise her as Sthenno, my one-time therapist who is also Grace's school counsellor. Her trouser suit, the same soft grey one she wore when we saw her dragged into the abyss, is filthy and torn. She stands in her bare feet, wrists shackled to a damp stone wall like something out of a medieval torture chamber. Despite the fear I can sense in her, she stands tall and proud, spine straight and chin held high.

The other woman – older, shorter, but no less elegant – is in worse condition. Her head droops, letting her long grey hair hang down over her face in tangled clumps. Her clothes are shredded, hanging off her frail body like rags of black jersey. She lifts her head, and I can see the resemblance. This must be Euryale, Gretchen's mentor Ursula.

The immortal gorgons, our ancient aunts, chained like animals in a dank, dark prison.

As I watch, a beefy bald guy with sweat running off him in rivers steps up to Euryale. He grabs a handful of her hair and yanks up.

Looking at Sthenno, he growls, "Where is she?"

Sthenno's eyes flash almost imperceptibly, but she doesn't respond.

"She alone can find the door," he barks.

The man raises a stick with a leather strip on the end, pulls back and then cracks it over Euryale's tattered back. She doesn't even have the energy to cry out. But Sthenno does. And I do.

"Again," the sweaty guy says. "Where. Is. She?"

With a roar, Sthenno breaks free of her shackles and surges towards their attacker. Before she closes half the

81

distance, a pair of massive guards grab her by the arms.

"Get her out of here!" the main guy shouts. "Put her in the impenetrable cell. Maybe that'll keep her."

As the guards struggle to drag Sthenno away, sweaty guy turns back to Euryale and lifts the whip.

"No!" I cry out before he can lash her again.

"Greer." Thane's voice, calm and reassuring, penetrates my vision. "Greer, come back to me."

I open my eyes. The vision is gone. No more dungeon, no more gorgons, no more…

I shake my head.

"The gorgons," I whisper, barely able to form the words. "We need to hurry."

He nods, his dark grey eyes steady on me.

"We will save them," he insists. "It will take more than lashings and starvation to defeat a gorgon."

I can't even try to smile.

I hope he's right. I hope that vision isn't happening right now, because it didn't look like Euryale could last much longer.

I can't imagine what kind of torture it takes to break down an immortal like that, but she looked as broken as anyone I've ever seen. Tears stream down my cheeks – for her and for Gretchen. My sister might put on a tough show, keeping her emotions locked up inside – I know a thing or two about that myself – but this will hurt her.

All I can do is hope we get there in time and that

Gretchen lets her pain loose on whoever has been keeping the gorgons prisoner in that horrible place.

When I tell the group about my vision, the anger rolls off Gretchen in waves – anger and also fear. Those emotions she keeps hidden away are dangerously close to bursting out.

I don't blame her.

She turns to Alaia.

"Which way?"

Alaia turns without words and starts walking down the hall. We silently follow. It's as if everyone comprehends that Gretchen is a lit fuse and we don't want her wrath exploding on us.

She's done with stealth. Her boots clomp on the marble floor, echoing off the sparkling surfaces around us. At this point, I don't think she'd mind inviting a fight, except that it would delay the rescue.

"Is it always so empty?" I ask the golden maiden. "I would have expected Olympus to be bustling with activity."

"A meeting has been called in the great hall," she replies. "The gods and their servants are all in attendance."

"That's a stroke of luck."

She glances at me. "We do not wish to be here when the meeting breaks."

I can only imagine.

We fall back into silence as Alaia leads us down one long, columned hallway before turning down another. Even in our haste, I can still appreciate the breathtaking beauty of the building around us. Every so often we pass a window that opens either to a courtyard on one side or a sprawling green hill on the other. Each time, the pure brilliance of the sunshine and the vibrant blue sky above shocks me.

It's like the air itself is purer here.

Which I suppose makes sense. If you're going to be an immortal god living in a magical realm, wouldn't you want the cleanest air around? Mother would be so envious.

Halfway down the second hallway, Alaia stops in front of an open doorway. It is wider than a normal door – at least six feet across – and is topped by a graceful arch. Through it I can see a landing and the start of a spiral staircase.

"This way lies the dungeon," she says, leading the way. Her voice quivers as she adds, "From here I go no further. I must return to my master's side before he notes my absence."

Gretchen reaches out and takes Alaia's hand. "Thank you for leading us here."

"You are most welcome." She turns to the golden maiden. "I wish you good speed, sister. We all hope you succeed."

The two women – creations – embrace.

"We shall be united," the golden maiden says.

Alaia nods and then turns and retreats silently back the way we came. Without a word, Gretchen walks through the doorway.

The winding staircase – again pure white marble – leads down into the bowels of Mount Olympus. We begin circling, leaving the brightness of the halls behind, and descending single file in a spiral that seems like it will never end. Down and down. We must have travelled at least five stories when Thane suddenly grabs my shoulder.

"Stop," he whispers, loud enough for Gretchen, Sillus and the golden maiden several steps below to hear.

We all freeze, waiting. My heart thunders in my chest, and I listen.

At first I don't hear anything – just the echoing silence of our combined breathing in the enclosed stairwell.

Then... I do.

It starts as a soft purr, like a cat contentedly lounging on someone's stomach – not my stomach, of course. I've never been allowed a pet. Mother is violently allergic.

Gradually the purring gets louder... angrier. It turns into something more like a rumble, a soft roar... and then a louder roar.

Then the creature reaches the top of the staircase. For a moment, there is silence, and I cross mental fingers, hoping that it moves on. The next roar echoes down to us, beating against us like a violent wind, the sound amplified by the solid walls and the narrow column of air, like a pipe in a church organ.

"Run!" Thane shouts.

No one stops to ask why.

In a clatter of shoes on steps, we pound down the stairs, heading down to I don't know what – danger? Safety? Uncertainty. Away from whatever is clamouring down the stairs above us.

I feel the heat first, blowing down from above like the waft of warmth radiating off a patio heater on a cool summer night.

Then another blast, this time hotter. The white stone around us glows red-orange with the light of flames.

"What is it?" I shout.

The welcoming committee, a male voice says in my mind.

"Thespian dragon," Thane answers, urging me faster and faster down the stairs.

Then, finally, in a rush, we're running out of the staircase and into the dark, low-ceilinged space of what is obviously the dungeon. The walls are covered with the same damp, dark stone I saw in my vision.

"Over here," Gretchen calls out, heading for an innocuous door in the wall opposite the stairwell.

She grabs the handle and pulls. When the door doesn't budge, she lets out a primal roar and twists the handle as hard as she can, and the lock gives way.

She jerks the door open, waves us all through and then joins us inside what appears to be an unused closet, pulling the door shut behind her with a solid clank. Once again, we're plunged into darkness. No one makes a sound, not even the whoosh of panting breath, as we wait.

The growling we heard in the staircase becomes louder. Closer. Beneath the crack in the door, amber light seeps in along with a hot puff of air.

The dragon is right outside the door.

I bite my lips to keep from shaking. The warmth of a hand on my back calms me. Even in the dark, I know it's Thane. I feel something stronger than touch whenever we connect, something there in my core. I reach around and take his hand in mine, squeezing as another burst of light and heat invades our little space.

Then, after an eternity of our not moving and barely breathing, the light is no more. The heat is gone, and the growling and purring are replaced by an eerie silence and the soft drip of water on stone.

Still, we wait. Just in case.

It feels like forever as we sit in darkness, wondering if the dragon is gone yet. The feel of Thane's palm against mine reassures me. His pulse, surging against mine, gradually returns to normal.

Finally, when I can't stand it any more, I ask, "How did it know?"

"Know what?" Gretchen asks, turning on her flashlight.

"That we're here."

She and the golden maiden exchange a look.

"What?" I ask.

"Too many," Sillus says. "Monster notice."

Thane frowns.

"Should we separate?" the golden maiden suggests.

With Grace back in our realm, we are already divided. Splitting up further can't be a good idea. I squeeze Thane's hand again.

"That won't help," Gretchen says. "We just have to move faster."

The door creaks as Gretchen pushes it open and peers out into the dungeon. It must be all clear, because she slips out and gestures at us to follow. On my way out, I glance at Thane. He is watching me and scowling.

I start to ask, "What?" but Gretchen notices my hesitation and snaps, "Hurry up."

Thane shakes his head and nudges me out of the closet. Then I'm running to keep up with Gretchen's breakneck pace, and I don't have time to think about anything except not falling behind – not the strange connection between me and Thane, the monsters that keep showing up wherever we go, or the little voices that are whispering in my mind.

CHAPTER 8

Grace

I can't stop shaking. Across the room from where Nick is holding me, his arm tight around my neck as if he's going to crush it like a bad guy in a spy movie, is a guy with a dog's head and flippers for hands.

Clearly Nick knows him.

This must be the boss.

"You need her," Nick says to the guy. "The Keys can't open the door if one of them is dead."

That's reassuring, I guess.

The guy claps his flippers together in mock applause. "Nice move, Niko. You play the game well." He jerks his head at the hulking dude with charcoal-coated feet who is hovering just to our right. "Too bad you're playing for the wrong side."

"That's a matter of opinion," Nick replies.

For a moment – it feels like an eternity – they stare each other down. I can't see Nick's face, but I can feel the tension in his body. He's coiled tight, ready to react. Or act.

My initial panic starts to wear off, and I realise that if Nick wanted me dead, he'd have broken my neck already.

I take a deep breath, trying to calm my thinking so I can help him get us out of here alive.

"I'd rather let the door seal forever," Nick says, his voice low and menacing, "than let you take her."

The boss studies Nick, maybe trying to judge his commitment to that threat. I know exactly what Nick is threatening. I don't approve. The door seals if my sisters and I can't open it in time. We can't open it at all if I'm dead. As much as I'd like to *not* go with this slobbering guy and his hulking bodyguard, I'd rather not be dead more.

"Nick," I whisper.

He squeezes tighter, just enough to get his message across without cutting off my air. I'm just not entirely sure if that message is, "Keep quiet and let me handle this" or, "Keep quiet or I'll crush your windpipe." Either way, I keep quiet.

"You want me to get her, boss?" the charcoal guy asks.

While the boss watches us through squinting eyes, Nick pulls me closer against his chest. His heart is racing almost as fast as mine.

"Nah," the boss finally says. "Let 'em go."

"You sure?"

"Yeah." He looks away, dismissing us. "Better not risk it. We need the Keys intact."

I feel Nick release a breath behind me.

"You go out first," Nick says, nodding at the door. "Make sure none of your goons get the wrong idea about the situation. We'll follow you."

The boss smacks his gums. "Whatever you say, Niko." He grunts at the charcoal guy, who starts for the door. "I'll enjoy making you pay for this later."

"I'm sure you will," Nick replies. Then, too quiet for anyone else to hear, he whispers, "If they try to pull something, run."

Although my heart is still thumping up into my throat, relief washes through me. I wasn't wrong about Nick – Gretchen wasn't wrong. He's on our side. And by threatening to take my life, I think he just saved it.

There are two more bad guys waiting in the hall outside my apartment. The boss waves them off, and they warily move to the side and let us pass.

"Head for the elevator," Nick says, nudging me forward towards the bronze door at the far end of the hall.

For the first time since my near-death experience in the rickety old elevator, I'm looking forward to stepping into the cage of death. It's actually the lesser of two evils here.

"Push the down button," Nick tells the boss.

When he can only smack at the button plate, he shrugs. "Can't. That's the trouble with flippers, you know."

"Grace," Nick says, ignoring the boss's attempt at humour, "push the button."

I reach out, hand shaking, and call the elevator.

I'm not scared that Nick will kill me, not any more – I'm pretty sure he wouldn't anyway, but the thought of what Gretchen would do to him if he did would probably give him second thoughts in any case.

Everyone is very tense. The boss, even though he's acting unconcerned, the uneasy goons watching the boss escort us to the lift, and Nick behind me.

No one wants me dead here, least of all me, but tension can make people do things they otherwise wouldn't.

As we stand there waiting for the elevator to arrive, I study the people around us, or rather the monsters – the creatures who appear human to the ordinary people in my building. These beastly bodyguards could crush me with their bare hands, never mind the various weapons each one is carrying. Our only protection is my value as part of the Key Generation.

My palms are itching to get us out of this situation.

The elevator arrives with a creak and a sad ding. As the bronze door jerks open, I feel Nick tense up behind me. We're almost home free – why is he getting more nervous? Something is about to happen, but I'm not sure what.

"Nick, what—"

He releases me, shoves me into the elevator car and lunges for the boss.

"Get out of here," he shouts. "Autoport as soon as the doors close. Find your mother and get safe."

"No," I scream as I stumble to the back of the car and brace myself against my crash into the mirrored wall. "Nick, wait!"

But as I dive back for the door, it slides closed. I try

to shove my hands into its path, to find the sensor that will reverse the motion, but I can't. It crashes shut, and suddenly I'm in the elevator, alone and afraid.

Before I can push a button – before my brain stops freaking out long enough to tell me to push the button for the floor we're on so I can go back and help Nick – the car starts moving. Up.

"Shoot."

I stare at the button panel. There are eight floors, with no way of knowing where the elevator will stop. Maybe it's just another resident in the building. People must call the death trap all the time, right?

But as the elevator slows to a stop on the floor above mine, I have a bad feeling in the pit of my stomach. The door starts lurching open, revealing a tiny sliver of the hallway beyond – just enough for me to see the gang of thugs waiting with their weapons drawn.

Without thinking, I shut my eyes and blink myself out of there.

My thoughts are muddled by the fear and confusion. I'm not thinking clearly as I autoport myself out of the elevator. There isn't a thought in my brain except for escape. *Get away, get somewhere safe.* That's the only explanation I can think of for my popping onto the soccer field at Milo's school.

Milo is doing ball drills a few feet away.

"Grace?" he asks, blinking as he lets the ball hit the ground.

Shoot, shoot, *shoot*.

"M-Milo—" Looking around, I'm relieved – beyond relieved – to see no other soccer players on the field. This is bad, but it could have been *really* bad. "What are you doing here?"

He gives me a look that implies that's not the most relevant question at the moment. But he answers it anyway.

"Coach wants me to improve my footwork." He crosses the short distance between us. "What the heck just happened?"

Yep, there's the relevant question. The one I don't want to answer.

I shake my head. The reality of the situation rushes in. I don't have time for this; I can't afford to have this discussion with Milo right now. I have to get back to the apartment to help Nick.

He just saved my life, and I have to return the favour.

I'll have to use my hypno-eyes on Milo. It won't wipe his memory altogether, but it'll give me a chance to get out of here without answering questions. It'll give me time to go save Nick.

Maybe when the gorgons are back, one of them can make him forget he ever saw me today. Either that or he'll act like he never saw me *ever*. Who wants to date the freak girl with magical powers?

"Did you just materialise on the field?" he asks.

"Milo, I—" This is so hard. "I can't explain right now. My friend is in danger, and I have to find him fast."

He studies me for a second.

"Okay," he says, grabbing the soccer ball off the ground and tucking it under his arm. "I'll help. I have my dad's car."

"You – you'll what?"

"I'll help." He nods towards the street. "Whatever you need."

I can't help grinning. "Seriously?"

"Just promise me answers later," he says.

I can't believe he's being so understanding. Maybe he's in shock. He did just see his – what am I exactly?

A girlfriend? A friend? A friend's sister? Whatever I am – appear out of thin air on a soccer field. He's entitled to some post-traumatic recovery time.

I follow him to his dad's car, a little brown thing covered in dirt and rust. He walks around to the passenger side, unlocks the door and holds it open for me. As I start to move past him to get in, he blocks my path with his forearm.

"But I will want answers, Grace," he says. "Eventually."

His dark curls are damp with sweat and his cheeks are flushed pink from his workout. He's cute and tall and he smells good, even now. He almost makes me wish I were still a normal, ordinary girl.

I duck under his arm and climb into the car without replying.

Either I'll be able to give him answers or I won't. As I sink into the ripped plastic seat, I wonder what he would do if I blurted out the truth, right here, right now, every last detail. Probably run as fast as he could in the opposite direction. He's an amazing athlete; he can run pretty fast. He'd dismiss me as the crazy girl who believes in ancient mythology, and he'd be out of my life. Forever.

That thought makes me ridiculously sad. We barely know each other, but I've learned enough to really like him. He's sweet and kind and – apparently – not entirely freaked out by something completely insane. Maybe there's hope. Maybe I won't have to get someone with stronger powers to brainwash the memory right out of his brain.

Maybe I can have the best of both worlds – for once.

He drops into the driver's seat next to me, jams the key in the ignition and asks, "Where to?"

Right. Girl on a mission, not girl on a date.

"My apartment," I say, refocusing my thoughts on Nick and my biological mother. Time is precious. "As fast as you can."

He shifts into gear, pulls out of his parking spot and floors the accelerator. I wonder what I'll find when we get there.

"Can I borrow your phone?" I ask.

He grabs it from the dash console and hands it to me.

I left mine at home when we went into the abyss – no signal in the monster realms – but I need to check on Mom and Dad. I try home first, and I'm not sure if I should be relieved or afraid when there's no answer.

I hang up and dial my mom's cell. She picks up on the first ring.

"Hey, Mom."

"Grace?" she gasps. "Gracie, are you okay?"

"Are you with Dad?" I ask.

"Yes, he's right here."

My entire body sighs in relief. They're safe. For now.

There are sounds, and then my dad is asking, "Grace, where are you?"

"I'm fine, Dad," I say.

"Are you—" He hesitates, trying to find the words. "Are you back?"

"No, it's not over yet," I say, avoiding the direct question.

Silence. "But you're okay?" he asks.

"Yeah, Dad," I say. "I'm okay."

"And your brother?"

I glance at Milo, as if he'd have the answer. "He's fine, too." As far as I know. Nick, on the other hand… "Look, Dad, you guys can't go home."

"What happened?"

How can I tell them without freaking them out? I can't tell them the truth. "The monsters know where we live,"

I say simply, hoping they won't ask too many questions. "Just find a hotel and wait for my call."

"Gracie, this is—"

"Dad, please!" I shout, my fear making me more assertive than usual. "Please," I say again, softer. "I need to know you're safe. Promise me you won't go home until I call."

He hesitates, and I can practically hear him thinking. In the end, though, he trusts me.

"Okay," he says. "We promise."

"Promise what?" Mom asks in the background, and I can hear the worry in her voice. I don't have time to reassure them.

"Thanks, Dad."

"You take care of yourselves," he says.

"I love you, Grace," Mom shouts, almost desperate. "Come home soon."

I bite my lip as I hang up.

They're safe, and I feel some of the fear leave my body. With a sigh, I drop Milo's phone back into place. He doesn't say a word. His hand is on the gearshift between the seats and I have the almost irresistible urge to lay my palm over his. *Almost* irresistible.

Until Nick and my biological mother are safe, my sisters are back with the gorgons and the looming war is over, I have to stay focused on the mission. Lives are at stake. My love life can come later.

CHAPTER 9

Gretchen

The dungeons of Olympus are a harsh contrast to the shiny white marble world above. Those halls – all sparkle and gemstones – are what I imagined Mount Olympus would be like. This is like a slumlord's boiler room compared to the high-rent high-rise above. The gods are sending a clear message that if you end up in their basement, you're in big trouble. It doesn't look that different from the abyss – dark, wet and foul-smelling; never-ending.

The main hallway at the base of the staircase branches off in several directions. I stop to listen. The place is eerily silent. It's starting to make me nervous. The sooner we get out of here, the better.

With no standout reason to choose one branch over the others, I lead us down the left-hand corridor, mostly because it's the biggest and there are torches lighting the way. It seems the most likely to lead somewhere important.

Or it could be a trap.

"Stay close to the wall," I instruct, "and right on my heels."

We follow the corridor around corner after corner, with nothing but stone walls to guide us. There isn't even a rat or a medieval torture device to break up the monotony. It reminds me of King Minos's labyrinth. If a minotaur is the biggest bad we run into down here, we'll be in great shape.

Then we round one last corner, and it all changes.

I hold up my hand, and everyone behind me stops.

The hallway spills into a vast open space. Encircling the outer wall of the chamber is a row of cells, cages closed in by iron bars. The rough stone floor stretches a few feet beyond the cell walls and then drops away. Smoke rises in its place, like a moat of fire. Across the gap, on a stone island floating amid the smoke, are more cages – dozens of cages with thick steel bars that overlook the flames.

Every cage I can see is occupied. The dungeons of Olympus are overflowing.

Somewhere in here, Ursula is suffering.

"Then she took off her dress and she had *eight* legs," a booming male voice bellows.

Another male voice cackles with laughter.

Swinging my backpack off my shoulders and dropping it on the ground, I wave everyone back and press myself against the edge of the wall. Looking towards the sound of their voices, I spot two guards tromping around the walkway.

"I'm like, what are you, a spider?" the first voice says.

"And she says, no, I'm a daughter of Arachne!"

That sends the other guard into a fit of laughter.

I turn to the group and gesture at them to move up against the wall. We wait, unmoving, as the guards draw closer. Bending at the waist, I reach down and pull out a handful of zip ties from a cargo pocket.

I hope they're continuing their perimeter walks, and not heading for our hallway.

They reach the juncture and – I hold my breath – keep walking. After a quick glare at my companions to keep them in place, I take off at a run. The guards turn at the sound of my footsteps, but I launch into a flying kick, nailing the talkative one in the gut and knocking him into his laughing friend. I land on my feet between them, quickly dropping to my knees and yanking zip ties around their wrists.

"You stupid bi—"

The talker doesn't have a chance to finish his insult before I knock his head into the ground and render him unconscious. His buddy silently shakes his head, but I can't risk it. An instant later he's just as unconscious as his friend.

I resist the urge to push them into the moat – I don't know what's down there, and the two morons aren't necessarily bad guys – so I just drag them out of the way.

With the guards dispatched, my focus shifts to finding Ursula. Running along the walkway, I twist my head left and right to check the cages on both sides of the moat, scanning for any sight of her and her silver hair.

I'm almost back around to the start when I finally see her.

"Ursula!" I shout. Then, using her true name, "Euryale!"

Through the haze of smoke and brimstone, I can see her in a cage on the far side of the moat, hanging limp from her shackles. She is chained to the wall, but her body is too weak to provide any support at all.

She doesn't move when I call her name.

"Ursula!" I scream again.

Thane appears at my side. "It's soundproof."

He reaches forward. Even though there seems to be nothing but air in front of us, his hand connects with something, sending a shimmering ripple through the empty space, like touching the surface of a pond, only without the water.

"What is this?" I demand.

"A shield," he says, "raised up by Nemesis."

I bang at the air, and my hand hits something soft but unyielding. Wave after wave ripples out in every direction from where my fist connects with the shield.

"How do you know that?"

He doesn't respond.

I fight the urge to punch him in the face. We don't have time for games and secrecy. As much as I want to pound the whole truth out of him, that's not the highest priority at the moment.

"Then how do we get across?" I ask.

He shrugs. "No clue."

I turn my attention to the little monkey. "Sillus?"

"Sillus no see," he says, his big brown eyes sad. "Never before."

I look at the golden maiden, who slowly shakes her head.

"There must be a way." Someone has to be able to get across the moat to feed the prisoners. Or beat them.

Leaving the group, I circle the perimeter again, this time more slowly, more observantly. I walk the full length of one side, then turn and walk another and another, and finally the last. Half of the prisoners call out to me as I pass by – some in English, some in other languages, some in nonhuman speech. The others are too weak to speak.

My inspection turns up no clues. No bridges, no paths, no sign that anyone has ever made it across to reach the prisoners within.

Even if we figure out how to get the shield down, there's still the matter of the moat – twenty feet of open space with the gods know what down below.

I turn my attention back to this side of the moat. If there's nothing directly over it, maybe there's something else around here that will give me a hint at how to gain access. A lever, a ladder, anything. I circle the moat a third time, now facing the outer ring of cells. They are spartan – nothing but a stone bench, rusty shackles and a disgusting bowl. And a downtrodden prisoner.

Men, covered in dirt and wearing nothing more than loincloths that look like they've been doing overtime as baby diapers. Pathetic, skinny beasts that look like they're being slowly starved to death. Their empty eyes glance up and follow me as I walk by. Even though I know some of them are bloodthirsty monsters, it's horrible to see them in such terrible conditions.

"What are you?" a hoarse voice whispers as I pass a cell.

The hair on the back of my neck stands up in warning, but I stop and look inside.

"What are *you*?" I throw back.

Inside the cell, a thin, haggard man lifts his head. He watches me with sagging, hollow eyes.

His tongue darts out over his lips before he says, "Innocent."

I scowl. "Isn't every convict?" I retort.

"I have been convicted of no crime," he says, his voice smoothing out as he uses it more. "I have been sentenced to a lifetime of chains and beatings without trial."

"For what?" I ask.

"For daring to disagree."

That sounds like a bum deal. On any other day, I might be swayed by his sad story and inspired to do something to help – argue his case, maybe, or break him out of jail. But not today.

"Sorry, bud," I say, actually meaning it even though it comes across as sarcastic. "Can't help you."

I don't have time for this right now. I don't have time for anything except saving Ursula from torture. But as I continue on my search, the image of his vacant eyes haunts me.

By the time I circle back around to the group again, I've exhausted every last inch of the walkway around the moat. I've studied every block of stone, every line of mortar, every keyhole and footing and iron pipe. Finding nothing but cells and prisoners, I am no closer to getting through the shield and across to the other side. There's no sign of a secret button, hidden lever, or magical key.

"What the hell?" I shove my fingers into my braid.

I pace back and forth, running over the space in my mind. There has to be a way across; how else would the prisoners get over there? How else would the torturers get to them?

A tiny voice at the back of my mind suggests that maybe the only way across is a magic I don't possess. I punch that tiny voice in the throat. That'll shut it up. I don't have time for negative thinking.

"There has to be a way." I face the golden maiden. "You seem to know everything. Didn't your sister mention this?"

She shakes her head. "I am sorry. Alaia would have no way to gain that knowledge."

Turning on Greer, I demand, "Tell me everything you saw. Every last detail of the vision."

Her eyes widen. "I did," she insists. "I only saw the cell. Nothing beyond. I can't even be certain it was one of these cells, or anything near this time. It could have taken place last week, or it might be going to happen tomorrow."

"What good are your stupid visions?" I fight the urge to slam my fist into the stone wall. "Why even have them if you can't figure them out?"

"I don't know!" she shouts. "All right? I have no idea how these visions work or what they mean. I can't even control them!"

"Then keep trying!" I shout back.

"What?!"

"Keep trying," I say. "Try again."

She blinks. "Try again?"

"Try. Again." I close the distance between us. "Have another vision."

"I—" She frowns and shakes her head. "I can't."

"Of course you can."

She just blinks at me. "I never have."

It takes me a moment to realise we're not shouting any more. With a calmer head, I start to think my idea isn't a bad one. I've honed my super strength with years of training. Grace has been practising her autoporting. Greer needs to do the same.

"Now's a good time to start, don't you think?" I place my hands on her shoulders. "Instead of waiting for a vision to come to you, go after it with a big stick."

"How?" she mouths.

Thane steps closer to her side. "I think I can help."

We both turn to look at him in shock.

He meets my gaze straight on. "Give us a few minutes," he says. "I'll teach her to draw down the vision."

"Draw down?" I question. He scolds me with a look. "Fine. Answers later. We'll give you some space."

With Sillus hurrying to keep up, the golden maiden and I walk away from my sister and my other sister's brother – my life has become too complicated by half – and back around the corner. If Thane thinks a few minutes alone with Greer will help us get to Ursula – Euryale – I'm willing to give it a shot. What other options do we have?

CHAPTER 10

Greer

When Gretchen and the others round the corner, Thane lifts my backpack off my shoulder and drops it and his on the ground at our feet. He steps closer so there are only a couple of inches separating us. He seems so calm and certain, but I don't know if I'll be able to do this. I'm not used to feeling afraid of failure – I don't generally fail, so what's the point in fearing it? But the pressure is overwhelming.

So much is riding on my ability to produce this specific vision.

"Thane, I've never—"

"You will."

His eyes are so deadly serious that I have to believe him.

I want to believe him, which makes him easier to trust.

"Close your eyes," he instructs.

I take one last look at his eyes, at his strength, before I comply – before putting my faith in him, in his ability to banish the unfamiliar helplessness.

"Imagine you're in an empty room." His voice drops

to such a low whisper I can barely hear him above the roar of the flames in the moat below. "A white room, with a white table and a white chair."

I smile. "I like white."

"Shhh." He smoothes his fingertips over my forehead. "Just listen."

I nod, enjoying the feel of his hands on my face, erasing the dull ache at my temples.

"You walk into the room." His fingertips dance across my skin, focusing on the spot right above my nose, between my eyes. "On the table there is a marble. It's small and round, made of bright red glass."

I picture it down to every last detail: the smooth surface of the table, the brilliant shine of the marble – even the aura of red from the light that passes through it. My mind is so intent on the room that the sounds and smells of the dungeon around me drift away.

"Walk over to the table." He rubs a soft circle over my forehead. "Are you standing in front of it?"

I nod, not because I remember I'm supposed to be silent but because I'm too relaxed to disturb the moment with speech.

"Don't do it yet," he continues, "but when you reach down to pick up the marble, have the gorgons in your thoughts. When you squeeze the marble in your palm, you will have a vision that answers our questions."

Mentally, I stare down at that marble like it's the

last piece of fresh sourdough at Boudin's; it's the most desirable thing I've ever seen.

"Are you ready for the vision?"

His hands shift back down to my shoulders.

"Now," he says, gripping me tightly. "Grab the marble."

In my imagination, I reach out and snatch the red glass ball from the table.

Immediately I'm slammed with the dizziness.

"Hold on, Greer," Thane soothes. "Keep it together, and the vision will come."

I force thoughts of the gorgons into my mind. I picture their faces, their elegance, their strength.

Then it comes, like an old home movie – dark around the edges, with bright lens flares and burned-out spots in the middle.

I see the dungeon – the moat and the cells and the shield keeping us from reaching the central island. I spin in the vision, searching for the answer. There must be an answer; otherwise, why have this vision? Movement catches my eye. Directly across the moat from Ursula's cell, the little monkey creature has climbed up to the ceiling. He sticks his tiny hand into a nearly invisible hole between two of the ceiling stones.

In a flash, a bridge shoots up from within the flames, and then the shield, the very air around the moat, flickers like a bad hologram and then cuts away.

I watch, thrilled, as the monkey drops gleefully back

to the ground and Gretchen races across the bridge. It worked. I know how to get us across. I know how to save Ursula.

Then, just as I'm about to shift my thoughts to Sthenno, my stomach swirls and my head explodes in pain. My vision goes black.

You have seen enough, the male voice in my head says.

"Leave her alone," Thane growls. "Greer, get out now."

No; I need to find Sthenno, too. She's in here somewhere.

As I reach for her, the pain magnifies. I whimper, but I refuse to give up.

Yes, the female voice says. *Push harder.*

No! Thane's voice says; then he shouts, "Greer!"

Through the searing pain, a vision begins to form. I struggle to focus. Just as I make out the space – a hallway lined with the same stone as the rest of this awful place – the vision jerks out of reach, like someone yanked it away before I could see the whole picture.

The next thing I feel is Thane shaking me. I blink against the pain, relieved when I see Thane and the world as it is, not the imagined world of my vision.

I draw in a shaky breath.

"Are you okay?" he asks.

I nod, even though I'm not really sure. I've never had that kind of feeling in a vision before. They've always come and gone without much fanfare, nothing more than an annoying dizziness before and a bit of fatigue afterwards. The nausea and the headache aren't exactly minor side effects. They're not pleasant, but I've felt worse.

That pain was something else.

And the voices in my head – Thane's and the other two – arguing over me… I don't know if that was part of the vision or not.

"Yes," I say, taking a deep breath to calm my nerves and my stomach. "I'm fine."

"You saw how to get across."

It doesn't sound like a question, but I smile and answer anyway. "What do you think?"

Gretchen is back around the corner and at my side in an instant, an expectant look on her face.

"What did you see?" she demands.

As the monkey and the golden maiden join us, I tell Gretchen, and she takes off running for the spot I indicated.

It's only a matter of moments before she's directing Sillus up the wall, his little furry fingers gripping spaces between stones like it's his personal climbing wall. He finds the hole easily enough.

I stand there, stunned. I can't believe the vision was real. Other visions have come true, sure, but this is one I *chose*. I sought it out. I knew what I wanted to see, and then I saw it. And I was right.

Now I'm eager to try again. I wonder if there's an easier way to get there than to go through the whole white-room visualisation. Maybe it's just a matter of practice. Hopefully practice will lessen the pain.

Knowing I can force visions of my choosing, I'm more than ready to try.

You must strengthen your mind, the female voice says. *You must control the power unleashed by the pendant.*

I blink and look around. No one else shows any indication of having heard the warning. But I heard her as if she were right here, speaking to me. Maybe I really am losing my mind.

"Gots it!" The monkey hops back down to the ground.

As he lands, a thunderous roar echoes throughout the dungeon. Stone screeches against stone and drowns out the sound of prisoners moaning.

I push thoughts of my fracturing mental state aside. As long as the voices aren't telling me to become a serial killer, dealing with their cause can wait until later – until after the gorgons are rescued and the world is saved.

I move to the edge of the moat to peer over, just in time to see the bridge from my vision lift up into view. Up, through the smoke, it glides until it's level with the ground.

Gretchen looks at me, her silver eyes full of appreciation and gratitude.

That stuns me more than anything else. Gretchen isn't one to give thanks easily. She'd rather do it all on her own and tell everyone else to go to Hades. That I could do something to make her grateful is kind of amazing.

In this moment, I truly feel like her sister.

I smile back.

Then she's running across the bridge, shouting her mentor's name. Sillus and the golden maiden hurry after her, and I'm about to follow until I see Thane hanging back.

"I'll stay here," he says. "In case there's trouble."

"Thank you." I slip my arms around his neck before he can protest. "I couldn't have done that without your help."

He shrugs, like he's uncomfortable with the compliment. But he hugs me back. He's almost as closed off as Gretchen, so this is a major victory. It's amazing how good that makes me feel.

"You're welcome."

"I—" I pull the image from the second part of my vision into my mind. "I couldn't see Sthenno. I tried to go further, to look for her, but it was too vague. Just a shadowy hallway."

"You went after a lot for one vision," he says. "You'll get better with practice."

I can only hope. If this is my power, my magical legacy from our ancient ancestor, I want to be able to use it to its full potential.

"At least now I know *how* to practise. You knew just how to help me get the vision." I shake my head. "How?"

His entire body tenses. That small muscle along

114

his jawline clenches and unclenches. Every last syllable of his body language says this is an off-limits topic of conversation.

I don't believe in limits. I'm getting tired of having these questions and getting no answers.

"Are you even human?" I ask. A few weeks ago that would have been a sarcastic question. Now, I'm deadly serious.

His grey eyes flash. "Yes."

"But you're not *just* human," I push. "You're something more."

His jaw muscle tightens and doesn't release.

"You'd better go," he says, not looking at me. "Gretchen will need your help."

I study him for a moment longer, trying to find some clue about what's going on inside. He's conflicted, and maybe scared. Whatever he's hiding, now is not the time for me to dig it out.

I'm not usually patient, but I am determined. Eventually, he will tell me his secrets.

Without another word, I turn and follow my sister and our friends across the bridge.

CHAPTER 11

Gretchen

The layout of cells on the other side of the bridge is a freaking maze – another labyrinth of stone and steel – and with the soundproof shields down, the groans and growls of the prisoners echo throughout the entire chamber. Euryale is being held in the outer ring, but we have to wind our way through all the others – *past* all the others – to reach her cage on the far side.

Between these cells and those beyond the moat, there must be two hundred prisoners being chained and tortured. And from what the golden maiden says, there are other dungeons, other labyrinths of cells, just as full. It's horrifying. Whether they are guilty of some crime against the gods or are political prisoners like Ursula, the treatment is inhumane.

When I finally get to Euryale's cell, I see her crumpled and beaten, hanging from her shackles like a piece of meat. My stomach lurches. If I'd had anything to eat in the past few hours, I'd be heaving.

I step up to the door.

"Ursula!"

I can't hide the pain in my voice, not even from myself.

"We have to get her out," I say without turning around. "Now."

I wrap both hands around a steel pipe in the door and yank. The door rattles but doesn't budge. I yank again, pulling with every last ounce of my super strength. Two more pairs of hands appear alongside mine – pale ones and gleaming golden ones. Together, we grunt and pull, to no avail. The door stays solidly in place.

"It's no use," Greer says.

"Ursula," I shout, louder. "Euryale!"

She stirs, but only slightly. There's the barest hint of movement beneath her flowing garments. My breath huffs out in a relieved sigh. She's alive.

That's all the encouragement I need.

"The steel is too strong," the golden maiden says. "It will not yield."

"Then we do it the easy way." I tap at the metal plate that shields the locking mechanism. It looks like a standard, old-style prison lock. It's big, black, rusty and – hopefully – vulnerable to picking.

"How?" Greer asks.

"Basic military strategy," I explain. "Attack the most vulnerable spot. The lock."

I bend down, pull up the flap on one of my cargo pockets and pull out a multi-tool – one that's supposed to have a tool for every situation. I hope it lives up to the salesman's promise.

Flipping through the seven thousand accessories, I finally decide on the flathead screwdriver. I shove the point into the keyhole, wiggle it around and pray something happens. I've never had to pick a lock before. Monsters aren't usually hiding behind closed doors; I find them in the open, on crowded streets, or in back rooms and alleys, hunting somewhere with easy access.

Now I wish I'd developed the skill.

After several jerks and pulls and twists and curses, feeling nothing but the scrape of metal on immovable metal, I give the door a solid kick.

"How are we supposed to get in?" I hate feeling helpless. "How are we supposed to get her out?"

"We simply have to think this through," Greer says. "There must be a solution – something obvious that we just aren't seeing."

"Sillus help huntress."

I turn to see the little monkey emerging from the labyrinth, running towards me, his teeth bared in a huge grin.

"How?" I ask.

He jams his fist into the air.

There, dangling from his little furry hand, is a set of thick black keys.

"Where'd you get those?" I demand, snatching the keys from him.

He shrugs. "Sillus find."

Right. The unconscious dungeon guards.

"Nice thinking," I tell him.

His little monkey face beams.

I choose one of the big metal keys, shove it into the lock and turn. Nothing. I choose another. The third key finally works. With a heavy clank, I feel the lock mechanism roll over.

"Yes!"

Everyone cheers.

Leaving the key in the lock, I yank the door open and dash to my mentor's side.

"Ursula," I say gently, kneeling down at her side. "It's Gretchen. I'm here. You're safe."

She makes a sound.

"What's that?"

I lean down closer, until my ear is right next to her mouth.

"Not safe," she rasps. "Too dangerous."

Yes, the world around us is dangerous and we won't be safe until we're home, but I can't help but take a moment to look at my long-missing mentor. Seeing her in such an abused state hurts worse than the burn of monster venom in my bloodstream ever has.

"Leave," Ursula whispers.

Warning tingles down my spine as everything falls quiet. Silence in a place like this is never a good thing.

"We have to move," I command. "Now."

Squatting down, I slip one arm under Ursula's shoulders and the other under her knees. I stand too easily. She's lost a lot of weight.

"Why?" Greer asks, panic in her voice. "What's wrong?"

I turn to face her.

"You hear that?"

She tilts her head. "I don't hear anything."

"Exactly." I hold Ursula a little tighter. "This place just got deadly quiet."

"Time hurry," Sillus says.

Without bothering to agree, I take off through the maze, heading for the bridge. I hear the others following me, but I don't take time to check. If something is happening, we don't have a second to spare. Someone could be on the way to intercept us right now. With our luck, someone already is.

"Oh noes." Sillus skids to a stop as he emerges from the labyrinth first.

Stepping out behind him, I see what's waiting for us on the other side of the bridge: a group of soldiers, heavily armed with golden weapons. There are at least a dozen of them. They carry golden shields and wear golden helmets that clearly mark them as the Arms of Olympus.

I mutter a string of curses.

This is just what we needed.

"Where's Thane?" Greer whispers.

He stayed behind to guard the bridge, but here's the bridge being overrun by our enemies and Thane is nowhere in sight. Did he abandon us? Or did he set us up? I don't have time to wonder about his loyalty right now.

How are we going to get out of this?

Then, as I'm just about to formulate a plan, I see a flash of quiet movement behind the group of soldiers. It's Thane, coming out of some hiding spot in the shadows. He takes a strategic position that puts the soldiers between us and him. I know exactly what he has planned. The boy has tactical skills.

I quickly – and carefully – hand Ursula to the golden maiden, who nods in understanding. Stepping up to our end of the bridge, I shout across the moat, "What's the matter? Afraid to come over here and fight a girl?"

"You are no girl," one of the soldiers yells.

"Now that is downright insulting." I squat down and pull daggers from my Doc Martens. "Looks like I'll have to defend my honour."

I step onto the bridge, blades at the ready. I just need to draw them forward a few feet.

A deafening roar echoes up into the chamber from the hallway beyond, shaking the very stone I'm standing on. The noise startles the soldiers, who look up and around as if the space has come to life, and I take advantage of their distraction. I rush forward, grab the lead soldier in a choke hold and pull his back tight against my body.

With a dagger to his throat, he's not too eager to struggle.

"Looks like I caught the prize," I call out, taunting his soldiers as I back away, across the moat.

They whip round, and instinct – their desire to save their leader – overrides good sense. In a rush, they hurry towards me, out onto the bridge.

Right where I want them.

"No," their leader shouts.

But it's too late. With a quick jerk, I spin him out of my hold and send him sailing off the bridge, into the fiery moat below.

His soldiers realise their error and start to turn back, only to find Thane blocking them in from the other side. They're trapped. Between my daggers on this side and Thane's sword on the other, we quickly toss most of the soldiers off the narrow bridge. They don't have much room to manoeuvre, and Thane and I have the tactical advantage. The soldiers never stood a chance.

Still, Thane's swordplay is impressive. For an ordinary boy, he is holding his own – and then some – against Olympic soldiers like he belongs in this world. He's dispatched at least as many of them as I have.

When it's down to us and the last two, they look at each other before taking a crazy leap, following their comrades into the unknown before we can send them.

Panting with exertion, I meet Thane's gaze across the

span of the bridge. Neither of us says anything; a nod is all it takes to thank him. No question where his loyalty lies now, is there?

No, the question is, where the hell did he learn to fight like that? Not from his and Grace's parents, that's for sure. The boy has serious skills, but the interrogation will have to wait.

"Let's go," I shout to the group, who are already stepping onto the bridge. "Time to get out of here, before reinforcements show up."

I just hope Ursula's up to the task of autoporting us home. She's our only way out.

"What about Sthenno?" Greer asks.

I freeze in my tracks. I'd been so focused on getting out of here and getting Ursula to safety, I'd completely forgotten our other immortal aunt. She's somewhere in this horrible prison, too.

I shake my head. "I thought they were supposed to be in the same cell."

"In my first vision," Greer says, "they were. But when I sought out how to get to Euryale's cell, I tried to see where Sthenno is too. It wasn't a clear vision, but I'm sure she isn't in this part of the dungeon. I think she's down one of the other hallways."

I nod. "Let's stash Ursula somewhere safe, and then we'll start searching." Quickly, before our bad luck sends another obstacle our way.

The only safe hiding place is the closet where we hid from the Thespian dragon. I don't like the idea of leaving Ursula here with nothing to protect her, but we have to find Sthenno. We need her, too, and I'm not leaving her behind.

Besides, as weak as Ursula is right now, there's no way she's strong enough to autoport us home. She's barely conscious. We're stuck until she regains some of her strength.

I manage to get her to swallow a few gulps of water and one bite of an energy bar. She is already improving.

Eyes bleary but open, she says, "I told you not to come."

I smooth a hand over her greasy, dirty hair. "I know."

"Never did heed authority well," she says with a small grin.

That makes me smile.

"We have to go find Sthenno," I explain. "Then we can go home."

Her elegant brow pinches into a frown. "My sister?"

"Yes," I say. "Haven't you seen her?"

"No, not—" She hesitates. "I'm not certain. My memory is… incomplete."

"Don't worry about it," I insist. "We'll find her."

The look she gives me is so full of pride that I almost cry.

"I know you will."

Emotion tightens in my chest. We've never been much

for showing feelings, but I'm overwhelmed by a whole bunch of them right now. I don't have time for that. I need to shove them away until later.

I hand her another energy bar and a bag of trail mix.

"You eat up," I say. "Get your power back so we can get home."

She takes the food. "Hurry."

I nod in silent agreement.

Using one of Sillus's other keys, I lock the door behind me when we leave. Trapping her in isn't ideal, but keeping other creatures out – even if only for the space of time it takes them to go find another set of keys – is worth it.

Thane and the golden maiden are standing guard while Greer digs through her backpack.

"Let's start searching," I say, pocketing the keys. "Sillus, you go back over every inch of the area where we found Ursula. Check every cell, double-check them, just in case there's some magic disguising her."

"Yes, huntress miss." He gives me a silly salute.

"The rest of us will spread out and search the rest of the dungeon. Those other corridors." I drop to a squat and pull a handful of flashlights out of my backpack. "Maybe there are other holding cells, other areas where they might be keeping her."

I don't like the idea of us splitting up, but I like the idea of wasting time even less. The faster we get out of here, the better.

"I have not seen the gorgon before," the golden maiden says. "Can you describe her?"

I shrug and look at Greer.

"She looks a lot like Euryale," she says, "but with blonde hair."

"And she's wearing a light grey suit," Thane adds.

Greer's eyes widen.

I'm feeling full of questions myself, but later.

"Good," I say. "Anything else we need to know?"

Greer shakes her head, like she's regrouping.

"We can use these" – she hands everyone a safety whistle on a lanyard – "to signal each other."

Clearly, she doesn't like the idea of separating, either.

Thane and the golden maiden slip theirs over their necks, and I do the same. Sillus swings his wide, letting the cord wrap around his waist until the whistle hits him in the backside, then swings it back around the other way. I ignore him.

"Good idea," I tell Greer. "When you find something, whistle once." I demonstrate with a sharp trill. "If you find trouble, whistle twice. If you don't find anything, then meet back here and wait for everyone else."

Hopefully Sthenno is being held in *this* dungeon, and not one of the others somewhere else on Olympus.

Everyone nods. Greer doesn't offer any argument or suggestion, which I take as a sign that she realises how serious our situation is. Maybe she's learning.

"And don't draw attention to Ursula's location," I warn as I hand flashlights to Greer, Thane and the golden maiden. "If someone or something comes, hide elsewhere."

I want all of us out of here, safe and in one piece. That includes Ursula.

Then, with my instructions delivered, we separate. Sillus heads back to the maze of cells to start his search. The rest of us each take different hallways. As my boots pound down the darkened corridor, I flick on my flashlight and cross my mental fingers, hoping that the search for Sthenno goes fast and easy. That would be nice for a change.

CHAPTER 12
Greer

As Gretchen and Thane disappear down other hallways, I hesitate before moving. I might as well try to make my power more useful. I need the practice. Eyes closed, I focus, searching for a feeling – anything that will tell me which hallway holds Sthenno.

"Sugar," I whisper when nothing comes to mind. But then, as I open my eyes, I see a faint glowing light in one of the hallways – one not chosen by the others. It's just a faint blue glow, but I figure it's as good a sign as any.

Ignoring the dull throb in my skull – I rarely get headaches, but lately I have had almost constant pain – I start forward, keeping to the side, near the wall. If anything shows up, maybe I will see it in the dim light before it sees me in the shadows.

My hallway turns a corner, and what light there is all but disappears. It's blacker even than the abyss; I can't even see my hand in front of my face.

I tighten my grip on the flashlight Gretchen gave me. Dare I risk the glow?

Then I remember a lesson from my self-defence

seminar. If I'm shining the light, I'll blind my opponents. I will be able to see them, but they won't see me through the beam.

I have to take that chance. Sthenno might be captive in here.

Turning the flashlight over in my palm, I take a deep breath and hold it as I push the button.

Light fills the space, which is just another hallway – another grey stretch of corridor with doors lining either side, like something from a psychiatric hospital.

I shake my head. What had I been expecting? Monsters hanging from the ceiling?

Doors are a good sign. That means prisoners might actually be held here.

I walk over to the nearest door. It's large and metal, a battleship grey devoid of anything resembling real colour. At face level there is a window.

There is no glass in the opening, just a grid of steel bars.

I hear growling from within.

"This can't be good," I mutter.

Then I catch myself. I never mutter. I never back down. That is how I've succeeded at everything in my life, and it's how I will succeed in this world of mythology.

Being a good Morgenthal, I suck in a sharp breath, straighten my spine and point the flashlight into the window.

The flashlight clatters to the floor as I leap back in shock. The creature inside is almost as large as the small cell – a big mass of clumping fur, sharp teeth and drool, something like a werewolf in a horror movie.

"Definitely not Sthenno."

My headache builds and I take a moment to rub my temples, hoping to keep the symptoms in check. I seriously wish I'd thought to bring some painkillers.

I retrieve the flashlight, quieten my shaking hand and move on to the next cell, and the next, and every last one until the very end. Then I start back down the hall on the other side.

Every room on the hall is occupied, filled with some creature or another. Most are more animal than human and only snarl and snap when they see my light. Some are almost half human, either on the bottom or the top. They don't look any happier to see me.

I've peered into every window, making sure Sthenno isn't within, and am about to concede defeat and return to the meeting place when my light flashes over a small reflective surface back at the far end of the hall.

I sigh.

"This is the place in the movie," I whisper, "when the audience yells for the heroine to run."

I don't have the luxury of choice.

Tracing my tongue over my teeth, I let my fangs drop as I make my way back down the hall. My headache grows into a persistent pulse, a throbbing pressure against my skull.

The reflecting surface, it turns out, is a tiny metal door sunk into the stone at knee height. About a foot wide and a few inches high, it's hinged along the top so an object can be slipped inside without risk of losing fingers or an inhabitant escaping, like an in-the-door mail slot.

"Can't turn back now," I tell myself.

Then, my hands shaking with fear of the unknown, I squat down on the balls of my feet and reach for the metal door.

It squeaks on its hinges, like it hasn't been used in a long time. Either the cell beyond is empty, or the thing inside hasn't been fed in ages.

I carefully push the door up and shine my light inside.

The opening is so small that at first I can't see anything but the glow of the beam on the opposite wall. I move the flashlight to one side of the slot and manoeuvre myself into position to get a better view.

I swing the beam around until I see her.

Sitting in the corner, back to the wall, wrists draped over her knees, her dove grey suit marred by what looks like dirt and blood, is Sthenno. Our immortal aunt. Grace's school counsellor. The therapist who at one time banished visions of monsters from my mind.

For an instant, I let myself indulge in the fantasy of having her do it again. I don't even know if she could, but there's a chance. The question is… would I want her to? After everything that's happened in the past few weeks – monsters and sisters and ancient prophecies – do I want to make it all go away?

The idea is tempting.

But, as any one of my friends or my smooth-talking ex can attest, I never succumb to temptation. And I never shirk a responsibility.

My light hits her eyes and she winces, holding a hand up to shield her eyes.

"Sthenno?" I ask.

"Who's there?" She squints, trying to see through the light.

"It's Greer," I say. "I'm Grace's sister. One of the triplets."

She's across the room and at the metal slot in a flash. And I thought Euryale was supposed to be the supernaturally fast one.

"Are you all here?" she asks. "All three of you?"

"No, Grace had to go back." I kneel down, glad I decided to wear my least attractive jeans. I'll be lucky if they survive all the wear and tear I'm putting them through on this expedition.

"Good," she says. "That's good."

"Why are you in here?" I ask. "Why aren't you in a cell like Euryale?"

Her laugh is full of pride. "The shackles and steel bars were no match for my strength." She demonstrates by yanking the metal flap off its hinges. "I broke out of three cells before they decided to contain me in here. If there was any exposed hardware, I'd have broken out of this place too."

"That's really—"

A sharp pain pierces my skull, right above my forehead. I rub at the spot, trying to do something – anything – to stop the pain. My migraines are usually triggered by bright lights; clearly not the case here.

I just have to push through the pain.

The pain is only the beginning, the male voice says.

No, not now.

Leave her, the woman says.

You dare defy me? he roars. *You dare violate the binds of ritual?*

No more than you fight the prophecy itself, she throws back. *You mock your own rules and—*

"Enough!" I shout. Hands pressing on my temples, I try to push the voices out of my mind. "Leave me alone!"

I clench my eyes shut, waiting for the argument to continue, but there's nothing but silence – blissful silence.

When I open my eyes, Sthenno is frowning at me through the small opening.

"You touched the pendant," she demands, "didn't you?"

She sounds furious.

"Yes," I reply, wary at her tone. "I had to. Gretchen

went into the abyss and we didn't know how to get her out. I had a vision that told me the pendant would give me the answers. And it did. If I hadn't touched the pendant, she wouldn't have—"

"Damn it! You are a walking trap," she says. "You'll get us all killed or captured."

"No," I argue. "We're going to rescue you." The pain is getting worse; my vision is starting to blur. I reach for the whistle hanging around my neck and lift it to my lips. "We already have Euryale safe. We're going to take you home."

Pain slices through my forehead. I suck in a breath to blow the signal.

As the ear-piercing shrill of the whistle echoes down the stone hallway, off the metal doors and into the dungeon beyond, my mind explodes like someone took an axe to my skull.

"Greer!" I hear Sthenno cry out as I collapse to the ground.

I don't even fight the black as I am yanked into another vision.

I am in a white room. It is made of marble, like the halls of Mount Olympus, and decorated with laurel branches and ravens. In the corner, a stand holds a golden instrument that looks like a miniature harp.

"Welcome, young huntress."

I spin to face the source of the familiar voice, the voice that has been whispering in my mind. It is a man – no, more than a man. A god. I don't know how I know; I just know.

"Who – who are you?"

I never stammer. But, then again, I've never come face to face with a god – not even in a vision.

He smiles, his beautiful face transformed into an angelic expression. "You do not know?" His smile fades, replaced by a scowl. "How charming."

I take it all in – the ravens, the lyre, the too beautiful face.

"You're Apollo."

He applauds softly. Mockingly.

"After all the time we've spent together, I would be hurt if you didn't know."

"Time together?" I shake my head. "We've never met."

"Not formally, I suppose." He studies me. "But I have been watching you closely since you touched my pendant."

"Watching me?" The air rushes out of my lungs.

If he has been watching me, he has been watching my sisters, watching our progress. No wonder enemies keep showing up everywhere we go. Apollo knows just where to send them.

Remembering the sensation of being pulled out of my body and pulled into this vision, I ask, "Why did you bring me here?"

"I thought we should have a chat. Please" – he gestures at the space in front of me, and a chair appears – "have a seat."

Something feels very wrong about this situation. I shouldn't be here. I shouldn't be having a conversation with a god while in a vision. They shouldn't work like this.

I slowly shake my head. "No thank you." I straighten my spine. "What do you want from me?"

"What do I want?" he asks, his voice deceptively sweet. "I want you and your sisters to walk away. I want you to let the door seal forever so my family has *something* else to talk about over dinner."

In a flash, Apollo is right in front of me, mere inches away.

"Since you do not seem inclined to give up," he says, "then I want you dead."

"You will have to find us first," I say with more bravado than I feel. My heart pounds like an earthquake in my chest. "You cannot kill what you cannot catch."

"You cannot hide." He smiles, and the expression knocks my breath away. "You and your companions have fought children until now. The wrath of Olympus is in motion against you. Not even one of my sister's wayward soldiers can save you. You will not know what hit you."

His sister's soldier? What does that mean? He is only trying to confuse and frighten me, and, well... I do not frighten easily. I've never faced down a god before, but I dig down deep and draw out all my courage.

"We are strong," I insist. "We can take whatever you dish out."

His smile is full of wickedness.

"And we will kill you," he replies. "You, your sisters, your friends and family... one by one, until no one who even remembers the Keys remains."

My hand strikes out without hesitation. My palm stings, the pain as real as if the slap had occurred in real life, not only in my mind.

And Apollo's rage is just as tangible.

That's my girl, the woman's voice says.

He reaches out to strike me, hard and fast, a blow that I'm sure will leave me bruised and bloody.

Not so fast, wolf god.

I'm gone before his hand can connect with my cheek, pulled back out of the vision, just as violently as I was pulled in.

CHAPTER 13

Grace

Avoiding the elevator, I run up the stairs to my floor, taking them two at a time. I don't have to look back to know that Milo is keeping up. As I step out into the hall, I can see that the door to my apartment is open – wide open. This can't be a good sign.

Milo follows me down the dark wood-panelled hall, but when we get to the front door, he pulls me back by the shoulder and steps in first. He pauses in the doorway, and I stand on my tiptoes to peer over him.

Everything looks normal.

"Are they gone?" I whisper.

"Let me check," he says. "Stay here."

I smile. The old Grace would have gladly waited in the hall while the boy went inside to search, but the new Grace has courage and confidence – and fangs.

As Milo moves left, through the dining room and into the kitchen beyond, I scan the living room on my way to the back hall. I duck a head in my bedroom, snatching my phone off the nightstand and slipping it into my pocket, and then check Thane's room and the bathroom we share. Milo meets me in the hall outside my parents' room.

He frowns but doesn't say anything.

Together, we walk into the last room of the apartment. Empty.

"They're gone," I say, defeated.

There is no sign that any kind of violence occurred here – no blood, nothing broken or disturbed. The monsters who were after me are gone. They must have taken Nick with them.

The earlier scene in the apartment plays through my mind. The boss and his goons hadn't looked too happy with Nick calling the shots. Nick threatened to kill me – and I'd thought he was betraying *us*. He actually betrayed *them*. I don't think they treat traitors like him very well.

"He's gone," I whisper. "He saved my life by sacrificing himself. They'll kill him for sure. Gretchen is going to hate me."

"Grace," Milo says.

I jump at the sound of his gentle voice. I was so lost in thought I'd forgotten he was here. Turning slowly to face him, I can't keep the despair off my face.

He lays his hands on my shoulders and ducks his head down to look me in the eyes.

"What's going on?" he asks.

I shake my head, either because I can't tell him or because I can't speak at all. I can't just confess what's going on. Besides the fact that humans aren't supposed to know that monsters and mythology are real and running wild on the streets of San Francisco, I don't *want* him to know.

I like Milo. I mean, I *really* like him, and I don't want to scare him away.

I don't want him to see me as anything other than an ordinary girl.

So I look away, unable to meet his steady gaze.

"Clearly you're freaked out," he says, dropping his hands. "I am, too, after you materialised out of thin air onto my soccer field and then you told your parents the monsters found your house—"

My gaze flies up. I hadn't even been thinking when I said that on the phone. I'd been totally intent on making sure my parents stayed safe; I hadn't realised Milo was listening.

"So why don't I go grab us a couple of sodas from the fridge," he continues, as if the world around him were still perfectly normal. "We can sit down at the dining table, and then you can tell me what's going on."

He turns and walks away before I can respond.

My heart races.

As much as I don't want to, as much as I think it's a horrible idea, he already knows too much. Right now I have no one else to trust. I have to keep my parents safe, my sisters and my brother are back in the abyss –

or, hopefully, by now, on Mount Olympus – and the supernatural boy who came with me to help is now a prisoner of my enemies. Milo is all I have.

As I sit across the dining table from Milo, my courage vanishes.

It seems like such a small thing, only a few words. But when it comes to actually getting them out… My mouth goes dry.

Our relationship, whatever it is, is still so new – just as new as the world of myth being part of my life. I remember how hard it was for me to process, and it's a part of me. How on earth will Milo understand?

"Listen, Grace," he says, not looking at me. He has his forearms braced on the table, fidgeting with a flyer for an outdoor movie series Mom left out. "We haven't known each other very long, so I get it if you don't want to tell me."

Oh, but that's not true. I do want to. I hate keeping secrets – I'm terrible at it. I want to tell Milo everything. I'm just afraid of what will happen once I do.

"You should know that I like you a lot," he says, not looking up from the bright yellow paper.

My heart does a little flip-flop.

"And that I'm a pretty open-minded guy," he continues.

"I—" I stare down at my hands. "This is a really hard thing to explain."

When I look up, he's carefully folding the flyer into smaller and smaller shapes – first a square, and then a triangle, and then a smaller triangle.

Two things connect in my mind. When I saw the unicorn in the abyss, I knew I'd thought about one recently. I'd chalked it up to something I read or Gretchen mentioning the one she met, but now I really remember.

Milo once gave me an origami unicorn.

The hair on the back of my neck stands up. I think about Nick suddenly appearing in Gretchen's life and turning out to be more than human. There's something special about Thane, too. Maybe Milo is more than he seems. Maybe he and Thane didn't become friends by accident. Maybe his interest in me isn't purely romantic. At least that would make sense.

"You make origami," I say dumbly.

He shrugs. "Yeah. When I'm nervous."

"You're nervous?"

I almost laugh. I'm the one on the verge of telling the boy I like that I'm a freak creature from mythology, and he's nervous. Of course, seeing a girl appear out of nowhere and hearing her say that monsters are after her is pretty scary. He probably thinks I'm mental.

"The other day," I say, "when we were at lunch, you made an origami unicorn. Why? Why a unicorn?"

He glances up at me through his thick lashes. "Honestly?"

I nod.

He holds up the piece of paper he's been meticulously folding. He tugs on both ends, and the paper pops up into the shape of a unicorn. "It's the only thing I know how to make."

This time I do laugh.

For a second, I'd started to believe maybe Milo had given me the unicorn as a hint that he's part of this mythological world, too. Maybe I was hoping that was the case. But it was only a coincidence – just my frightened brain trying to see a connection that isn't there.

I take the unicorn from his outstretched palm.

The relief that Milo is a normal boy – with a normal interest in me – relaxes me. For some reason, that makes this easier.

"You're sure you want to hear the truth?" I ask.

"Without a doubt."

I hope he still feels that way in a few minutes.

"In case you didn't already know," I begin, "Thane and I are adopted…"

Milo watches, focused, as I explain everything. I tell him about my sisters, about our mythological heritage, about the door and the legacy and the brewing war that might turn San Francisco into a battleground.

"One group," I say, "wants to stop us before we can open the door. We think Zeus, Hera, Apollo and a few other Olympians are on that side."

He doesn't flinch when I start naming gods. I'm impressed.

"Another group wants to take us out after the door is open." I lower my gaze as I trace figure eights on the tabletop. "That's most of the monsters. We don't know who else is on their side. Maybe Hades and Ares because, well, they like to stir up trouble."

He shifts in his seat, and I glance up to see if he's ready to bolt. Not yet.

"We're kind of caught in the middle," I say, describing the third and final faction. "A handful of gods, spirits and even some monsters want us to open the door and guard it like it was meant to be guarded." I shrug. "That group is the smallest one."

I lay it all out for him – every last detail. Through it all, Milo watches me intently.

Then I tell him about Nick being taken prisoner and my mission to find my birth mother.

"I managed to find her name in our adoption records, and I wasn't in that big of a rush to find her. But now our enemies are trying to kill her," I explain, "because they think that will destroy our powers."

"Powers?"

Oh yeah. That.

"Um, I can kind of…" I can't think of an easy way to tell him about autoporting. I'll have to show him.

Closing my eyes, I focus on the space behind his chair.

There's a light and then, when I open my eyes, I'm looking at the back of his head.

"I do this," I say as I tap him on the shoulder.

He spins around in his seat, his pale eyes wide and unblinking. He stares at me for several long, torturous seconds before he says, "So you *did* appear out of nowhere on the soccer field."

"Yeah," I say, "I did."

I pop back to the other side of the table, back into my chair. Milo turns back around to face me, his features frozen with shock.

He finally blinks and swipes his tongue across his lips. "Grace, I…"

I close my eyes. This is the part where he decides that he didn't see what he just saw, that I'm nuts, completely delusional – dangerously so, probably, since I'm talking about biting monsters and coming war – and that he should be as far, far, far away from me as he can possibly get. Like in Japan, or on Mount Everest.

"It's okay," I say, pushing back from the table. "I know it sounds crazy. Believe me, I know."

I start to stand, but Milo's hand wraps gently around my arm before I can push up.

"Wait."

I sit, frozen, staring at the spot where he holds my wrist.

Then his other hand slides forward, under mine,

so I'm sandwiched between his palms. I look up, uncertain but hopeful.

"It does sound crazy," he says, his pale eyes watching me, "but you're not. You're as far from crazy as anyone I've ever met."

I swallow hard, waiting for the other shoe to drop.

"So if you're telling me this is true" – he lifts his brows – "then it must be true."

I shake my head. "Are you…" Surely I heard him wrong. "Have you lost your mind?"

"Maybe." He stands and tugs me up and forward. As he leans over the table, he whispers, "Definitely."

His lips are soft and warm and everything I need right now. They're a gentle connection to something real, something not dangerous or deadly or out to kill me, my sisters, or my friends – something… perfect.

When he pulls back, his eyes are glowing – like a normal, excited human glow, not a demon monster from the abyss or anything.

"Now," he says with a dimpled smile, "what's the plan?"

CHAPTER 14

Gretchen

When I hear the whistle, I run.

There was only one short burst of sound, which means someone found Sthenno, and it echoed all the way through the dungeon.

My hallway was a dud – nothing but empty cages and cells filled with crates of supplies or something, most of them with bright yellow Xs spray-painted on the sides. No gorgons hidden there. No prisoners at all.

When I get back to the fork where Thane, Greer, the golden maiden and I split up, I pause to listen for another whistle burst. I hear nothing except the echoing sound of booted feet running on stone. I back myself up against the nearest wall and wait until I see Thane emerge from his hallway.

"Was that you?" I ask.

He shakes his head.

The golden maiden arrives, looking just as expectant.

Thane and I simultaneously say, "Greer."

"You stay with Ursula," I tell the golden maiden. I toss her the keys. "She needs to be ready."

Thane and I take off running down the hall my sister chose.

Behind us, I hear metal clanking against stone – a whistle dragging on the floor – and Sillus calling out, "Wait, huntress wait."

I don't stop.

"Hush, little one," I hear the golden maiden say as I race out of earshot.

Greer's hallway is dark, with no torches or lights or magical whatevers to illuminate it, but there is a low beam of light spraying across the floor at the far end of the hall – her flashlight on the ground. I break into a sprint.

Thane beats me to her.

He skids to the ground on his knees right next to her head, reaches under her shoulders and cradles her in his lap. I kneel at her side.

"Greer," he says, gently shaking her. "Greer, wake up."

She doesn't move.

A scratching clank announces Sillus's arrival. "Oh no, huntress."

I ignore him, scanning my gaze over Greer, looking for an injury or a wound. She doesn't look hurt, and there are no signs of—

"Gretchen?"

I twist around at the sound of my name, searching for the source. There are doors on either side of the hall, so I grab Greer's flashlight off the ground and peer inside.

"Down here," the voice says. "The door is hidden."

"Here huntress," Sillus cries out. "Look here."

I spin back, the flashlight beam swinging back and forth as I follow the direction of his excited gesture. Then I see it, just a couple of feet off the ground, in the middle of the wall that ends the hallway: fingers reaching out and wagging at me from a narrow opening. Non-monster fingers.

"It's me," the voice says. "Sthenno."

"Sthenno," I whisper, relief washing through me. I drop to my knees in front of the opening. "What happened?"

"I'll explain that later," she says, "once we're out of here. Apollo will have raised the alarm. The soldiers won't be long now."

I scan my gaze over the wall around the opening, tracing the beam of light over every stone, every joint of mortar. There is no sign of a door at all, let alone a way to open one. It's like she's sealed in.

"How?" I ask. "There's no door."

"One of the stones is a false front." She gestures to the left of the door. "Somewhere over there. It pushes in to release the catch."

With the flashlight in one hand, I start running my other hand over the wall. I push on every stone, waiting for one that gives way. Push after push, and nothing.

Finally, I get to the smallest stone – only about four inches square – and when I press on its surface it sinks back into the wall.

"Got it," I exclaim.

The words are no sooner out of my mouth than I hear a metal-on-metal sound and the entire wall around the opening – maybe four feet across and six feet high – pops out from the rest. Thane gets to his feet, Greer hanging limp in his arms, and moves them out of the way. I try to get a handhold on the stone edge to pull the door the rest of the way open.

"Stand back," Sthenno says.

Sillus scrambles to my side.

I find a rough spot where I can get a grip. "I've almost—"

The door moves suddenly, swinging open like a tetherball on a string. It knocks me a few feet to the left, but I manage to keep my balance.

Sthenno appears in the doorway, dirty and bedraggled, but otherwise intact. That was an impressive display of strength.

"We must hurry," she says, stepping into the hall. "They know you're here, and they're coming."

We run down the hall, the light from Greer's flashlight guiding our way. Sillus's whistle drags on the ground, but I don't yell at him to pick it up. We'll be gone before it matters.

The golden maiden is waiting for us at the fork, a serious look on her face.

Gesturing at us to be quiet, she hurries to meet us.

She whispers, "There are soldiers guarding the closet door."

"Ursula?"

"They know someone is inside," she says, "but the door is locked. They have sent someone to retrieve a key."

Hugging the wall, I move to the end of the hall and peer around the corner. There are only a few of them, but they are bigger than and just as armed as their friends who took a dip in the moat earlier. It's only a matter of time before they open the door. Ursula is so weak, she's virtually helpless. We have to get the soldiers away and us back home.

"Maybe," I say, thinking out loud, "if we—"

"As soon as they are gone," the golden maiden says, "get to the closet and get home."

Then, before I can ask her what she means, she's stepping out of the hallway and calling out to the gathered soldiers.

"Great Zeus," one of them says when he sees her. "It's a golden maiden."

"There hasn't been one on Olympus for centuries," another says.

A third grins. "Not since Hephaestus threatened to melt them all down for their insubordination."

"Those are the lies he spread," she mutters quietly. The golden maiden places herself between the soldiers and the staircase that leads back up to the shining halls of Olympus. "What was his offered bounty again?"

"A sword that never misses its mark," one shouts.

"And, as I recall," she says, with a teasing tone, "a helm of immortality."

In a glint of gold, she's racing across the hallway and disappearing up the stairs.

The soldiers chase after her, abandoning their posts for the promise of reward. She's fast; I'm sure she can outrun them. I *hope* she can.

We don't have time to wait around to find out.

The golden maiden has bought us a few precious minutes, a narrow window of opportunity. I rush to the closet door and unlock it. Ursula steps out, looking far more like herself. Guess I come by my fast healing honestly.

She looks at her sister. "Are we too late?"

Sthenno shakes her head. "But we must hurry."

"I'm not sure I have the strength."

Sthenno steps up to her and places a palm on either side of her face. "I shall give you the strength."

"What about her powers?" Thane asks. "Are they still tethered?"

Sthenno studies him appraisingly. I can't guess her judgement.

"No," Sthenno says. "Once free from the cell, her powers are released."

"Hurry," Ursula says. "Everyone gather close. Make sure you are touching one of us."

I start to pocket the dungeon keys, but something stops me.

"Give me a sec," I call out over my shoulder as I head down the hall towards the maze of cells.

"Gretchen," Sthenno shouts. "We haven't the time."

I don't stop to argue. They won't leave without me, and this will only take a moment.

Back in the vast, smoke-filled room, I hurry to the cell of the man who'd talked to me earlier. He looks up as I toss the keys into his cell.

"Everyone deserves a trial," I say.

I don't wait for a response before sprinting back to the group.

Sthenno scowls at me, but we'll have that discussion later.

Sillus jumps onto my back as I wrap a hand around her forearm. I can feel power – strength – surging through her beneath the fabric of her jacket. Thane steps to my side, Greer still cradled in his arms. He turns to press his shoulder against Ursula's.

I'm not convinced that's enough, so I grab Greer's hand with my free one.

"It will not come." Ursula's voice is weak, and she sounds like she's given up.

"It will, sister," Sthenno says. "Concentrate."

Ursula opens her eyes. "It is no use. I am too weak."

I'm not sure what scares me the most: the threat of

our enemies coming back for us, or the defeat in Ursula's grey eyes. Since that day four years ago when she pulled me off the street, talked me out of the warehouse I was calling home, and gave me a bed, a future and a destiny, she's been nothing but strong – nothing but certain that I could succeed in whatever I tried.

To see her give up like this ignites a fire in me.

"The hell you are," I shout.

She looks at me, eyes wide.

"You are going to get us out of here," I say. "You're going to autoport us the hell out of this mountain. Right now."

Her grey eyes light up and I see the first spark of hope – of belief.

She closes her eyes again, focusing, and I tighten my grip on Sthenno's arm. I channel whatever powers I have into Ursula. Together, we can do anything.

The bright light is already blinding me before I remember to tell her not to autoport us to the loft.

When the world stops swirling, I open my eyes. We're standing in the hollow shell of what used to be our home. The building still smells like barbecue and burnt rubber.

Releasing my grip on Sthenno and Greer, I say, "I might have forgotten to mention that—"

Ursula collapses to the ground.

"Ursula!"

"We must get her to the healer," Sthenno says. "Who has a vehicle?"

"I do," I say. "But not here."

My car is halfway across town, parked in front of Greer's house.

"Where is the healer?" Thane asks. "Greer needs help, too."

Sthenno looks at Greer, frowning with concern. "I am afraid," she says, "that a healer cannot help her."

The muscles in Thane's jaw clench. If I didn't know Sthenno was the gorgon with super strength – like me – I'd be worried for her health. Thane looks like he wants to destroy something, or someone.

I know the feeling.

"I'll go get my car." I glance at our two unconscious companions. "It will take me a while. Maybe twenty minutes."

"There is no time," Sthenno says. "Can you carry your sister?"

"Of course," I reply without hesitation. Sillus climbs off my back.

Sthenno smiles like a proud teacher. "And I can carry mine. We can be at the healer's in a matter of minutes."

I reach for Greer, but Thane holds her out of range. "I have her."

Our eyes meet and, for a moment, I feel like we're going to have a stare-down. Then his look softens, and his brows dip just a little, turning his expression into a plea. I don't have to be a social genius to know what that means.

"Fine," I say, pulling the monkey back onto my shoulders so he won't slow us down. "Let's get moving. Sthenno, you can lead the way."

The healer is in a tiny storefront in Russian Hill, a short uphill trek from the loft. Unlike the oracle's abandoned-looking shop, this place is all lights and neon; only a plastic 'Closed' sign on the door gives a go-away message.

Sthenno knocks on the door.

The painted notices in the window invite customers to get acupuncture, acupressure, massage, facials and aura readings inside. A glowing neon sign advertises aromatherapy. There is a special discount – free aura reading with the purchase of six acupressure sessions.

"Who is this quack?" I ask. "How can they help us?"

Sthenno looks evenly at me. "This quack," she intones, "is a child of Panacea, a goddess of healing."

My cheeks burn, and I try to disguise my embarrassment with cooperation. "Oh, that's good, then."

When the door swings open, I want to take back my words.

"Sorry," the short, wiry man says, "we're—"

When he sees Sthenno, his jaw drops.

"Gorgon," he says, inclining his head, "you are most welcome."

He steps back and waves us inside. Sthenno goes in first, carrying Ursula in her arms as if my mentor weighs nothing. I wave Thane in before me, and Sillus and I bring up the rear.

The healer takes one look at the two unconscious bodies and says, "Come this way."

We follow him through the space, into a large room in the back with twin massage tables set up in the centre. It smells like herbs and essential oils, and the air is filled with music that sounds like the soundtrack to some tragic movie where everyone dies.

"Lay them down," he says, walking over to a stereo sitting on the counter and punching off the music. "What happened?"

"Euryale is but weakened," Sthenno exclaims. "She autoported us from Olympus while her energy stores were still quite low."

The healer pumps liquid sanitizer onto his hands and then walks over to Ursula. He runs his hands around her, not touching her – his palms hover just above the surface of her body. When he gets to her wrists, he swirls his hands in small circles. She groans and tries to sit up.

"Hold still, gorgon," he says to her in the gentle voice of a therapist or kindergarten teacher.

He crosses to the cabinet, pulls open one of the bottom drawers and takes out a small brown vial with a black top. Unscrewing the cap, he squeezes the bulb on the top, drawing up a dropper full of orange liquid. Returning to Ursula's wrists, he squeezes one drop on first her left and then her right. He replaces the cap and then proceeds to rhythmically rub the stuff into her wrists.

"This nectar of Iaso will restore her," he says. "She will need to rest for a few hours. When she wakes, she will be healed."

"Thank you, friend," Sthenno says. She sounds relieved.

"What about Greer?" Thane asks.

Sthenno studies him. Maybe she sees the same thing I saw in his eyes when he told me he could carry my sister here. He cares about Greer. They may not have known each other for long, but he has feelings for her.

Sometimes it doesn't take much time. I haven't known Nick for long, but I still dived into the abyss to save him.

Sthenno turns to the healer. "These are my…" She glances at me, like she's trying to figure out how to define our relationship. "Nieces."

There are too many "greats" in there to keep track of, so I suppose "niece" is simpler.

"Your nie—" The healer's eyes widen. "Oh, wonder of wonders. They are of the Key Generation?"

Sthenno only stares at him.

The healer turns his attention to me. "Are you?" When I nod, his old face cracks into the widest grin. "Such miraculous news. The rumours are true."

"Yeah, it's great," I say. "But right now my sister could use your help."

He glances at Greer and then back at me. "Of course, of course."

He turns to stand over Greer's table, muttering to himself.

For several minutes, he pokes and prods at Greer. She doesn't stir, doesn't react, doesn't even wince in pain. That she's not hurting is good, I guess, but my heart is racing. She's so… still. The longer he evaluates her, the higher my blood pressure goes.

But it's when he finally places his hands over her scalp that I really panic.

"Oh dear," he says with a heavy dose of worry in his voice.

"What?" I ask. "What's wrong?"

"Am I correct that she has the second sight?" he asks.

Sthenno answers, "Yes. She has Medusa's power."

"That is what I was afraid of." He turns to face me, frowning. "Your sister is in an astral lock."

Now it's my turn to frown. "What does that mean?"

"It means her consciousness is anchored in a vision," he explains. "When beings with second sight seek a piece of the future, they journey to the astral plane. In ordinary circumstances, the visit is short and uneventful – there and back without incident. With the power of a god magnifying her access, her mind can be overwhelmed by the sheer volume of information, not unlike a computer trying to process more data than it has the capacity to handle."

"What can we do?" Thane asks.

"Very little," the healer says. "With adequate rest, however, she will return to her body."

I sigh with relief. "Good," I say. "That's good."

"Why is this happening?" Thane asks. "Is it a normal side effect of her powers?"

The healer shakes his head. "I'm afraid not."

"Then what?" I demand.

"She has become a beacon of Apollo," Sthenno answers for him.

Sillus gasps.

Thane curses, multiple times.

"A beacon of Apollo?" I echo. "What does that—"

Oh, no. Now I remember. When Nick and I found the pendant of Apollo in the oracle's storefront, he explained what would happen if Greer came in contact with it. Because of her psychic ability, it would forge a direct connection between her and the god of prophecy. It would give Apollo a direct connection with her brain.

"She touched the pendant?" I guess.

"Yes," Sthenno answers.

"Why would she do that?" I demand. "She knew it was dangerous."

"She did it to save you," Sthenno replies. "She sought the knowledge necessary to rescue you from the abyss."

To save me? And all because I had to dive in after Nick. If I had known the cost...

I look around at the faces in the room, all studying me with varying degrees of sympathy – except for Thane, who just looks furious.

"Then we undo it," I say, matter-of-fact. Seems like an easy answer to me. "We disconnect her. Unplug her like a computer in a thunderstorm."

Sthenno and the healer exchange looks.

"It is not that easy," the healer says.

"There is no magical undo," Sthenno adds.

"Why not?" I argue. "The oracle did it. She left the pendant and abandoned her powers."

"The relationship between Apollo and his oracles is governed by ancient law and precise ritual," Sthenno explains. "Greer's connection with the god of prophecy was created outside the bonds of ritual. That is what makes her situation so dangerous."

"Apollo can do whatever he wants." Thane flexes his fingers, like he wants to strangle someone. Maybe Apollo. Maybe me.

Sthenno nods sadly. "He has unrestricted power in his connection to Greer."

That sounds bad. That sounds really bad.

"I don't accept this." I start pacing. "There must be a way."

"There is only one way to break this connection," the healer whispers.

"How's that?"

Sthenno shakes her head, and the healer drops his gaze.

"How?" I repeat.

Thane looks me straight in the eyes. "The human has to die."

CHAPTER 15

Greer

Everything around me is grey – hazy and misty and unclear. I feel like I'm jogging on the beach at Crissy Field when the fog rolls in off the Bay.

Only when I'm on Crissy Field, my head doesn't usually feel like it wants to explode into a supernova.

"Oh god," I moan.

"Greer," someone shouts.

"She's waking up!"

"Shhhhh," I complain, trying to lift a hand to my aching head, but my arm is tied down. Both of them are. "Stop yelling."

"We're not yelling," a voice says, not quite as loud as before.

"Where am I?" I ask. "Why are my hands tied down?"

"You're in the healer's room," the voice, which is starting to sound more and more like Gretchen, says. "And your hands aren't tied down. See?"

I feel something wrap around my wrist, and then one of my arms lifts up.

I try to pull it away, to guide it to my throbbing head, but it remains frozen as before.

163

"Don't try to move," Gretchen says, her voice getting softer. "The healer says your brain needs time to restart."

"Restart?" I try to remember… something, anything. The last thing I can recall is a beautiful white hall, more glorious than anything I'd seen before. It feels like a long time has passed since then. "Why?"

"That's not important right now," Gretchen says. "Just relax. Close your eyes, and everything will be back to normal when you wake up."

She sounds like she's trying to convince herself.

I don't always choose to do what Gretchen tells me to do – I hate following orders – but just this once…

The next time I wake up, my head still hurts like someone is crushing it in a vice, but my arms seem to work. I lift one to my forehead, expecting to find a bloody gash or pieces of skull sticking out. The way I hurt, I wouldn't be surprised if half my brain was missing. I'm disappointed when I only feel my normal, unmarred skin.

"Obviously we can't kill her," a hushed voice says. "What's plan B?"

My ears perk up.

"There is no plan B," another voice replies. "If she were stronger, had more training, perhaps she could withstand him for a time."

"We have to do something," a third voice whispers. "Anyone with Apollonian blood or one of his amulets can track her wherever she goes."

Squinting against the blinding light, I force one eyelid open just a fraction. I'm in what looks like a spa room; I've been in enough to recognise one on sight. There is soothing sage green paint on the walls, a stack of fluffy white towels on a rack by the door and a collection of massage oils and lotions on the counter. I'm also completely alone.

"We need to get to the safe house," the second voice says. "It is only a matter of time before they show up here."

"We stay here as long as we can," the first voice insists. "She needs the recovery time."

"Huntress recover."

The voices are coming from the other side of the dark wood door.

The conversation sounds important; I need to be out there with them.

I push my palm against the surface I'm lying on, trying to get myself in a sitting position. Fierce pain sparks from my wrist, up my arm and down my spine.

I cry out.

Wave after wave of pain washes through my body, and I scrunch up my face as my stomach coils in knots. I can't remember ever feeling this kind of pain. Of course, right now I can't remember much of anything. I force my brain to work. I remember the loft exploding, the mythological armies showing up at my tea, going into the abyss and then

Mount Olympus beyond that. The brilliant white hall.

"Sthenno," I whisper, my voice dry and cracked.

Memory slides into focus, and I remember.

I'd been searching for Sthenno, had just found her in some invisible cell and blown on the whistle to call Gretchen and Thane back to my side, when I blacked out – got pulled away. By Apollo.

As the god of prophecy's warning echoes in my mind, I can't stop the shiver that chases down my spine. How can someone so beautiful be so malicious?

A warm hand slips beneath my palm and gives me a squeeze.

I smile. I hadn't even heard the door open. "Thane?"

"How do you feel?"

"Like someone threw me off the top of the Transamerica building." His soft laugh is like a balm to my pain. "Where am I?"

"At a healer's," he says. "Sthenno brought you and Euryale here."

"We did it?" I ask. "We got them both out?"

"We did."

"And they're all right?" I ask.

"Yes. They're outside with Gretchen," he says. "Are you?"

"Yeah, I—" I shake my head, not sure how to explain the vision with Apollo. "When I blacked out," I say, "I saw Apollo."

Thane scowls. "Like in a vision?"

"Yes," I explain, "but not like any vision I've had before. We were… talking."

"About what?"

This is the part I don't want to think about. "About—"

The door to the room flies open and Gretchen bursts in.

"We need to go," she says, rushing to my side and grabbing me by the ankles. "Now."

With one rough thrust, she spins me around, yanking my legs to the side, letting them dangle off the table. Pain shoots up my spine, but I ignore it.

"Can you walk?" she demands.

"What's happening?"

"*Can you walk?*" she repeats.

She reaches for me. Before she can manhandle me off the table altogether, I slide down to the floor and test out the stability of my legs. There is some pain, but only a little wobble. I pronounce myself able to stand.

"Yes," I say, pushing away from the table to balance on my own two feet. "Now, care to tell me what's going on?"

"No time." Gretchen grabs our backpacks from the chair next to the door. She shoves one at Thane, pulls one onto her back and threads her arms through the third so it rests on her chest. "First we move, then we talk. Sillus and the gorgons are waiting at the back door."

She's gone from the room before I can ask again.

I look at Thane, but he's stone-faced.

"Walk," he instructs. "If you need help, I'll carry you."

"I can walk." The first few steps from the table to the door are a little unsteady, but I make it. "When we get where we're going, I want answers."

"You'll get them," he says, guiding me out into the hall in front of him. "Even if you don't like them."

Gretchen leads us into a back alley strewn with garbage cans, loose trash and abandoned furniture.

"I shall delay them as I can," the healer whispers as we exit into the daylight. "May the gods be with you."

I hear Sthenno mutter, "Only the ones on our side."

Then Gretchen is running down the alley, keeping to the side and dodging behind whatever obstacles can provide us some protection. We follow as closely as possible: the gorgons first, then the furry little monkey and finally me with Thane right at my back. When Gretchen gets to the end, she holds up a fist that I interpret to mean 'stop here'. She waves us behind a dumpster, and as much as I don't relish the idea of hiding behind a container of garbage, I dislike the idea of being found by whoever is after us even more.

She steps around the corner to investigate.

Thane leans close from behind. "Are you okay?"

My head is killing me, but that's becoming a standard state of being.

I nod, wishing we weren't in this life-or-death situation so I could enjoy the sensation of his breath on my neck. I may not understand this connection between us, but I cannot deny that I like it, a lot.

Gretchen runs back to join us.

"There aren't many," she whispers. "Half a dozen soldiers, maybe. And they're entering through the front."

Sthenno asks, "Arms of Olympus?"

Gretchen nods.

"We could fight them," Thane suggests.

"That would be unwise," Euryale replies.

Gretchen shakes her head. "They're heavily armed." She skims her gaze over me and Euryale. "And our forces are not full strength."

I want to argue, but I know she's right. Just staying upright requires all of my strength.

"Getting to the safe house is our only chance," Sthenno says. "It will buy us time to find a solution."

"Right. We're going to walk out of the alley, single file," Gretchen explains. "Head right and don't look back."

"I'm not leaving Greer's side," Thane insists.

Gretchen studies him for a second and then concedes. "Fine – in pairs. We'll regroup at the bookstore four blocks south and then make for the safe house."

We all agree.

"On my mark," she says.

She moves back to the head of the alley, leaning up

against the wall and peering around onto the street beyond. She raises her arm and waves us forward.

We'll make quite the parade.

Thane grabs me by the forearm and pulls me out from behind our hiding spot. "You're going first."

We walk past Gretchen, stepping out onto the sidewalk and trying to look like normal people. Thane releases his grip on my arm, dropping his hand to clasp mine. He threads our fingers together, securing our hands palm to palm. To anyone else on the street, we must look like an ordinary couple out for a walk on a grey afternoon, happily enjoying each other – except for the tension in every muscle of our bodies.

I start to look back over my shoulder, but Thane tugs at my arm.

"Don't," he says. "Eyes forward."

I scowl at him. "What is your problem?"

He flicks a glance at me. "I'm trying to keep you alive."

"If you hadn't noticed," I argue, "I'm not incapable."

His mouth quirks into a half smile. "No, you're not. But you are a beacon of Apollo. You are in the greatest danger of all."

"What does that mean?"

"When you touched the oracle's pendant," he explains, "you created a direct connection between your mind and the god of prophecy."

I give him a blank look.

"Apollo has unlimited access to your brain." Thane scowls. "He can track you, communicate with you, and see your visions."

Sugar. Well, that explains the conversation with Apollo in my vision, and why Sthenno seemed so upset that I had touched the pendant. At the time I didn't think we had another choice; otherwise I would be upset with myself as well.

As it stands, I did what I had to do, and I will live with the consequences. I will figure out a way to fix the situation.

Seconds later, the sound of footsteps smacking on the pavement clatters around me.

"They're coming!" Gretchen shouts, rushing past us with the monkey on her shoulders. "Let's go!"

Thane doesn't wait for me to respond. He breaks into a sprint, dragging me along with him. My weakened legs struggle to keep up, but every time I start to lag behind, Thane pulls harder. He keeps me upright and moving. It feels like we run forever, even though it's only a few blocks.

Inside the bookstore, Gretchen is standing by the front door, watching, while Sillus hugs her calf. She waves us inside, gesturing us deeper into the shop. Thane and I move between the wooden shelves of local travel guides and books by Bay Area authors, heading for a side room with a big window facing the sidewalk.

He leads me up the few steps and into a place behind a short bookcase where we can watch the street. The gorgons hurry by, heading for the front door. Moments later, they all join us.

"Get down," Gretchen whispers urgently.

I bend my knees but keep my eyes glued on the window. I see the half dozen men run by, sporting golden armour and carrying vicious-looking weapons. They must not have seen us duck inside, because they don't stop or alter their course.

No one says a word for several minutes.

"They will return," Sthenno warns, "as soon as they recalculate our position."

A sharp pain pierces the dull ache in my brain.

The bookshop goes blurry around me as my mind drifts into a vision.

Apollo stands before a full-length mirror in his all-white chamber. As I watch, his reflection in the glass fades, and instead the mirror reveals the interior of a bookshop – the interior of *this* bookshop, with all of us inside.

"You cannot hide," he says. "I thought I made that clear."

The vision ends, and I gasp.

"They already have." I look around at my companions, at the very image I just saw in the mirror. "Apollo knows we're here."

Sthenno huffs out a tight breath.

"It's uncanny," Euryale says, tears glistening in her soft grey eyes.

"What?" I ask. I glance at Gretchen and Thane. "What?"

Euryale beams. "You are exactly like her."

"Exactly like who?"

"Our sister," Sthenno says. "The late gorgon queen Medusa."

Now that I did not expect. They have just compared me to a legendary woman, a woman whose legacy has been distorted by myth and history, a maiden turned monster by those who would end our line. What am I supposed to say?

That I carry her power, her gift, is an honour and a burden. I am no stranger to pressure – it's almost as if Mother was grooming me for this all these years. I have to believe I can live up to the responsibility.

"It should not be surprising," Euryale says. "You have her power, her gift. And it manifests itself in but one way."

They both stare at me for a long time. I can imagine what they're feeling: pain, over the long-ago loss of their sister; pride, to see her power within me; and probably a slew of other emotions that I couldn't even begin to put into words.

It's touching, and I hate to interrupt the moment we're having, but—

"We need to go," Gretchen says, doing the interrupting for me.

"Yes," Euryale says. "Let us get to the safe house before Apollo has time to redirect his soldiers."

I am a bit overwhelmed by the situation – by the knowledge that a Greek god is reading my mind and tracking me through our mental connection, that this connection might be having an adverse effect on my brain, that I have visions in the same way as my ancient ancestor. If I thought therapy would help, I might sign myself up for a few sessions.

But what therapist would ever believe a word of this?

Gretchen is at my side as we walk out of the bookshop. Thane walks silently on my other side.

Both of them are strong and silent, determined to protect me. Between them, I feel completely safe. Neither of them will let anything happen to me. If only their protection didn't put *them* in danger.

CHAPTER 16

Grace

"You should go home," I tell Milo after the twelfth Cassandra Gregory in the city turns out to be a young stay-at-home mom with twin two-year-olds.

"Why?" Milo asks, opening the passenger door to his car. "It's just getting fun."

He's being generous. After I printed out the directory results for every woman in the city with our mother's name, Milo and I spent hours canvassing last night and more this morning. Since I couldn't just go home, I spent half the night online in a twenty-four-hour internet cafe, trying to narrow down our list of targets, with no success. None of these women have online social profiles. After catching a couple hours of sleep in the safe house, I met Milo at a coffee shop, and we started again. He doesn't need to be here. He's wasting his time.

I stand in the open space between the door, the car and Milo. "This is pointless. There are three dozen Cassandra Gregorys in the city. She might not even be here any more."

She might not even be alive any more.

Maybe our friends in the abyss got the message wrong. Maybe they aren't trying to kill our mother; maybe she's already gone.

I don't say that last part out loud, but I've been thinking it, a lot. Sthenno said they'd lost contact with our mother a long time ago, and the last mention of her in our adoption file was when she tried to make contact four years ago. A lot can happen in four years.

Heck, a lot can happen in four *days*.

"It doesn't hurt to keep looking," Milo says.

"You've already spent all of last night and this morning." I stare at my shoes. This isn't fair to him. "I can keep searching on my own."

"You need my car."

"I have a bus pass."

"Grace." His tone is so serious that I look up. "Did you ever think I might like having an excuse to spend more time with you?"

My cheeks burn, and I can't keep the smile off my face.

His gaze drops to my lips. I don't wait for him to lean in. Heart racing, I curve my hands around his neck and lift my face to his.

When I drop back onto my heels, I'm in a daze.

"Now," he says with a lazy smile, "if you're done trying to get rid of me?"

"For now," I tease.

"Then where's the next Cassandra Gregory on the list?"

I pull out the printout of search results and scan past all the ones we've already crossed off. I draw a line through number twelve before reading the next entry to Milo.

"That's in the Richmond," he says as he walks around the front of the car. "We'll be there in five."

I sink into the passenger seat and pull the door shut. As I click my seat belt into place, Milo puts the car in gear and takes off for the next mom-hopeful.

My hand shakes as I press the doorbell.

This isn't new; it's been shaking ever since Nick and I autoported into the middle of a bad-guy meet-up. It was shaking as I knocked on the doors of the previous twenty-two Cassandra Gregorys, so it's no shock that it's shaking now.

Though after going through this so many times, I really should be past that.

Footsteps echo inside, followed by the sound of a deadbolt retracting.

The woman who opens the door has freckled alabaster skin and flame-red hair, but she's the right age, and that's an improvement over two-thirds of the other contenders.

"Cassandra Gregory?" I ask.

She scowls. "I am."

"Did you by chance give your triplet daughters up for adoption sixteen years ago?"

My heart thuds in anticipation.

"Honey," she says, placing her hand dramatically at her waist as she scans me from head to toe, "take a look at these hips. No child has ever passed their way."

Another strike. "I'm very sorry," I say. "Thank you for your time."

As I turn to walk back to Milo and the car, she calls out, "I hope you find her."

Me, too.

I look back over my shoulder. "Thanks."

When I get back to the car, Milo guesses, "Not her?"

I shake my head.

"Maybe the next one," he suggests cheerfully.

"You say that every time."

He shrugs. "It's always true."

"Number twenty-four," I say, scanning the list, "is in Chinatown."

I settle in for the drive, listening to Milo's crackling radio and hoping – desperately – that the next Cassandra will be the right one. At this point, the chances are getting pretty slim.

I try to imagine what I think she'll be like. Do we get all of our features from her, or do we look more like our dad, whoever he is? Does she have powers and fangs? Is she tough or elegant or good with computers? Is she like all three of us or none of us?

Milo pulls to a stop in front of the address I gave him, jarring me out of my wondering.

"Be right back," I say as I climb out of the car.

We have this down to a science now.

"Maybe not," Milo calls out.

I smile. I hope that eventually he's right.

This building has a set of buzzers with the residents' names written in thick black marker next to the corresponding apartment numbers. I locate the one that says Gregory – 4B – and push the small black button.

I wait patiently but get nothing but silence.

I buzz two more times, with no response.

Oh, come on.

I really don't want to leave this Cassandra Gregory as a question mark on the list. Maybe her buzzer's broken, I reason. She might be up there waiting for friends or pizza or long-lost daughters to show up and not even know they're ringing her bell.

She might be grateful.

So, with my delusion in place, I start pushing every buzzer on the panel. Normally I would never do something like this. My only excuse is that my patience is in short supply and this is a desperate situation.

Someone finally buzzes me in.

I hurry inside and head for the stairs. Elevators aren't exactly my favourite method of transportation after the situation at my apartment. I pound the steps two at a time until I'm on the fourth floor.

I'm so winded and tired that my hand doesn't shake at

179

all as I knock on the door to 4B. I'm too worn out to be nervous, I guess.

I listen carefully.

Maybe she's really not home. Maybe I was making up that story about her buzzer not working – okay, I *definitely* made up that story. But maybe she's just out.

Then I hear it: the soft shuffle of feet on a hardwood floor.

I get goosebumps.

I duck down, out of sight of the peephole. If she wants to know who's at her door, she'll have to open it.

I realise what a dumb thought that is – who in the city is just going to open their door to any old knock? – half a second before I see the handle turn. I bite my lips together, waiting, hoping… fearing.

As the door swings open, I bring myself back to my full height. I'm straightening my legs at the same moment when Cassandra Gregory's face appears in the opening.

It's like looking in a mirror.

Well, a fast-forward mirror in which I'm looking at my future self, but a mirror nonetheless. I'm frozen, gaping at this woman who is so obviously my biological mother.

And she, too, is frozen and staring at me.

This is her, the woman who brought me and my sisters into the world, who gave us up for adoption to protect us from those who want to kill or control us because of the blood that runs through our veins.

Ancient, powerful blood. *Her* blood.

It's a surreal moment.

A phone rings somewhere else in the building. The spell is broken.

"Cassandra Gregory?" I say, not able to keep the question out of my voice. "I'm Grace, your—"

The door slams in my face before I can finish.

" – daughter."

Well, this is not a good start to our reunion.

My knuckles are going to go raw from knocking.

"Please, Cassandra," I say – I can't call her Mom. I already have a mom. "Just let me in. We need to talk. I have something to tell you."

I turn my back to the door and sink to the ground. Why won't she even talk to me? She must realise who I am and what's going on.

Well, if she won't let me in, then I'll wait for her to come out. She'll have to leave eventually.

"Please," I whisper.

My phone dings in my pocket.

I pull it out and silence it so it can't ding again; maybe if Cassandra thinks I'm gone she'll come out sooner.

It's a text from Milo.

Success?

I text back, Yes and no.

I stare at the screen, waiting for a reply.

Be right up.

I start to smile, wondering how long it will take for someone to let him in, but when I hear the lock above my head moving I scramble to the side and press myself against the wall. I keep silent and out of direct view. The door starts to open.

Today I'm doing a lot of things I would normally never do: tell Milo the truth about me, push every buzzer in an apartment building, and – apparently – force my way into a stranger's apartment. But she's not really a stranger, is she? She's my mother. Before Cassandra has time to react, I jump in front of her and block the door with my foot.

She doesn't even scream.

"I'm sorry if this is a shock," I say when I see her wide-eyed stare, "but this is important. Life or death, even."

She watches me, her pale grey eyes unblinking. I can't guess what's running through her head, but, honestly, today I don't care. Today, I put my hand in the doorjamb and take a step forward.

She's in danger, and she's as much a key part of this war as my sisters and I are. She needs to let me in. She needs to listen to me.

"You can't be here," she says. "Please, you have to go."

When she backs up, I advance again.

"Leave the city." Tears fill her eyes. "Before it's too late."

Two more steps and I'll be inside the apartment.

"I can't do that," I explain. "You're in danger.

How much do you know about the legacy?"

She sucks in a breath. "The legacy?"

"Medusa and monsters and—"

"No," she says, her voice cracking at the end. "It's already begun."

Then, she's lunging towards me. I brace myself for the attack, and my fangs descend on instinct.

When her arms wrap around me, I don't know how to react.

"You shouldn't have come," she says. There is so much tightness in her voice that she can only be crying. "I separated you to protect you, to prevent the prophecy from coming true." She leans back to look at me. "But I am a selfish creature, and I'm glad you're here. I never thought I'd see you again."

There are so many thoughts and emotions bombarding me I can barely think. I can only hug her back.

"So I guess this one is your mother?"

I twist to look over my shoulder and give Milo what can only be a very confused look.

"Yeah," I say. "I guess so."

CHAPTER 17

Gretchen

The safe house hasn't been home for long – just enough time for it to feel weird having other people sit on the ratty couch and rickety chairs.

"A priestess of Apollo might be able to break the bond," Ursula suggests.

"*Might*," Sthenno echoes, "if she didn't want to exploit the connection for herself. And just where would we find one? There hasn't been a priestess of Apollo in North America for more than a century."

Ursula shakes her head. "I know." She frowns. "Even if there were, Apollo could track her even more immediately than he is tracking Greer. We would have no chance."

Sthenno gives her a look that says, *Precisely*.

I stand in the kitchen, my back against the peeling white countertop.

Ursula – after four years it's hard to call her anything else – sits on the shabby couch, looking much more like herself with clean hair and fresh clothes. I can't stop staring at her. It feels like a century since I last saw her. She's back, safe and sound.

It's like a missing piece of my life has fallen back into place. As much as I hate to rely on anyone but myself, I never realised how much I had come to depend on her. She's been my mother, my trainer, my boss and my friend since I was twelve.

Even the new sisters in my life couldn't quite fill all those voids the way having Ursula back does.

Her sister, Sthenno, stands in front of the small yellow-lace-curtained window. She, too, has bathed and changed clothes, although she chose a pair of my backup cargoes and a tank over Ursula's flowing top and trousers.

The two immortal gorgons are busy debating how to break Greer's open connection with Apollo.

Greer and Thane are each sitting on one of the chairs from the dining table. I didn't miss how Thane scooted his chair closer to hers after they sat down, or how Greer leaned towards him when he did.

Sillus sits on the counter next to me, his furry feet swinging back and forth.

This is finally the moment of opportunity I've been waiting for. Pushing away from the kitchen, I walk over to the dining table, spin one of the chairs around backwards, and drop into the seat with my arms draped over the back.

"So, Thane," I say with a falsely sweet smile. "Want to tell exactly how you're involved in this big mythological mess?"

Thane lifts his dark eyes to study me.

Next to him, Greer scowls. I'm not sure if it's an I-was-wondering-the-same-thing scowl or a why-are-you-accusing-my-boy scowl. I don't care either way.

"Grace is my sister," Thane says slowly.

"She's my sister, too," I reply, "and my first job is to protect her. Now" – I level my fiercest huntress glare at him, pulling my hypno powers to the front of the class – "tell me who you are."

I watch his eyes carefully, looking for signs that he's as immune to my Medusa eyes as Nick. But, to my shock, his eyes grow unfocused.

"Who are you?" I ask.

He replies, "Thane Whitfield."

"Why are you fighting in this war?"

"For Grace," he says, his voice hollow and distant. "For Greer."

Greer looks from me to Thane and back again. "Satisfied?"

I shrug. Not entirely, but at least that's one thing off the list. Thane has no mythological blood. He's just a truly amazing human fighter.

Well, I can't be right *all* the time.

I pull out my phone and try texting Grace again.

That's two unanswered phone calls and twice as many text messages since we reached the safe house. Nick isn't responding, either. They were supposed to find our mother and meet back here. I hope it's only a matter of a bad signal or taking longer to locate Cassandra than Grace guessed, and not that they've run into trouble looking for her. Much longer and I'm going to go looking for them.

"Huntress no answer huntress?" Sillus asks.

I give him a sideways glance. "Not yet."

"Huntress will," he says. "Huntress always okay."

I pat him on the shoulder. I hope he's right.

"What about the Bacchanalia?" Ursula glances at her sister. "Perhaps an out-of-body experience is enough to disconnect her."

"And just where do you think we'll find a dozen Dionysian goats?" Sthenno replies. "Or a trio of innocent maidens, for that matter?"

"Enough!" I blurt.

I am so sick of this back-and-forth of bad ideas and ridiculous suggestions. Dionysian goats? Seriously? It's time we come up with a practical solution. The protective mojo on the safe house won't last forever, and I want Greer safe before it runs out.

"We think Apollo is on the side with Zeus, right? The side that wants us dead before we can open the door, right?" I ask.

The gorgons exchange a look.

"We are certain," Ursula says. "He was among those who held us captive on Olympus."

"Along with Zeus, Hera and more than half of the Olympians," Sthenno adds.

"Why didn't one of the others set you free?" Greer asks. "We have Olympians on our side, too, right?"

"We do," Ursula answers, "though not many."

Sthenno says, "They could not have aided us without the risk of exposing themselves. For many, secrecy is their only protection."

"We need them in place," Ursula explains. "When the time comes, you will need their help more than we ever did."

That seems to appease Greer's curiosity, because she sinks back against the chair and crosses her arms over her chest.

"So," I say, getting back to my point, "I'm going to state the obvious here."

Everyone turns to look at me.

Apollo and Zeus and who knows how many other gods and godly players are on the side that wants to stop us. They believe the best thing for both gods and man is for the door to be sealed permanently, and the only way they can ensure that happening is to kill us so we can't open it. Which means there's an easy way to get that side off our backs.

"Let's open the door."

Five pairs of eyes blink blankly at me.

"If the only reason he's connecting with Greer and tracking her is to prevent us from opening the door," I explain, "then he'll stop once we do – or at least stop trying to kill us."

That still leaves the monster side eager to kill us *after* so they can have free reign in this realm, but that's a whole other issue. One enemy at a time.

No one answers.

I clench my jaw. It may not be a spectacular idea, but it's certainly the most useful one offered up yet. "It's better than covering Greer in head-to-toe Hephaestian gold."

Including over her eyes, nose and mouth. What good is getting her off the gods' radar if she suffocates in the process?

"You are correct," Ursula says. "Opening the door would eliminate Apollo's desire to see the three of you dead."

Thank you. At least I'm not the only one who can see reason.

"I know there are other options," I say. "I know we can seal the door, killing every creature inside. But I'm not okay with that."

I already know Grace feels the same way. I glance at Greer, and she shakes her head. We don't always agree – meaning never – but we're on the same page about that.

I lift my brows and give Ursula a then-what's-the-problem look.

For a moment, I feel like it's four years ago. When Ursula first started training me, I questioned everything. I argued all the time and went toe-to-toe with her about the smallest things. The only difference now is this time

I'm not doing it because I have something to prove. I'm doing it because I'm right.

"I am glad you have chosen to take up your destiny," Ursula says, smiling. "Not all believed you would welcome the responsibility."

As if there were another option, at least not after meeting some of the non-monstrous creatures in the abyss.

"And what is the responsibility, exactly?" Greer asks. We turn to look at her. "What does guardianship entail?"

Actually, I've wondered about that, too.

The gorgons exchange a look. At first, I'm worried they're afraid we won't like what we hear. Ursula should know me well enough to realise I don't get frightened off. Greer's not exactly one to back down, either. Then I see the looks in the gorgons' eyes: pain and memory.

They're thinking back to *their* time as guardians, when Medusa was still alive.

"With three standing guard," Ursula says in a sad voice, "it is a pleasure."

"The door must be opened daily," Sthenno explains, "or the seal will lock and all inside will die."

I tense at the thought of my friends, of the innocent monsters in the abyss, dying by default. There are plenty of not-so-innocent ones in there, but taking them out in one fell swoop isn't worth the cost. I will never let that happen, even if I have to take on the job all by myself.

"Continue to patrol as you already do," Ursula

goes on, "to keep order amongst the monsters in this realm."

"Send the transgressors home," Sthenno says, "and keep the bad sort from coming through."

They make it sound almost easy – too easy. I'm sure something more is involved – that there are complications and difficulties – but we don't have time to go into the nitty-gritty. We'll deal with those details when they come up.

We need to act fast. Who knows how long the protection of Ursula's magical safeguards will keep Apollo out of my sister's head?

"Then let's do it," I say, exchanging a look with Greer. "Let's open the door. We're ready."

"There is a flaw in your plan," Sthenno says.

I scowl. We already agreed to open the door and accept whatever responsibility follows. This is no time for negativity.

"What's that?" I reply, with more attitude than Ursula would approve of.

Sthenno's voice is flat as she replies, "No one knows the door's location."

"Explain it to me again," I say, still not understanding.

How can the door be lost? How could all of mythology forget where it put one of the most important things it has? I've lost my keys plenty of times, but I never lost the door to my place – well, except for when it blew up. But I still knew where it was, technically.

"Few knew its location in the first place," Ursula says with the serenity of the most patient being ever on planet Earth. She doesn't let on that this is, like, the tenth time she's gone over the same facts. "For the obvious reasons, the fewer who knew how to reach the abyss, the better."

"Yeah," I reply. "That makes sense."

"Then, those of us who knew – those who eagerly awaited the prophesied days of the Key Generation – tried to maintain our distance, so as not to draw attention."

I nod. "Yeah, fine. I get that."

They didn't want the bad guys to find the door so they could try to break the seal by themselves or be there to kill us when we did.

"And then, the human world grew up around it." She makes a sweeping gesture, meant to encompass this room, this building, this neighbourhood and even the entire city. "The landscape changed. The land itself changed. Even those who knew what the location once looked like would not recognise the spot now."

"I don't get—"

"Oh, for heaven's sake, Gretchen," Greer snaps. "Does it really matter why or how? The bottom line is the same: we don't know where the door is. No one does. We have to find it before we can open it."

"Fine!" I glare at my sister. She certainly has a feisty

streak. If we weren't in the middle of a mythological crisis – with her sitting dead centre – I might compliment her fire. Right now, I just want answers. I ask the gorgons, "Tell me what you remember about it."

They both shrug.

"It was so very long ago," Sthenno says.

Ursula adds, "And so very much has changed."

"I get that," I say, trying not to roll my eyes. I could really use some of Ursula's patience right now. "But you must remember something? Anything, even the tiniest detail, might help. Was it big or small? Red or black?"

Sthenno laughs, almost a snort. "The door is not, in fact, a *door*," she says. "It is more of a location."

"What do you mean?"

"It is not a physical portal," Sthenno says.

"It is just a place where the realms connect," Ursula explains. "It could be anywhere – in a park, a building or the middle of a street."

Greer rubs her forehead; she must be as confused as I am.

"There must be some way to identify it," I say. "We can't just wander around the streets of San Francisco hoping to stumble onto it."

"No, of course not," Ursula replies. "There are ways."

"We just don't know what those ways are," Sthenno adds. "When we guarded the door, it was defined by stone markers."

I perk up. That's something.

"Sadly," Ursula says, "those markers are long gone."

Damn it. Just once in this mess I'd like to catch a break.

"What about our mother?" Greer asks, dropping her hand from her temple. "Whoever put you in the dungeons thinks she can find it."

"Why would the godly faction think that?" Ursula replies.

"I had a vision of you being tortured," Greer explains, taking Thane's hand like she needs the support. "I saw you being tortured. The man wielding the lash asked you where *she* was, that *she* would know how to find the door."

"And our friends in the abyss said Olympus was looking for our mother," I add. "That's why Grace came back to search for her."

Ursula looks confused, but Sthenno just shakes her head.

"It is not your mother that Olympus seeks," she says.

"It's not?" I ask.

"No." Sthenno crosses her legs. "It is the oracle."

"The oracle?" I echo. "As in *my* oracle? The one who told my fortune four years ago and told me where to find you last week? *That* oracle?"

Sthenno nods.

"Yes," Ursula replies. "The very same."

I ask, "Why?"

"Because," Ursula explains, "she has powers that will render this entire war obsolete."

This seems like information I should have known before now.

I cross my arms over my chest. "What does that mean? I thought she only told futures."

"An oracle is so much more," Sthenno replies.

"At our invitation, she was there at the original sealing," Ursula explains. "She witnessed the ritual and contributed words of her own to the ceremony."

"She is responsible for the prophecy about the Key Generation," Sthenno adds. "She wove in the threads that led to you."

The door was sealed centuries ago – *millennia* ago. I try to imagine the oracle, the little old woman with the flowing robes and the dusty old storefront, being alive and well and participating in the sealing ritual. I knew she was old, but I didn't know she was *ancient*.

"An oracle with enough power can *create* futures," Ursula says.

"Or if not create them, at least *direct* them." Sthenno rolls her shoulders like she's trying to loosen a tight muscle. "This oracle is one of the most powerful who ever lived."

"Because her magic is entwined in the very fabric of the prophecy," Ursula says with a grave tone, "it can also be used to unravel it all. She is the only one who can alter the prophecy."

"If the monster faction wants her," Sthenno says, "they believe they can use her to reverse the seal with the Key Generation."

"Can they?" Greer asks.

"They have tried for millennia," Sthenno replies.

"Until recently, I would have said no," Ursula says, "but the magic is weakening in preparation for the fulfillment of the prophecy. Perhaps now they might actually succeed."

To think the oracle could – with a snap of her gnarled fingers – undo this whole mess... It might have been nice if she'd mentioned that. And it's not like she's around to tell me now.

"I don't think she can help us," I say. "She's been missing for weeks. We searched the entire city and didn't turn up a clue."

The two gorgons exchange a worried glance.

"She must be found," Sthenno says.

"There were signs of foul play at her storefront." I picture the destruction Nick and I found at her place. "Her furniture was busted up, and there were drag marks on the floor. What if she was taken?"

They could already be using her, torturing her into changing the prophecy.

"She left her pendant," Sthenno argues.

Ursula nods. "She has gone into hiding."

"I can look for her," Greer says. "Now that I know how

to control my power, maybe I can find her in a vision."

"No!" the gorgons shout at once.

Greer jerks back, stunned by their vehement response.

"What?" I ask, confused. They should be happy that my sister is honing her second sight. "Why not?"

Ursula lays a hand over Greer's on the table. "With the connection to Apollo in place," she explains, "any attempt to seek out a vision allows the full breadth of his power into your mind."

Yeah, that doesn't sound good. The last thing I would want is some god peeking around in my thoughts. I don't know how Greer stands it.

"Human brains were not meant to contain the powers of a god." Sthenno crosses her arms over her chest. "There is a reason so few have been elevated to that status."

"So... what?" Greer asks, her cheeks pale. "I can't use my powers or I'll..."

"You've already been in an astral lock once," Ursula says, "for a short time. Each further attempt will only result in a longer and longer lock, until..."

"Until what?" I demand.

"Until her consciousness gets frozen there," Sthenno answers. "Permanently."

I suck in a tight breath and huff it out. Greer looks just as terrified as I feel.

"Permanently?" Thane growls.

"Not even Apollo could free her," Ursula answers.

"Some things are beyond the powers of the gods," Sthenno says. "The astral plane – the source of all magic, power and prophecy – is not theirs to control."

The thought of Greer with her consciousness trapped in some bizarre place and her unconscious body stuck here is awful. I will do whatever it takes to keep her from that.

"Fine," I say, shaking away the image of my sister in permanent astral lock. "No more seeking visions – not while Apollo has full access to your brain."

"No." Greer's voice is barely a whisper. "No more visions."

Thane laces their fingers together and squeezes tight.

"It is, however, imperative that we locate the oracle," Sthenno says. "She wrote the prophecy. She created the idea of the Key Generation."

"It is the oracle they wish to kill." Ursula clasps her hands together. "Destroying her could unravel everything, from the sealing ritual to…"

She trails off, and my gut tightens.

"Let me guess," I say, already sure I know the answer. "To the Key Generation."

"What?" Greer asks. "What does that mean?"

I look my sister in the eye as I say, "I means it could unmake *us*."

Her jaw drops in a look of unprecedented shock.

"Well, we won't let that happen," I insist. "There must be another way to find her."

"I know some places she might have gone," Sthenno says. "Havens for those seeking a break from their magical lives. I will seek her out there."

I could use one of those havens myself sometimes – like right now. Maybe, when this war is all over and things have settled down, my sisters and I can visit one for a while.

Ursula smiles at Sthenno, her eyes shining with pride and joy. I'm sure she is happy to see her sister after their long separation, after they kept out of touch in order to keep me and *my* sisters safe. They have made a lot of sacrifices to keep us safe.

Generations of our ancestors have made sacrifices to make fulfilling the prophecy possible. There is no way we're going to let them down.

"I, too, must leave. I have other assistance to convene," Ursula says, pushing back from the table. "As the time of prophecy draws near, our allies need to rally to the cause."

I just got Ursula back. The last thing I want is for her to leave again. Sthenno is going off to find the oracle. Even if I decide to trust Thane, he has no powers beyond killer fighting skills. I can't leave my sisters alone in the city without supernatural protection, which means I can't go with Ursula to protect her. "Can't you call them or something?"

She shakes her head. "Such methods of communication are too vulnerable. I must collect them in person."

"As the appointed time approaches," Sthenno says,

already heading for the door, "it becomes more critical that our forces be united."

Ursula smiles at me. "We must go. But we shall return."

"With help," Sthenno adds.

I have a little mental chat with myself. It's selfish to care more about keeping Ursula close by than about succeeding when we open the door. If the gorgons think we need the oracle and those other allies in order to win – to live and save the lives of those in the abyss – then we must need them. They haven't been wrong yet.

"Fine – while you two go after the oracle and our allies," I say, checking my phone to make sure I haven't missed a call or message from my other sister (nope), "I'm going to find Grace."

If it's the oracle the monster faction is after, there's no point in Grace continuing this wild goose chase for our mother. And there are only three people who are absolutely necessary when the time comes to open the door: me, Greer and Grace. She needs to be back at our side. We are stronger together.

Greer stands like she's going to come with me.

"No," I tell her. "You need to stay here."

"I want to help."

"You coming with me won't help."

Her face pulls into a scowl that probably makes normal people cower. I just give her a think-about-it look. It only takes a second for her to understand.

"Oh, right," she says quietly, tapping her temple. "Beacon of Apollo."

I nod. "Sillus, with me." Then, looking at Thane, I ask, "You'll protect her?"

He replies with one curt nod, and then Sillus and I are out the door, following the gorgons down to the street below. While they go off hunting for friends, allies and an oracle in hiding, I'm going to find my missing sister and bring her back to safety.

My first thought is to look for Grace at her apartment. If she hasn't found our mother yet, maybe she's back home researching. I'm halfway there from the safe house when my phone rings.

I check the caller ID.

"Grace." I click to answer the call. "Where the hell have you been?" I demand. "I've been trying to call—"

"Gretchen," she says, her voice equal parts excitement and fear, "I found her."

"What?"

"I found our mother!"

"Where are you?" I demand. She tells me the address. "I'll be right there."

I floor the gas and head for our mom's house. Our mother. Guess it wasn't such a wild goose chase after all. I hope this doesn't complicate an already crazy situation.

CHAPTER 18

Greer

The safe house is one of the most disgusting spaces I've ever inhabited. Every object and surface in the tiny apartment is worn, rotten, or stained. Some are all that and more. The plastic chair from the too-vintage-to-be-cool dining set looked like the safest place to sit.

It's not comfortable, but it's probably not harbouring bedbugs or bacteria.

I glance down and see a small puddle of dark brown liquid seeping out of one of the legs. Perhaps I was wrong.

Pushing to my feet, I cross to the lace-covered window and pull the brittle curtain to the side. The sun outside is bright, and even though my head still hurts, it feels good to stare out into the light.

It is an odd feeling, knowing that my brain is somehow connected to a god. On the one hand, it makes me feel powerful. How many people can claim to have ever been telepathically joined to an Olympian? But on the other hand… it's terrifying. My brain – always a source of pride and power, the means to all of my success – is suddenly my enemy. It is bringing my enemies to my side, to my sisters' sides. And I hate it.

The thought of being in any way the cause of harm to Grace or Gretchen makes me nauseous. I turn away from the window.

"You know," I say to Thane as I try to shake off my morbid thoughts, "I'm still waiting for those answers of yours."

"Answers?" he asks, as if he doesn't know what I'm talking about.

"Do not play games with me, Thane Whitfield." I cross the small apartment, careful to not trip over the frayed carpet. "You will not like the results."

Arms folded over my chest, I am so not going to let him get away with not filling in some of his blanks. The world around me is going to Hades and back, but I can still hold my own in a one-on-one with a cute boy.

All right, perhaps cute isn't the right adjective. Hot, handsome, ruggedly sexy – all of the above apply.

But I will not be swayed by a hot, handsome, ruggedly sexy boy, either.

His stormy grey eyes darken with longing and shadows… and fear.

Thane is so strong and tough; seeing him suffer is like a jolt of electricity. He lifts his hand like he wants to reach out and touch me – my face, perhaps, or my hair. Then he lets his hand fall away.

My approach is all wrong.

I am more than willing to take the gentle initiative. Slowly, I trace my fingertips over his furrowed brow, smoothing out the tense muscles of his forehead. His eyes drift shut.

I resist the urge to lean up and press my lips to his.

"I don't know what kind of girl you're used to dealing with," I whisper as my fingers flutter down over his cheeks, "but the strong and silent thing doesn't really work for me. I like a guy who can communicate. You don't need to confess your feelings, but you do have to be able to answer seemingly simple questions." My touch drifts along his jaw, temptingly close to his mouth. "If you can't do that, then let's just agree right now that this thing between us goes no further."

His eyes blink open and he stares at me for several long moments. I can't get a read on his thoughts – can't determine if I've used the right tactic. Maybe he likes the pushy, aggressive Greer. Maybe I need to bring the diva attitude back out.

Finally, he says, "None."

"Excuse me?"

"None," he repeats.

"What does that mean?" I frown. "None what?"

"Girls," he answers. "The kind I'm used to dealing with is none."

I'm stunned, and it takes me a few seconds to comprehend what he means.

"Are you saying… ?"

"There have been no other girls, Greer," he says quietly. "Ever."

"Thane… why?"

I'm not sure what I'm asking – whether I mean why no other girls, or why now, or why me.

On any given day, I'm quite aware of how exceptional I am. Both socially and academically, I am at the top of the food chain at Immaculate Heart. When I graduate next year, I will have my pick of Ivy League universities, and I already have my pick of wealthy, powerful friends and boyfriends.

This, however – right here, right now, with this boy – is almost enough to floor me. I think I'm close to tears, and for once I don't know if I want to hold them in.

"My life is complicated. My future is…" He rubs a hand over his short hair. "Uncertain."

I take his hand in mine. "Whose isn't?"

He shakes his head with a sad half smile.

"I'm not good with words, Greer," he says. "I like you, more than I should, and I want to be at your side for as long as I can."

"Why?" I repeat.

"Does there have to be a reason?"

"Yes," I say. "No. I don't know. But there must be. We're so different."

"I can't explain it." He tilts his head slightly to one side.

"I look in your eyes and I… belong."

I blink.

"I love my family, and they love me," he says, although he flinches when he says the second part, "but I've never really fitted in."

He may not be good with words, and he may not use them a lot, but when he does… they work.

I stare into his eyes, enchanted, because when I do I feel the same way. I belong – in a way I never have with my friends or parents, and in a different way than I belong with my sisters. He supports and understands me. And, for the first time in my experience, he makes me the priority. Not what I can do for him; me.

"Thane," I whisper, leaning forward.

He meets me halfway.

The moment our lips touch, the dizziness slams into me.

I cry out.

Then I'm standing in an alley. My sisters are there, along with Sillus and a boy and a woman I don't know. The boy, I would guess from the way Grace is grinning at him, is her crush – Thane's friend Milo. He has the look of a cheerful soccer player. The woman looks like us, with dark blonde hair and pale grey eyes – obviously our mother.

Everyone is standing awkwardly, like it's an uncomfortable reunion. Our mother steps forward and pulls Gretchen into a hug, and my sister tentatively pats her on the back. Grace looks up at Milo, joy and stars in her eyes.

The little monkey kicks a pebble across the alley.

I want to enjoy the moment, but the stench of fear soaks the air around them. My stomach lurches. In a flash I feel like I'm going to throw up, to vomit violently all over the scene.

Something catches my attention – a movement or a sound or a flash of light. I turn to look.

Everything slows down.

Grace gasps, her face frozen in a wide-eyed look of shock.

A knife floats through the air towards her.

Gretchen dives in front of her, but it's too late.

The knife slips between Gretchen's open arms, hurtling towards its target – towards Grace's chest.

"No!" I scream.

The scene speeds up.

From the omniscient perch of my vision, I watch Grace crumple to the ground, clutching at the knife sticking out of her chest. Milo kneels at her side, his hands hovering around the hilt, unsure what to do. Grace looks at him desperately, her face contorted with pain and confusion.

Gretchen takes off after the assailant while Milo shouts at our mother, asking her what he should do. Our mother is frozen, her face drained of all colour, like a ghost.

Grace's eyes look around wildly, desperate. Then they glaze over.

All the tension leaves her body.

Sillus wails.

Our mother finally screams.

"Grace," I shout. "No!"

"Greer, let me in!" Thane's voice yanks me out of the vision. "What happened? What did you see?"

I stare at him, in shock. I shake my head. I can't make the words come.

There's no time.

I shake off his grip and race out the door to save my sister's life.

Fear drives me. I don't know how I know where they are, but from the moment I come out of the vision I go on autopilot, like how I knew how to find Gretchen's loft the first time. I race through the streets, heading towards Chinatown, as if I'm following a GPS beacon to my sisters.

When I reach the alley, the group is at the far end. Grace is still standing, talking to Gretchen – introducing her to our mother.

I nearly cry with relief.

"Grace," I shout as I sprint towards them.

I have never run so fast in all my life.

They turn to face me – Grace and Gretchen and Milo

and our mother and the little monkey – all five, just like in the vision.

Everyone but Gretchen looks confused. She looks furious, probably because I've left the protection of the safe house – because I've risked danger to everyone, including myself, by leaving the safe house's shield.

Apollo is the least of my worries at the moment.

"Get down," I yell. "Hurry—"

Before I finish the words, that something catches my attention, just like in the vision. Only in reality, I can pinpoint the disturbance as the flash of a knife blade in sunlight.

Am I already too late?

"No!"

I dive for Grace, desperate to knock her down before the blade reaches her.

What I don't take into consideration is that by doing so, I put myself in the dagger's trajectory. At first it feels like a sharp bee sting in the chest, between my collarbone and my rib cage. Then the pain radiates out, overwhelming, and I collapse to the ground.

No! Apollo's voice roars in my mind.

My last thought is that I'm glad it wasn't Grace. I'm glad I could do that much for her.

CHAPTER 19

Gretchen

Everyone always says that time drops into slow motion in the heat of a crisis. In reality, it all happens in the blink of an eye. One second, Grace is introducing me to our mother. The next, the world erupts in chaos.

Greer gasps, a soft intake of breath.

The knife speeds past my ear – small and shiny and glinting in the sun.

I twist my head to follow its path.

The sound of metal sinking into flesh.

Another gasp from Greer, this one with a harsh gurgle at the end.

Thane shouts something – in *Greek* – and then takes off, lightning fast, chasing down whoever did this, down the alley and out onto the street beyond. I almost go after him, terror and fury urging me to join him in the hunt. But Grace cries out, and I turn back to watch our sister collapse to the ground, a wide-eyed look on her face – wide-eyed, and vacant.

"Greer!" I dive to my knees at her side, feeling my cargoes tear across the pavement. "*Greer!*"

The blade sticking out of her chest shines like a gold coin in the sun. I grab her by the shoulders and pull her up, lifting her so I can cradle her in my arms, careful not to touch the knife, not to push it further into her body.

My arms are shaking, flooded with fear and adrenaline. Grace drops down next to me, her face eerily pale.

"Is she – ?"

"No," I insist. "No!"

She isn't. She can't be. I won't let her.

My hands are wet and sticky, coated. I don't look at them because I already know what I'll see.

"Here," our mother – Cassandra – says, dropping to my side and wrapping her palm around the hilt of the knife sticking out of my sister's chest. "Quickly."

"No!" I shout, grabbing her wrist. "It might be staunching the blood."

"There is no time," she replies, placing her other hand over mine. "I'm a trauma nurse and a Sister of the Serpent. I've trained for this."

Sister of the Serpent? What? I can't make sense of her words.

For a moment, our grey eyes meet. I see confidence and determination in hers, along with the fear. I let her unwrap my hand from her wrist. Turning her attention to Greer, she slowly pulls out the knife. I stare at the flow of blood. It gurgles out of her like a bubbling brook.

I struggle to keep from throwing up.

"Give me your right hand," our mother says.

I just stare at Greer, shocked and numb. She can't be gone. She can't.

"Gretchen!" Cassandra barks.

Jerking up, I look at her.

"Give me your right hand," she repeats.

With jerky motions, I lift my right hand and hold it out to her. She takes the knife – a small dagger, no more than a four-inch blade, with intricate gold carvings on the hilt – and holds it above my palm.

"This will sting."

Like I care. All the emotion in my body – all the emotion I ever let myself have – drained away with Greer's life force. I hear Grace sobbing in the background. I wish I could find release like that, a way to let it out. I wish I didn't care so much that it feels like the knife landed in *my* chest.

Sillus is wailing. "No, huntress. No."

Cassandra presses the blade into the flesh of my palm, but I scarcely feel it. I'm numb. I don't feel anything.

She tosses the dagger aside and yanks my hand forward, over Greer's chest. Turning my palm over, she presses it to the wound.

The action yanks me out of my disconnect.

"What are you doing?" I demand.

She doesn't respond, just watches the spot where my

blood and my sister's mingle. Unmoving, she looks like she's willing something to happen.

"What are you doing!" I shout, practically screaming in her ear.

I'm losing it, I know I am. But I've never lost a sister before. I've never lost anyone I cared about. I've never even cared about anyone before, and now all of a sudden it's all happening at once – the caring, the losing. My brain – my heart – can't take it.

Grace's sobs get louder.

"Shhh," Milo soothes

I turn and see him kneeling at Grace's side, his arms wrapped around her in comfort. As much as I don't allow myself to care about many things, Grace cares easily and deeply for the people in her life. This must be hurting her even more than it hurts me.

And that magnifies my pain.

Sillus huddles against my side, his little body hiccupping with sobs.

The tears come, flooding my eyes and spilling over. Beneath my palm, I feel... nothing. No movement, no breath, no heartbeat. She's just gone.

I don't know what Cassandra thought she was doing, but clearly it wasn't enough.

I look up, and my eyes meet Grace's. Hers are red and puffy, full of tears.

I'm sorry, I mouth.

Grace shakes her head. She doesn't blame me – not now, anyway. Maybe she will later, after the raw emotions are gone. But I blame myself. I should have done more. I should have known something like this would happen.

I hang my head. I've failed Greer. I've failed Grace, too. I was supposed to protect my sisters – I'm stronger than them, and I have more experience with monsters and mythology. I failed, and now Greer is dead.

Everything is over: the Key Generation, the door, the prophecy, the war and the restoration of balance and the lives of every creature within the abyss. One less heartbeat in the world, and everything changes.

Something pulses beneath my palm.

I jerk back. I must have imagined it. There is nothing there. Greer is gone. She—

It pulses again.

"She moved," I gasp.

"What?" Grace asks, her voice barely a whisper.

I look at Cassandra, who is smiling through her tears.

"She moved," I repeat. "There! She did it again."

"See it, see it!" Sillus cries.

Cassandra sighs with overwhelming relief. "She did."

"Impossible," Milo gasps.

I ask, "How?"

Grace scrambles to my side and presses her palms to Greer's face.

"Your blood," she explains. "From the left vein it has

214

the power to kill, and from the right it has the power to heal."

"Yeah, I know that."

"The healing blood," she continues, "can – in very rare instances – also return life to the dead."

My mind reels. "What?"

Cassandra smiles. "When administered within moments of death, your blood has the power to save a life."

Grace sobs. "Oh my god, she's breathing."

"How do you know that?" I ask our mother.

As far as I'm aware, Cassandra hasn't been a part of our lives or the mythological destiny we carry since she handed us over for adoption. She shouldn't know about the blood.

"There is another legacy," she answers. "The Sisterhood of the Serpent. From the moment of the prophecy, the women in our line have known this time would come. While we do not have your powers, we pass on the knowledge from generation to generation so the truth is not lost."

"That's amazing," I reply, trying to imagine how hard it was to carry that information forward through the centuries.

"When you were born," she continues, "I knew the time would come when my daughters would need even more from me. In addition to the knowledge of the Sisterhood, I've studied every piece of Medusa lore I could get my hands on. I went to nursing school, volunteered for the emergency room and the trauma ward. I've had sixteen years to get ready."

I shake my head, stunned. I thought she had abandoned us. All this time, she's been preparing for this moment.

And it paid off by saving Greer's life.

I feel frozen, like I can't draw breath into my lungs.

But beneath my palm, my sister is not having that problem. Her chest rises and falls with the steady rhythm of resting breath.

If I were the kind of girl to cry at happy news, I'd be sobbing right along with Grace. Even so, I find it almost impossible to keep my act together. I wrap an arm around Sillus's shaking body and hug him tight. It's only the knowledge that my other palm needs to stay steady on the wound and my mind needs to stay focused on revenge that keeps me from collapsing onto Greer's life-filled body.

CHAPTER 20

Grace

Greer is alive. I can't stop staring at her, can't stop watching the rise and fall of her chest, can't stop my heart from pounding in *my* chest with unparalleled joy.

A minute ago, she was dead. I didn't have to feel her pulse fade away to know. The look on Gretchen's face was enough to tell me everything. She was gone.

And now she's back.

My brain can't quite accept the reality of it. In the space of a couple of minutes, I've experienced just about the biggest possible roller coaster of emotions. My sister – my triplet – came back from the dead. And my other sister brought her back.

Greer is still unconscious – maybe in another astral lock – but she's breathing easily, and the wound has stopped gushing blood. There is so much blood. Her clothes are covered with dark red – she's going to be upset when she wakes up. The ground, too, is soaked in blood, as is Gretchen's hand – the hand that saved Greer's life.

Gretchen looks stunned, and I suppose I do, too. The idea that my sister is back from the dead – however briefly she was gone – is beyond comprehension.

"You saved her," I whisper.

Gretchen glances at our mother. "Cassandra did," she says. "I mean, our mother."

Cassandra shakes her head with a weary smile. "I only knew the lore, and hoped it was true."

"It's still amazing," I say.

"It's impossible," Milo says, reminding me that he's still here – that he witnessed all of this.

If he wasn't freaked out before, he is now.

"We need to get her back to the safe house," Gretchen insists.

"Yes," Sillus says. "Go."

Rough footsteps echo down the alley an instant before Thane comes running around the corner, covered in sweat and with a bleak look in his stormy grey eyes. "Bastard got away."

He took off after the murderer – well, attempted murderer – almost the instant the knife hit Greer's chest, and it had looked like he and Greer had run all the way here from the safe house in the first place.

He should be exhausted, but he doesn't show it.

Ignoring everyone else, he crosses to Greer's side and drops to the ground. He reaches out, reverently tracing his fingertips over her brow.

There is such sadness in his eyes – Thane has always had a bit of sorrow in him, just beneath the surface –

but this is so much worse. He looks… bleak. As I open my mouth to tell him the good news, Greer coughs. He lurches back.

"She's—" He swivels to stare at me. "She's not dead?"

I shake my head. "Gretchen saved her."

Thane looks at Gretchen, uncharacteristic emotion on his face. He doesn't usually let this kind of feeling show, but the gratitude is unmistakable. He looks like his soul aches with relief.

"How?" he asks.

"Our blood," Gretchen says, holding up her right hand. "It… has that power."

He nods, as if that's all the explanation he needs. I shouldn't be surprised that he just accepts it. If his blood had been able to save Greer, to bring her back from the dead, I think he would have drained every last ounce to try.

"Cassandra showed her how," I tell him.

As he turns back to face me, he sees Milo standing off to the side. He scowls and then turns to me. "Grace?"

"Um, yeah, I…" I flick a desperate glance at Milo, but he gives me a helpless look. That's okay; now isn't the time anyway. "Can we talk about this later?"

Thane considers it for a second and then nods. "Get Greer back to the safe house."

"We were just about to do that." Gretchen looks at Cassandra. "Can we move her?"

Our mother's brow furrows. "Let me examine her."

While Gretchen, Thane and Cassandra figure out how to get Greer off the ground, I walk over to Milo.

"So…" he says.

As much as I don't want to do this – I want to talk to him about this and find out if he's really freaking out – things are far too serious. I won't put him at risk.

"Milo, I—" I lower my gaze, because I don't want my hypno powers involved. "I think you should go home now."

After a hesitation, he says, "Okay. If that's what you want."

He doesn't sound freaked out.

"I don't," I say, "but things are very dangerous right now."

"I can help."

I look up, giving him a grateful smile. "I know. But for now, my sisters and I have to handle it."

He nods. "Okay. For now."

He casts a quick glance at Thane and then presses a brief kiss to my lips. "Call if you need me."

"I will," I say, smiling as he waves goodbye to my brother and heads out of the alley.

Maybe things will work out between us despite all the crazy in my life. Maybe.

As I'm walking back to my sisters, the glint of gold and steel catches my eye. I walk over to the dagger that our mother discarded after slicing open Gretchen's palm and pick it up. Such a small, pretty thing to cause so much pain.

It might have caused even more, if Cassandra and Gretchen hadn't acted so quickly.

"Shiny," Sillus says.

"Can I see that?" Gretchen asks.

I hand her the blade.

"Can you tell who it belongs to?" I ask. "Or maybe who sent him?"

She turns the dagger over in her hand. The blade is short, double-edged – like the black ones Gretchen carries in her boots – and pretty unremarkable. The handle, though, is quite unusual. There are intricate carvings, swirling patterns of what look like antlers in gleaming gold, now covered in bright red blood.

Gretchen wipes the handle off on her trousers.

Woven into the golden antlers are gems, mother-of-pearl inlays in the shapes of crescent moons. There must be two dozen in total.

"No," Gretchen says, staring at the dagger as if it might have an invisible 'property of' label hiding somewhere. "I've never seen anything like it."

"It looks like it comes from Hephaestus's forge," our mother says, stepping closer to examine the blade. "But as to the owner's identity, I cannot hazard a guess." When Gretchen and I stare at her, wide-eyed, she shrugs.

"I have studied a lot of books on Greek mythology."

"I know whose it is." Thane's voice is low and hard.

"You do?" I ask.

He doesn't look at me, keeps his eyes steady on Greer. "It belongs to an assassin sent by Artemis, the goddess of the hunt."

"Artemis?" I echo.

Thane nods. "Apollo's twin. She's on Zeus's side in this war. She's been working actively against you for years."

"How do you know that?" I ask.

Gretchen demands, her voice low and full of warning, "How do you know the dagger is hers?"

"Because—" He swallows hard, his jaw muscles clenching like he has to force himself to speak the words. He reaches down and pulls up the leg of his jeans, revealing an ankle holster. Glinting in the sun is a dagger just like the one Cassandra pulled out of Greer's chest. "It is standard issue."

Cassandra pronounces Greer stable enough to be moved, and Gretchen carries our sister back to the safe house, back to a magically protected, comfortable place to recover without worrying that monsters are going to break down the door at any moment. There was no way she was letting Thane touch her.

Then, once Greer is settled into the deceptively soft bed, we gather around Thane in the living room – me,

Gretchen, Cassandra and little Sillus. I listen intently as he tells his story. We all do.

"As a little boy, I was given into the service of Artemis," he begins. "My parents were poor, and the goddess gave them great wealth in return for me."

I can't remember him ever stringing this many words together at once, especially about his past. He *never* talks about his past. Mom and Dad would be in shock.

"As part of my service to the goddess of the hunt," he continues, "I trained as a warrior. As an assassin."

"Assassin?" I echo, my voice barely a whisper.

He gives me a curt nod. "Even as a child. I was her star soldier. Could handle any blade with deadly precision."

He casually flips the dagger he pulled from his ankle holster into the air, letting the golden hilt spin several times in the gleaming sun before landing squarely back in his palm. He turns and, faster than my eye can follow, sends the blade speeding through the air. It is quivering, blade-first, in the narrow strip of wood between the window panes. A fraction of an inch to either side and it would have shattered the glass.

"Could best anyone in her army," he says, not sounding proud of his achievement, "even the teenagers."

"But you were only eight when we found you," I say.

An eight-year-old being trained as an assassin? Fighting other soldiers, even the ones way older than him? I can't imagine what it must have been like, little boy Thane being taught to fight and kill. He'd seemed like such a fragile thing when he came into our family, small and hungry after living on the street. Had that been a sham? Was it all a setup?

"One day, the goddess came to me with a mission." His eyes cloud over. "It was a very special mission, one that would bring me glory and my parents even more wealth. If I failed, it would bring us death."

I gasp.

Gretchen just glares at him.

"For three weeks prior, she starved me. I was given two slices of bread and a glass of water each day." The haunted look in his eyes says he remembers that time as if it were yesterday. "When I was ready, she sent me to the city. She arranged events so that I was found, so that our parents" – he looks at me – "would be the ones who adopted me."

"What was your mission?" Gretchen demands.

Thane turns to her. "My mission was, and remains," he says, his voice chilled, "to kill the sister of the Key Generation who possesses the far-roaming power of the gorgon Euryale." He doesn't look at me as he says, "To kill Grace."

Sillus gasps.

I can only stare and blink.

Gretchen launches herself at him before anyone can react. She has him on the floor, her palms tightening

224

around his throat. His arms spread out, palm up. He's not resisting her. If what he says about his training is true, he could probably pin Gretchen in a flash. He's letting her choke him.

"Do it," he whispers. "I deserve it."

That stuns her. She doesn't release his neck entirely, but she sits back on his chest.

"Why didn't you?" she asks. "Why did you abort your mission?"

He shakes his head from side to side. "I—" He glances at me, and in that look I see everything I need to know. He loves me, unconditionally. He's my brother, however that came to be, and he loves me. "I couldn't."

"Couldn't?" Gretchen echoes.

He returns his attention to her. "I wouldn't."

She releases his neck.

"They know?" she asks. "Your keepers know you're not their boy any more?"

Thane nods. "I told them." He looks away. "Stupid. That's why they sent another."

"Is that where you went?" I ask. "When you disappeared, you went to tell them you wouldn't kill me?"

He doesn't nod. He doesn't have to.

"That's who beat you up," I say.

"I shouldn't have gone," he says. "I thought if I told them about you, about how you are a good person and you only want the best for everyone, maybe they would change their minds about the whole operation. Instead, they planted a bomb."

"Bomb?" Gretchen growls. "The one that destroyed my loft?"

The pieces fall into place.

"*You* made the call," I blurt. He doesn't answer, but I know it's what happened. "You saved our lives."

"Too bad you're the one who put us in danger in the first place," Gretchen says. "You should have told us sooner."

He winces in pain. "I know."

She climbs to her feet, knocking him in the ribs with her boot as she steps over him. Sillus runs over and kicks him in the thigh.

I don't know what to say. I don't even know what to feel. The big brother I have looked up to for most of my life, who taught me how to knee a guy who got too handsy and who always made sure I got the biggest brownie on the plate, is suddenly a stranger. One of the people I trust the most, and he was the one I should have been afraid of.

He's still my brother, but he has also been my enemy. I feel like I don't know him at all.

Thane lies there for a moment before finally getting up. He looks defeated. I don't know what to say. I want to tell him everything is okay, but is it? How can I tell?

Greer coughs, sputtering breath into the air.

I rush into the bedroom and sit at her side.

"Hush, Greer," I soothe. "We're here. You're okay."

226

Our mother sits at her other side, checking Greer's pulse and smoothing fingertips over her forehead. She's been watching over her ever since we got back to the safe house.

Greer is still unconscious, though I'm sure that's not surprising. I wonder how long she'll be out. I wonder what death, even a brief one, will have cost her.

I glance up as Thane steps into the doorway. He looks at Greer, and then, reassured that she's okay, he turns and leaves.

In that moment, I know everything is going to be okay. Whatever happened in the past, whatever secrets Thane kept from me my whole life, he is still my brother in every way that matters. He risked his own life to defy his mission. How can I hold him accountable for something he had no choice over in the first place? The important thing is that he's made his choice now.

He chose me.

Leaving Greer's side, I return to the other room to reassure my brother that everything is fine. "Hey, Thane, I—"

He's gone.

CHAPTER 21

Greer

The smell is terrible, revolting, like decaying flesh and skunk and vomit all combined into one. It's worse than the abyss, even worse than the trash bins behind Fisherman's Wharf – and that's saying a lot.

At first my eyes won't open, like they're glued shut. Maybe I should be grateful for that. If the smell is this bad, I can only imagine what it looks like – and I'd rather not.

Instead, I try to move. My chest explodes with a white hot pain.

I collapse back down, struggling to keep my breathing even and to maintain consciousness. The last thing I want is to hyperventilate and pass out here, wherever here is.

"Is this really her?" a young female voice whispers.

An older woman says, "Couldn't be."

"Looks like her," another says. This one sounds as old as great-grandmother Morgenthal. Something slimy pokes at my foot. "She has the mark."

"And the fangs."

I trace my tongue over my teeth and discover that,

yes, my fangs are showing. Maybe they're reacting to the stench.

"Sorry," I say, my voice a harsh whisper.

Shrieks pierce my eardrums and I force my eyes open to see what terror is approaching. At the rate my week is going, it's probably a giant flesh-eating tadpole or something.

No, just a trio of human-looking women, ranging in age from a teenager to an octogenarian. Their eyes are shut, but I get the distinct impression that they are shrieking at me. Like *I'm* the scary thing here.

I close my eyes and take a deep breath, trying to quell the nausea and pain that keep washing over me. When I open my eyes, the old woman has moved closer and is shoving her hand towards my face. Cupped in the palm of her hand is an eyeball.

I can't stop the scream.

Three women and one eyeball. Oh my heavens, I know who they are. The Fates.

This can't be good.

"What's going on?" I demand, trying to control my panic. Looking around, I add, "Where am I?"

"She doesn't know," the young one on the left says to the other two.

"You tell her," the middle one says.

The old one on the right says, "Yes, you."

"I'm not telling her," the first one argues.

"Tell me what?" I ask.

"That you're in Hades," the middle one quips. Then she slaps a hand over her mouth when she realises she just told me the thing they didn't want to tell me.

"Hades?" I frown. "That's not possible."

All three of them glance down at my chest. I'm about to feel insulted – there's a sharp barb on the tip of my tongue about it being rude to stare – when I look down. They're not looking at my breasts; they're looking at the ragged gash in my chest, right next to my sternum.

"Oh," I say.

It comes back to me in a flash: The vision. The alley. The knife.

"No. This can't be happening."

But it is. I'm dead because I dived in front of a blade heading for Grace. And it's not like if I could go back in time I would do anything differently. If I hadn't stepped between her and the dagger, she would be the one waking up in Hades. That is not a trade I'm willing to make. If I have to die, doing so in the process of saving Grace's life is a pretty honourable way to go. I have to say I'm quite proud of myself.

I am not, however, thrilled to find out this is where I'm ending up. I would prefer somewhere warmer, with more sun and maybe a beach.

I sit up and look around, relieved that the white hot ache in my chest is fading. I would hate to think I'm spending the rest of eternity living with the stinging pain – well, not *living* with it, precisely.

"So this is Hades?" I ask, recalling my mythology lessons on the ancient Greek afterlife. "Where is the ferryman? Cerberus? The lord of the underworld himself?"

The trio shrugs nervously.

"What?" I ask.

"You aren't going to meet them," the middle one says.

"Not yet, anyway," the young one adds.

"We were sent to give you a message," the old one explains, "to take back."

"To take back?" I repeat. "I thought there was no going back from Hades."

The first woman shrugs. "There are always exceptions."

"What's the message?" I ask.

The old one steps closer, holding the eyeball close to my face. I try not to shudder in disgust. "Fight not alone."

"Fight not a – what?" That makes no sense. "What does that mean?"

They shrug again and shake their heads.

"We weren't told."

"We're just the messengers."

"We give the message."

"Well, who sent you?" I ask, hoping maybe that will be a clue.

"That is not part of her message."

As if that's an answer. "Her?"

"Hush, youngling," the old one snaps at the first one.

"You share more than we are meant to. We cannot interfere in these matters."

The middle one explains, "We are only supposed to deliver the message."

"Before," the first one adds, nodding.

"Before what?" I ask.

The light around me suddenly brightens.

"Before this."

"Befo—?"

As one, the three women snap their fingers. The air around me crackles with energy.

I glance down and see my skin glowing, brighter and brighter. My entire body has turned into a fluorescent bulb. I look radioactive.

"Wha—?"

Suddenly I feel like I'm being pulled in every direction at once. My body struggles to stay together in one piece. My legs go in one direction, my arms another. Everything starts swirling, like a funhouse mirror in the middle of a tornado.

Then the smelly world around me fades away and I'm hurtling through space.

When I wake for real, I'm relieved to inhale a breath of air that only smells like dust and greasy Chinese food. I never thought I'd appreciate the disgusting smells of the city, but in comparison they're like designer perfume.

Hades is not a marketable scent.

"She's waking up," a woman's voice says.

"Greer!"

Grace's cheer brings me back into the world – into the real world. I hold my hand up before my face and am relieved to see the glow is gone. My skin is back to normal. *I'm* back to normal. Back to *life*. Is that what the Fates meant?

The group standing over me here looks a lot better than the trio in Hades.

"How do you feel?" Grace asks, dropping down next to me on the bed.

I scan the room and find I'm back in the safe house. I suppress a shudder at the knowledge that I'm lying on that ratty, stained coverlet in the bedroom. After dying and going to Hades, the thought of dirt and bedbugs should be the least of my worries.

"I feel…" I try to sit up, bracing myself for the pain – I took a knife to the chest, after all – but I'm surprised to find none. "Great, actually."

The bed bounces as Sillus jumps up by my feet.

"Welcome," he says with a toothy grin. "Huntress come back."

How I got to Hades isn't much of a mystery. I took that blade that was meant for Grace, and I went to the underworld. That shouldn't be any more surprising than the idea that I'm a descendant of Medusa who fights monsters and is trying to defeat the Olympians who want her dead. Mythology is now something entirely normal in my life.

How I got back to the realm of the living is less clear.

"What happened?" I ask. "How am I still alive?"

"Gretchen saved you," Grace says. "She brought you back from the dead."

"With Cassandra's help," Gretchen adds.

I shift my attention to the third woman at my bedside. She gives me a little wave.

Cassandra is our mother – our biological mother, anyway. Grace found her, apparently. There is no question that we are genetically related. We have the same natural hair colour, the same silver-grey eyes and the same high cheekbones. It's funny how I never before realised how little I resemble my adopted parents. I should have discovered my adoption much sooner.

"Where did you go?" Grace asks, her voice whisper soft. "Were you... aware of anything?"

I look into her eyes, so full of hope and wonder. So curious. I would be, too.

As much as I want to hold this inside, to keep this very private thing to myself, something makes me want to tell them. I think the trip to Hades was not as accidental as it seemed at the time. I was supposed to die; I was supposed to get that advice from the Fates. And now I'm supposed to share that with my sisters.

"I went to Hades," I say bluntly.

"Really?" Grace gasps.

Gretchen asks, "What was it like?"

"It was…" I close my eyes, remembering, but the memory is too raw, too real, and I have to open them again. "Awful. It smelled like a garbage dump."

"Oh." Grace sounds disappointed. Like I was going to say it was full of puppies and smelled like candy floss. Not quite.

"I was in more of an antechamber," I explain, hoping to make her feel better. "I didn't see Hades proper or anything."

She visibly relaxes.

"Were you alone?" Cassandra asks.

I flick my grey gaze to hers. "No, I wasn't."

I take a deep breath. Despite all the crazy, unbelievable things we've all seen, this is one step beyond. My visit to the underworld and advice from the human-looking personifications of destiny is another level of mythology.

"I saw the Fates."

"The Fates?" Gretchen echoes.

Grace's eyes get as wide as saucers.

"They were sent to give me advice."

"Sent?" Gretchen scowls. "By who?"

I shake my head. "They didn't say."

"What was the advice?" Grace asks.

"They said, 'Fight not alone.' "

Grace's mouth falls open, her brows furrowed like she's completely confused. Gretchen, just as puzzled, twists her head to the side.

"Fight not alone?" Cassandra repeats.

"That's it." I shrug. I don't have any better explanation for it than anyone else. "Kind of disappointing, right? I expect more from a trip to the underworld."

We sit in silence for a minute. As simple and anti-climactic as it seems, I have a feeling that their advice will become really important before this war is over. It just seems kind of silly now.

I hope it's more valuable than that. I would hate to have died for no reason.

A very important reason, the woman's voice in my mind says.

Well, good to know *that* hasn't changed. Still losing my mind. I mentally roll my eyes.

Finally, Cassandra breaks the silence. "I'll bet you could use some water."

She stands and walks out of the room, heading for the kitchen.

"I suppose I should thank you," I say to Gretchen.

She scowls. "I suppose you should."

Grace smacks her on the shoulder. "No," she says to me, "I should thank *you*. If you hadn't shown up just in time to jump in front of that knife, it would have been me bleeding out in the alley."

"And it would have been you being brought back from the dead," I reply.

"Why did you come, anyway?" Grace asks. "You were supposed to stay at the safe house."

"You saw it, didn't you?" Gretchen asks, though it's more of a statement. "You had a vision of, what, Grace dying?"

I look at her. She's too perceptive by half.

I love my sisters – apparently more than I love myself – but I can't bring myself to tell them that. I don't want Grace burdened by any guilt over the situation. I saw something about to happen, and I reacted; end of story. No regrets.

"No," I say, feigning boredom. "I couldn't stand to stare at these hideous beige walls a minute longer."

Grace laughs at me, but Gretchen glares. She studies me, probably looking for some sign that I'm lying. If she looks too closely, she'll find one. I meet her glare head on.

Cassandra returns with a glass of water, and Gretchen finally breaks eye contact. I'm not sure if she got her answers or if she's decided to give me a little breathing room. Either way, I'll take it.

As the group around me falls silent, my mind quiets. For the first time in days, my head feels normal and there is no pain – no ache or throbbing. In that instant, I realise one very important thing.

"Well, at least there's one good thing about my demise."

Gretchen frowns. As if any good can come from my death – other than saving my sister's life, of course. But I feel the truth.

"What's that?" Grace asks.

"The bond to Apollo has been severed."

"It has?" Grace looks hopeful.

"How can you be sure?" Gretchen asks.

"I…"

I don't know how to describe the feeling. It's not as if anything has changed – I still feel like myself – but there is an underlying sense of… emptiness. Of loneliness. I may not have been consciously aware of Apollo's presence, but I can certainly feel his absence.

It's like the difference between wearing a pair of genuine Louboutins and an extremely well-done knock-off. They might look identical, but there are subtle differences to the feel. You just *know*.

Good girl, the woman says. *Your powers are indeed great.*

Thank you, I answer.

I'm shocked when she replies, *You will soon have the opportunity to do so.*

I shake off the imaginary conversation. My brain might be Apollo free, but that clearly hasn't affected my schizophrenia.

"Trust me," I say. "He's gone."

I keep my voice neutral, not betraying my sense of loss.

"Life will be easier now." I try to sound cheerful. "No more running through the city streets and hiding in bookshops."

Although some parts of running weren't so bad. The parts with Thane, for example, were quite nice – especially the parts where he kissed me. I could do with more of those.

I scan the group around me, suddenly realising that Thane hasn't spoken since my return. Probably because he's no longer here.

"Where's Thane?" I ask.

I thought it was a simple question. But when I see the look of fury on Gretchen's face and the pain on Grace's, I worry.

"Oh, Greer," Grace says. "There is something we have to tell you."

CHAPTER 22
Gretchen

Greer surprises me. The look on her face is not what I expected. As Grace tells her about Thane's confession, the truth about him and his involvement in this big ugly war, about why he is a part of our lives in the first place, I expect to see confusion, doubt, betrayal even.

Instead, she looks thoughtful.

I'll never understand her.

I can hear the emotion in Grace's voice. A whole rainbow of feelings is running through her, I'm sure. She just found out her brother was sent to kill her; that'll mess up a girl's mind.

But Greer... she just tilts her head to the side and says, "He is not responsible for this."

"I know," Grace says, swiping at her tears. "But he lied. His whole life has been a lie. He's a liar."

Greer gives her a half smile, a gentle and peaceful look on her face. "Aren't we all?"

She looks so serene, relaxing back on the bed with a handful of pillows propping her up and Sillus curled at her side.

Normally, I would call her out for being stupid and naïve – something I didn't think her capable of – but after everything she's been through, I'll cut her some slack. She just came back from the dead to find out the boy she's getting involved with is an assassin sent to kill her sister. She might still be in shock.

Besides, I know all about boys who walk that fine line between devotion and betrayal.

"Do you have any Hestian serum?" Cassandra calls out from the bathroom.

"If we do," I reply, "it's in that tin of vials."

Where is that boy of mine, anyway? Between everything that's happened since we came back from the abyss – the nonstop running and worrying – I haven't had time to think about anything but survival and keeping my sisters safe. I didn't notice until now that Nick is nowhere to be seen. He should have been at Grace's side. The hair on the back of my neck stands up.

"Found it," Cassandra shouts.

"Hey, Grace," I ask. "Where's Nick?"

The air in the room stills. She turns to me, and her jaw drops. My stomach tightens into a knot.

"Oh, Gretchen, I didn't even think – I should have told you sooner," Grace says hesitantly. "But with everything that happened…"

She waves her hands around.

"Tell me now," I say through clenched teeth.

"When Nick and I autoported back to my apartment," she begins, "we found it overrun with bad guys."

Cassandra returns to the bed with a vial in one hand and a cotton ball in the other. She sits down next to Greer and starts dabbing the wet cotton ball on her forehead. "This should help you relax."

My heart pounds. Old fears and doubts seep up into my brain. Once again, our enemies show up where Nick goes. Another coincidence? What if she tells me he betrayed us? Again. I trusted him with the thing I value most: Grace's safety, her life. At least she's unharmed. He had better not have turned against us if he knows what's best for him.

"He saved my life, Gretchen," she says quickly, as if she can sense the direction of my thoughts. "But he sacrificed himself."

My stomach plummets to my feet. "What do you mean *sacrificed*?" He can't be dead. He just... can't be.

Every moment of our rocky relationship flashes through my mind: The first time I ran into him in that dim sum place. When he showed up in my biology class at school. Fighting the griffin and the skorpios hybrid. That kiss before the monsters dragged him into the abyss. Going in after him. Him letting me beat him to a pulp when I found out he knew more than he'd let on – before I knew everything about his involvement.

We've been through a lot together in a short amount

of time. He can't be gone. We have a lot more to go through before I'm done with him.

"Oh, no, that sounded bad! I'm sorry. He's not dead," Grace says. "I just meant he stayed behind to delay them so I could get away."

"Stayed behind?"

"He threw me in an elevator and told me to autoport away. Then he attacked the bad guys to keep them from coming after me." She shakes her head. "I think he was taken prisoner."

That sounds like Nick.

If he's been taken prisoner, then the odds are in our favour. The boy is a genius at talking himself out of situations – he's done it with me at least three times. He'll be fine until I can rescue him. I hope.

"Who were the bad guys?" I ask. "Did you recognise them?"

"No, but I think he did," she explains. "One – the lead guy – had a dog's head and flippers for hands."

Bad news. I know exactly who she means. "The boss."

Last time I saw that creep was in his office in the abyss, with half of monsterkind bearing down on him. Too bad he got out of that alive.

"Yeah, that's what they called him," she agrees. "The boss."

Maybe Nick won't be fine. One run-in with that flippered freak was more than enough for a lifetime. He's creepy with a capital everything. The boss learned Nick was a double-agent mole when I went in the abyss the first time. Nick said the guy would have killed him if I hadn't shown up to save him. I don't doubt that he would have.

I can't imagine his opinion of Nick has improved in the meantime. And I'm not there to stop him.

I hope Nick can sweet-talk him enough to buy us some time again.

"Bad?" Grace asks, her face twisted in concern.

"Yeah," I say with a nod. "Bad."

"Well, then," she says, pushing to her feet, "let's go get him."

I laugh. Just like that. *Let's go get him.*

Sometimes I envy her naïveté. Everything is so simple for her; "go get him." As if we'd even know where to look. They could be anywhere. It's been how long since he and Grace came back? One day? Two? More than enough time to get well and truly lost.

The sad thing is, that naïve response is also my gut reaction.

Part of me – the girly part that was just getting used to having him around, to feeling that connection with another person, to the idea that maybe fulfilling my legacy doesn't have to mean going it alone – wants to drop everything and go rescue him, if it's not already too late.

But the rest of me knows that's not possible.

"It's not that easy," I say.

"Why not?"

"Because we *can't*," I bark.

She jerks back, and I immediately regret the outburst. From the corner of my eye, I see Greer and Cassandra flinch on the bed. Even Sillus stirs in his sleep. I shouldn't take my anger out on them – especially not on Grace. She didn't take Nick. She didn't start this war. None of us did. But we can finish it. That's our priority. "Because we have other priorities. We have responsibilities that are bigger than one boy. Bigger than one life."

He of all people would understand.

As a servant of justice, he knows the cause is more important than rescuing him. He knows our first duty is to restore balance. It's what he came here to do; it's why he sacrificed himself to save Grace. The best thing we can do to help him, to save him – if it's not too late already – is fulfill our destiny.

I turn to the group. "We have to find the door."

"The gorgons think the oracle is the only way to find it," I say, "but clearly they haven't located her yet, or they'd be back already."

I look around the table: Grace, Greer – who is recovering quickly – Sillus and our mother. They are two girls who didn't know until a few weeks ago that mythology wasn't myth, a furry monkey creature, and the woman who brought us into this world but is herself powerless. Not much of a think tank, but it's what we have to work with while the gorgons are out searching.

"They might never find her," I continue. "We need to figure out how to find the door on our own."

"I wish I could help more," Cassandra says, "but the knowledge passed down to the Sisterhood through the generations did not include any information about the door, and human research only describes it as a cave."

I smile at the term *human research*.

"Well, we know it's not a cave," Grace replies. "The gorgons said it wasn't a physical portal."

I push to my feet and start pacing. The oracle sure picked a pretty inconvenient time to go missing, assuming the gorgons are right about her staging the scene at her place. Nick was pretty certain she left of her own accord, too. Our friends didn't mention seeing her in the abyss or the dungeons of Olympus.

Maybe she did just take off.

"The least she could have done was leave a clue," I snap, spinning on my heel in the kitchen before pacing back towards the table. "An X-marks-the-spot treasure map would have been nice."

"Maybe she couldn't," Greer suggests. "Maybe she didn't have time."

Grace gasps. "Or maybe she *did*."

"What?" I ask.

Her face beams with excitement. "What did you find in her shop?"

"No treasure map," I reply. "The pendant of Apollo and—"

"The riddle," Greer finishes.

"Sillus love riddle," the little monkey chimes in.

"The riddle?" I parrot. "The one written in ancient Greek?"

Grace nods. "Greer and I got it translated."

She pushes to her feet and pulls her phone out of the back pocket of her jeans. After a few clicks on the screen, she starts reading:

> In the space beneath the sky, between harbour
>   and haunted ground,
> Where graces and muses weep at gentle
>   water's shore,
> Be three within three, join life with death in thee,
> To find the lost and take up destiny.

She looks up when she finishes, a hopeful look on her face.

That's our big clue? I've got nothing. It does sound like directions for finding the door – for opening the door and accepting our legacy – but beyond that… it's so vague. It could be a map to the moon, for all I can tell.

I stare back blankly. "What does it mean?"

Her face falls. "I thought you might know."

We both look at Greer, who shrugs. Sillus and Cassandra are just as clueless.

"It certainly sounds like a clue to find a location," Greer says, giving me a scolding look for being unsympathetic. "It's quite likely it leads to the door."

"That's true. And if it's a clue to find the door, then at least now we know what the riddle means," I say, trying to make Grace feel better. "That's something."

She stuffs her phone back in her pocket. "Yeah. I guess."

We fall silent.

This is not the kind of puzzle I excel at solving. If the problem involves breaking into a high-security office building to take down an ekhidna, I can totally do that. I can kick through doors and scale chain-link fences, but I can't find someone who doesn't want to be found, and I can't solve a crazy old woman's riddle.

Greer clears her throat. "Am I the only one who sees the obvious here?"

We all turn to look at her.

"Apparently," I say. "What's the obvious?"

She glances around the room. Then, as if it truly is the most obvious thing in the world, she says, "*I* can find the door."

CHAPTER 23

Greer

Everyone turns to stare at me. "I can *try* to find the door," I clarify. "Or at least the oracle."

My powers are still raw, so there's no guarantee I'll find out what we need to know. I can try, though. I would be a coward not to.

"No way," Gretchen says.

"You heard what the gorgons said." Grace fidgets with the metal edge of the table. "You shouldn't be seeking out visions."

"That was before," I argue, "when I was still a beacon of Apollo. Now that the connection is severed, that isn't a problem any more."

Grace looks thoughtful. "That's true."

"It's too dangerous," Gretchen insists.

"It's my gift." I turn my palms up on the table in a helpless gesture. "I can't just abandon it."

"Remember what happened last time you went after a vision?" Gretchen pushes away from the table and starts pacing. "I'm not eager to see you in an astral lock again."

"That won't happen," Grace says, coming to my aid. "It was a side effect of her connection with Apollo."

"All the more reason to stay away from amateur attempts at prophecy," Gretchen argues, "in case she rekindles that connection."

"She won't," Grace insists.

"You don't know that." Gretchen gives her a stern look.

I sit there, watching my sisters argue over whether or not I should use my gift. I know they care about me. They are worried about me and don't want me to have any more problems. Neither do I.

But I refuse to be afraid of my powers. The visions are a part of me, and I'm going to embrace them, whether my sisters like it or not.

"This might be our only chance at finding the oracle or the door." I give my sisters a determined look. "I don't need your permission. But I would like your help."

It's time I learned how to use my power without losing myself in my visions. I don't have control over them, and when I've tried to control them there have been painful consequences. Maybe that was just because of the connection to Apollo, but what if it wasn't? What if it's just part of the bargain, a pesky side effect of second sight?

The truth is, I'm scared.

I push up from the table and start walking. I don't want to look like I'm pacing, so I walk to the window and look out through the curtain. When I turn back to face the table, four sets of eager eyes are watching me, expectant. I'm afraid I can't do it.

250

But I have to try.

Cassandra gets up from the table and crosses to me.

"I can tell you are frightened," she says, quietly. She stands before me, placing her hands on my shoulders. "I cannot imagine what the process is like. But I admire your willingness to embrace the gift. The world has been waiting countless generations for you to be born." Her hands cup my jaw. "And you, my darling daughter, bear the greatest responsibility of all."

"I—"

"You have the honour of carrying forward Medusa's legacy," she continues. "You alone hold her power of second sight, and you alone can seek the answers that will return the world to what it should be."

I can do it. I have to. This is my chance to prove myself worthy of Medusa's gift.

My mother's eyes hold my gaze, strong and certain. Her confidence feeds mine, soothes over my fears and the bad memories of the recent past. She calls on my sense of duty, and that is something I can't ignore. Duty is what convinced me to join this fight in the first place. Duty will get me through my fears.

I straighten my spine, lift my chin and say, "Thank you."

Cassandra looks just like Grace when she grins. "This time," she says, "we shall do it right."

"What does that mean?" Grace asks.

"Fetch me a bowl of water," Cassandra instructs, "and a length of cloth or a scarf."

"There's a bowl under the bathroom sink," Gretchen says, "and Ursula has a ton of scarves in the dresser."

"I'll get the bowl." Grace hurries out of the room.

Gretchen heads to the bedroom to find a scarf. Sillus follows her.

Cassandra pushes to her feet. "Hopefully there is some chilled Delphic oil in the refrigerator."

"What is that?" I ask as she crosses to the kitchen.

Cassandra smiles. "It is a prophetic aid," she says, pulling open the door and searching the shelves, "from the waters around the famous Oracle of Delphi."

Glass vials clink against each other as she lifts each for inspection. "Ah, here it is," she says, holding up a small purple vial with an eye painted on the side.

Gretchen returns with the scarf, a long, narrow, navy blue number with flecks of silver thread sparkling like stars in the silk. Sillus has another scarf – with bright red and orange stripes – wrapped around his neck. Grace sets a bowl full of water on the table.

Cassandra asks Gretchen to turn out all the lights but the one above the kitchen sink.

"Please," Cassandra says to me once the lights are off, "take a seat at the table."

I sit in one of the chairs at the dirty dining table, and Cassandra takes the one next to me. My sisters stand a few feet away, as if they're afraid to be in the way. Sillus hops up onto the counter for a better view.

"This ritual has been passed forward through the generations," Cassandra says as she twists the cap off the purple vial. She shakes several drops of clear liquid into the bowl of water. "It is said that the immortal gorgons used to help Medusa achieve her visions in this way."

Medusa – my ancient ancestor, the origin of my powers. To think she once sought visions in the same way I'm doing now. What kinds of things did she see? Was it easy for her, or did she have to practise?

Thinking about her naturally makes me wonder about her death. She was the only mortal gorgon, but also the one with the gift of second sight. Did she see it? Did she have a vision of her own demise?

It was awful enough seeing Grace's death in my vision. How could I live with the knowledge of my own death? Seeing it happen without necessarily knowing *when* it would happen, not being able to prevent it – that would be torture.

I would rather be immortal.

"According to tradition, the key to a successful summoning," Cassandra says, staring into the water as she swirls her fingers through the surface, "is controlling the atmosphere, controlling the five physical senses, so the sixth sense can rise to the forefront."

She dips the scarf in the water and then wrings it out over the bowl.

"Close your eyes," she instructs, and I do.

I feel a cool sensation on my face as she presses the scarf over my eyes, tying it loosely behind my head. When I inhale, I smell something rich and earthy.

"Juniper berry," she says. "It is an excellent cleansing scent."

I smile and inhale again.

"Now," Cassandra says, her voice dropping to a near-whisper, "I want you to clear your mind of all concerns, and focus only on the sound of my voice."

Cassandra's soothing words guide me out of the safe house, out of my body and into another place. Honestly, it reminds me of Hades – dark and misty, like the fogged-in shore at night.

This isn't like my previous visions. I have no dizziness, and I'm not immediately in the middle of the event. This feels more like a waiting room.

"Now," Cassandra soothes, "direct your thoughts. Seek that which you most need to know."

Direct my thoughts? That's easier said than done.

There are many things on my mind right now. It's tempting to let my mind drift.

But rather than complain, I focus. I have a mission. I start with the oracle. I've never seen her, but Gretchen described her. Plus I've seen the oracle's storefront. That gives me a place to start.

I narrow my thoughts onto that spot, onto the oracle I've never met, onto...

The door. That's what we *really* need to know. Everything else just leads to that. The oracle is a means to an end. My sisters and I need to find the door and open it so all this danger goes away – although how you open a door that isn't a door and isn't even really a place is beyond me.

Not that I think opening the door is going to magically make everything all better right away. I'm sure there will be plenty of people – and gods and monsters – who will want to keep stirring up trouble. But we'll be able to handle it with the gorgons, our mother and our friends at our sides – with Nick and Milo and Thane.

Thane.

Yes, Thane, the woman's voice says.

Where is he? Why did he leave? After finally revealing the truth about himself, he must have been worried about what we would think of him.

He should never have left. He should have known we wouldn't hold his past against him – that I wouldn't judge him for something that was beyond his control. Rather, I judge him for taking control of the situation, for standing up to his keepers to protect Grace. To protect me. I judge him as one of the bravest, most honourable people I've ever known. That he didn't want us to know his secret only means he cares about our opinions.

I need to find Thane, so I can tell him everything is all right.

Then I see him.

He sits on a bench in front of a pond. There are trees all around, and flowers. In the pond, a family of ducks swims to an island of reeds in the middle.

The mist parts, and suddenly I can see Thane's face. He looks pained. Not in pain – not physical pain, anyway – but aching, angry at himself and afraid of what he might have lost.

I reach out, but my hand goes right through him.

I look around, trying to see where he is. Through the mist and trees I see planes of brick and glass. This could be anywhere in the city.

"Thane," I call out. "Where are you?"

He looks around, like he can hear me.

I reach for him again, and this time when I do, I'm transported.

I'm back in the dungeon of Olympus, surrounded by that damp dark stone and the persistent drip-drip-drip of moisture from the ceiling. There is nothing around me, nothing but the black stone and the dim glow of torchlight.

I can practically feel the smoke in my lungs.

I start walking, surprised to find I can move around in this vision. Another first.

"I won't," I hear Thane say.

Then the snap of leather on flesh.

"Thane!"

I rush towards the source of the sound, around a corner and into a small space with three solid walls and a drain in the centre of the floor. Chained at his wrists and ankles, Thane stands in the centre of the room, shirtless, with his arms and legs spread wide towards the side walls.

An exquisitely beautiful woman with flaming red hair – literally flaming, as in on fire – stands before him.

"You have a mission, *stratiotis*," she says, leaning close to speak next to his ear. "Your goddess will not be pleased if you fail her."

Thane stands silent.

"You must kill the girls," she says. "All three of them. You are so commanded."

"No."

"You would refuse a direct order?"

The flame-haired woman looks almost gleeful when he says, "I will."

She holds up her hand, revealing long claws at the ends of her fingers. Then, her dark eyes sparkling, she drags her claws across Thane's chest. She leaves a ragged trail of three parallel marks on his muscular chest.

Those marks – I've seen them before, in the vision I had in our storage closet of Thane standing before a mirror, applying green liquid to cuts on his chest. This is how he got those wounds.

Has this already happened? Or is it happening now?

"The poison will take time," the woman tells him. "If you carry out your mission, I might give you the antidote."

Thane growls in pain.

Then I'm gone, back in the safe house with the scarf over my eyes.

I reach up and yank the scarf off, struggling to keep my panic from rising as my breath huffs out in ragged puffs. Those images, those events… I'm terrified for Thane.

But as I stare around the room at my sisters, at my mother, at sweet little Sillus, I can't tell them. They expected me to seek out a vision of the oracle. They would have been happier with a vision of the door.

I can't tell them I had a vision of Thane being whipped and poisoned. I don't know when it happened – or will happen – and I don't know if we can do anything about it. That helplessness will break Grace's heart.

"So?" Gretchen prods when my gaze lands on her. "What did you see?"

I shake my head, forcing my breathing back under control. "Nothing."

Not nothing, the woman says.

Gretchen frowns.

"Nothing?" Grace repeats, looking skeptical.

"No," I say, wishing I were the sort of girl who believed that crossed fingers counteracted a lie. "Nothing at all."

I draw in a deep breath and, turning to Cassandra, say, "Let's try again."

CHAPTER 24

Grace

Greer isn't telling us everything about her lack of vision; I'd bet my laptop on it. But what I can't figure out is why. What could she have seen that she wouldn't want us to know?

Then again, she's been through a lot today – I mean, she *died*; maybe she just didn't have a vision. Maybe I'm wrong. It's possible.

Gretchen isn't so accepting.

"How could you not see anything?" she demands. "You were out for ten minutes."

"I don't know." Greer's eyes slide away. "Maybe my energy is drained."

"I don't believe you."

"Do you want a soda?" I ask her.

"I'll get one," Cassandra offers.

"What I really want," Greer says, "is to try again."

Gretchen jams her hands on her hips, staring Greer down across the table.

"You're lying," she accuses.

For several long, tense moments, they have their battle

of wills. I'm glad I'm not caught between the two of them. My sisters are powerful – and stubborn – girls. Finally, Greer gives up. She rolls her eyes and relaxes back into the chair.

"All right," Greer says with a sigh. "I saw something. But it's not relevant. It wasn't about the door or the oracle. It was personal."

Cassandra sets a glass of fizzing orange soda on the table.

"Fine," Gretchen says, gesturing at the bowl of water. "Try again. Maybe focus harder this time."

"I was focused," Greer bites out. "In case you don't remember, I died this afternoon. My apologies if it takes me a minute to recover from that."

Gretchen pounds her fist on the table, sloshing some soda onto the already dirty surface.

"Maybe you should take that nap." I nod towards the bedroom. "Your focus will be better when you're rested."

"I *was* focused," Greer shouts. The outburst is so unlike her that we all jerk back. Even Sillus scampers away, wedging himself into the corner by the front door.

"I'm fine," Greer insists, calming herself with a deep breath. "I'll just go splash some cold water on my—"

A knock at the door interrupts our conversation.

Gretchen is instantly on alert, her body tense and her ear cocked to the door. Sillus's eyes are so wide they take up half his furry face.

"Maybe it's the gorgons," I whisper. "Maybe they found the oracle."

Gretchen scowls at me. "They have a key."

She scans her gaze around the room, a finger pressed to her mouth.

I bite my lips to ensure my silence.

She walks stealthily to the front door, her boots barely making a sound on the old shag carpet. Sillus moves behind her. After lifting up to peer through the peephole, she says, "Who is it?"

"Landlord," a bored male voice replies. "Doing my annual inspection."

She hesitates. "Everything's fine in here."

"Don't matter," the landlord says. "Gotta check it out firsthand. I got forms to fill out."

Gretchen looks to us like she's seeking an opinion. I keep my lips between my teeth while Greer lists to one side in exhaustion. Our mother moves to her side and places supportive hands on her shoulders.

"There's no alarm system?" Greer whispers, shaking off her fatigue. "Security cameras?"

"This is a safe house," Gretchen hisses, "not a vault. Ursula's magical protections are supposed to keep others from finding it. Secrecy is its security."

Gretchen bends down and pulls a dagger out of her boot. Sillus reaches into her other boot and palms the dagger hidden there. With one hand on the knife,

Gretchen twists the deadbolt with the other. She throws us a be-prepared look. Then she reaches for the handle, twisting slowly before pulling the door open an inch.

The door bursts open inward, knocking Gretchen back into Sillus.

"Run!" she shouts as she shoves her shoulder into the door, holding back the intruders.

The landlord pushes in first, and I can see at least a dozen more bodies behind him. I don't look long enough to tell if they're man or monster. It doesn't matter.

"Not landlord," Sillus says, jumping up and down.

I grab Greer by the hand and yank her off the chair.

"We have to go!" I shout at her.

"Come," Cassandra says, hurrying across the room to the small window on the exterior wall. She yanks the curtain back, flips a couple of latches and then pulls the window open wide, revealing a fire escape just outside. "Hurry."

She waves me and Greer towards the window, but I hesitate. I glance back at Gretchen, who is struggling – with Sillus's minimal help – to hold the door against the army outside. They're barely maintaining their ground.

"Here," I say, pushing Greer at Cassandra. "Take her and get out of here. I'm going to help."

Cassandra looks like she wants to argue.

I cut her off. "Go!"

She nods.

As soon as she is guiding Greer out over the windowsill, I rush to the front door.

"What are you doing?" Gretchen demands.

I shove my shoulder next to hers up against the door. "Helping you, stupid."

She actually laughs.

"You're getting a bit of an – oof – defiant attitude, Grace Whitfield," she says.

I smile back, pushing all of my weight into the door. "I'll take that as a compliment."

"Good," she says, "because it was."

"Huntress talk later," Sillus says. "Push now."

Together, we all shove, and the door moves. Almost closed. Sillus jumps up on Gretchen's shoulder and leans down to the narrow opening where human and inhuman fingers are struggling to get a grip on the door. Opening his jaws wide, he chomps down on the fingers.

When the hand jerks away, we give the door one more solid shove, and it connects with the jamb. Gretchen quickly flips the deadbolt.

"Go," she says. "Now!"

She shoves me away from the door, towards the fire escape. Sillus scampers out ahead of me. I don't bother looking back. I know she will be right behind me. Placing a palm on either side of the window, I climb out onto the metal platform.

Far below, I can see Greer and Cassandra climbing

down the ladder to ground level. I release a tentative sigh of relief as I start down after them.

I drop to the ground, wishing for once I'd worn shoes with more cushion than my standard uniform Chucks. They're awesome for pretty much everything but shock absorption.

As soon as I'm down, I move out of the way so Gretchen can follow.

"Jump huntress, jump," Sillus calls out.

Gretchen leaps down, landing hard on her combat boots.

"We need to move," Gretchen barks. "Head around back in case there are more of them waiting out front."

"You cannot escape, huntress!"

We glance up and see the fake landlord leaning out over the fire escape railing.

"Go," Gretchen shouts.

I don't wait to hear what else the man shouts. Taking Greer by the hand, I set out at a run, around the back of the building and into yet another alley. Gretchen passes me and takes the lead as she reaches the head of the alley. She stops just long enough to make sure the coast is clear and then takes off down the sidewalk.

Cassandra takes Sillus's hand, and they run after Gretchen. Greer and I struggle to keep up. I'm panting by the time we catch them, stopped at a red light two intersections later.

The five of us huddle up next to the lamppost.

"Where do we go?" Cassandra asks.

I shake my head.

"I don't know," Gretchen says. "They're still finding us wherever we go."

"Who were they?" Cassandra asks.

"Soldiers of the Arms of Olympus." Gretchen's expression turns dark. "I'm getting sick of those jerkwads."

I can't help but giggle at her calling the army of the gods a bunch of jerkwads – then I immediately cover it with a cough when Gretchen gives me the look of death.

"I thought things were supposed to be better," I say, "now that Greer's disconnected from Apollo."

Gretchen frowns. "They should. Between that and the magical protections, they should not have been able to trace us there."

"Clearly they have other means," Cassandra says.

"Well, we need to go somewhere," Gretchen says.

"Grace's," Greer whispers.

"My place?" I ask. "Why?"

Greer's brow twists. "Because…"

"Numbers," Gretchen says.

I ask, "What?"

"Your apartment building is huge," she explains. "If they track us there, it will at least take them a while to find your unit."

"They already did," I insist. "They were there when Nick and I autoported in."

"The monster side knows," Gretchen argues. "They're probably not sharing their intel with Olympus."

I suck in a breath. "You're right."

"Come on," Gretchen urges. "Let's go."

CHAPTER 25

Greer

When I suggested we go to Grace's apartment, I hadn't actually been thinking it would be good cover to be in a multi-unit building. I hadn't been thinking about the best or safest place to escape to. I had only been thinking about Thane.

Despite the vision I had, I was secretly hoping he'd be here, that he'd have come home.

But as Grace and Cassandra get drinks from the kitchen, I peer down the hallway to where the bedrooms are located. There isn't a sound other than Cassandra humming and the drumming of Gretchen's fingers on the dining table. It's clear that Thane is nowhere around.

He's off somewhere feeling guilty.

I take a seat next to Gretchen in the dining room, clasping my hands in front of me. For the first time in days – weeks, maybe – I feel like I can take a breath. I shouldn't feel safer here than anywhere else, but for some reason being in this apartment, in this home, is calming. I can pause and reflect and think about everything that has happened.

Then again, most of what's happened recently isn't worth dwelling on. It's not like I want to look back on that time I died with great fondness. It's not like I have some great life lesson to learn or divine wisdom to bring back and share with the human world.

No, I got the brilliant advice from the Fates to *fight not alone*.

What is that even supposed to mean?

You shall see, the woman says.

Who are you? I demand. I'm getting sick of having people in my head, real or not.

That too, she says, *you shall see. Soon. Until then…*

All right. If the voice in my head isn't going to help, then I'll figure it out on my own.

Well, at face value, it means we shouldn't do this by ourselves. It means we shouldn't face the coming war without help. The three of us can't do it alone – not facing all the enemies who are out to stop us, one way or another.

We need as many friends on our side as we can get.

The gorgons are gathering our allies, but what if they aren't enough? If I stop too long to think about the odds against us, I'll crumble.

This is the absolute worst time for Thane to take off. I don't care if he's upset or pouting or beating himself up for everything he's ever done; we need him, and he bailed.

Unacceptable.

I smack my palms on the table. "Enough."

I'm all for him taking a little while to pull himself together, especially after something big like seeing the girl he likes die or telling his sister he was sent to kill her. Thane gets a little leeway for that. But we're in the middle of epic things right now, and we don't have time to indulge in self-pity. We don't have time to indulge in anything.

None of us do.

There are too many things – too many gods and monsters – working against us. We need to be gathering numbers, not letting them spread out.

I turn my attention on Gretchen.

"You should go find Nick."

"What?" she asks, twisting her head and gaping at me like I'm a talking dog.

"We might need him," I explain, "and you obviously care about him."

"I—"

"Don't deny it; we can all see it." Now that I've started, I'm gathering steam. I resist the urge to pat her hand. "I saw the look on your face as he got dragged into the abyss. I saw you dive in after him without a moment's hesitation."

"We needed him."

"*You* needed him," I correct. "You still do."

She stares at her hands. I wonder what she sees there – the hands of a girl who's hunted more monsters than she can count? Or the hands of a girl who cares about a boy more than she'd like to admit, even to herself?

"If it were me or Grace," I say, "you wouldn't stop until you'd found us."

"It's not you," she argues.

"He's just as much a part of this," I continue. "Only he's in it by choice, which makes him all the more valuable."

She finally lifts her head, and the look in her eyes is a tumultuous mix of hope and fear, doubt and certainty. For someone like Gretchen, with her history, the kind of emotion she feels for Nick is dangerous, a liability. But she's tempted.

One little push could send her over the edge.

I think a little subtle manipulation is called for here.

If she thinks I had a vision about Nick, implying that I've already seen how important he will be, then maybe she'll stop fighting her feelings and go after him. Besides, how do I know that we *don't* need him? He could be the crucial piece to the final puzzle.

"We still need him," I say, choosing my words carefully. I casually rub my finger across my temple. "He's important."

She scowls at me, and at first I think I've gone too far. She looks angry, like she might shove back from the table and storm away.

Then she shocks the sugar out of me by saying, "I know."

"You do?" I flinch, then regroup and say, "Good."

"But I don't even know where to start." She tilts back

270

in her chair. "He could be anywhere. He could be—"

She shakes her head, not willing to say her worst fear out loud.

"Hey, girls," Grace says, returning to the dining room. She and Cassandra are carrying trays of drinks and sandwiches. "Lunch is served."

While Grace hands out the drinks, Cassandra sets a plate before each of us. Sillus grabs a sandwich and takes a giant bite.

"You said you met the boss guy before, right?" I ask Gretchen.

Grace freezes, her glass halfway to her lips.

"Well, did you" – I'm not sure how to say this without sounding disgusting, so I just say it – "*smell* him?"

Gretchen frowns for a second, like she's not sure why I would ask such an odd question. "Yeah. I did."

"What are you talking about?" Grace sets her glass back on the table.

"Who's the boss?" Cassandra asks.

Grace turns to her. "A bad guy. A really bad guy."

Cassandra makes a pained face.

"Can't you track him, then?" I ask Gretchen. "Sniff him out like a monster?"

She drops her chair back down on four legs. "Never had to pick out a specific scent before. I've always just followed whatever beastie stink was in the air at the moment. It's worth a shot."

"Um, *why* are we tracking the boss?" Grace asks.

"Gretchen's going to save Nick," I say.

"Really?" Grace cheers, sitting up straighter in her chair.

Gretchen mutters, "I'm going to try."

"Who's Nick?" Cassandra asks, and Grace leans over and whispers in her ear. A proud smile spreads across her lips. "You should definitely rescue him, then."

"Right," Grace says. "Let's get started."

"Actually," I say, staring at my sandwich, "I'm going after Thane."

"Thane?" Grace echoes.

"My vision," I explain. "It was about him. I need to go find him and bring him back. You guys go find Nick."

"*I'll* go after Nick," Gretchen says. "He is my mission. Grace can go with you."

"That's not practical," I argue. "Thane isn't being held prisoner. You'll need backup. I won't."

"Greer's right," Grace says, dropping her fangs and pulling back her lip to display them. "You're not going without me."

Gretchen nods. "Fine. Grace comes with me. Greer looks for Thane."

"Where Sillus go?"

"With me." Gretchen rubs the little monkey's head. "Of course."

"And me," Cassandra says. "I want to help."

272

"You can." Gretchen pushes back from the table. "But not with this. If the boss has kept Nick alive, he's hoping I'll come after him. It might be dangerous."

"But—"

"You'll get in the way," Gretchen snaps, cutting off our mother.

The words were harsh, but I can see the worry in Gretchen's silver-grey eyes. It's not so much that Cassandra would get in the way; it's that her presence would distract Gretchen from the mission. And that would be dangerous for everyone.

"You should go home," Grace tells Cassandra. "We'll all feel better knowing you're safe."

"I'm not ignorant of this world," she says, her silver-grey eyes steady and serious.

"We know." Grace throws Gretchen a look. "And I'm sure we'll need you before this is over."

"Yeah," Gretchen grumbles. "This is a simple smash-and-grab job. No mythology required."

Cassandra looks at each of us in turn. "If you're sure?"

We all nod.

"You know where to find me," she says to Grace. "And I'm always at the other end of the cell number I gave you."

Grace smiles and squeezes her hand. "We'll call."

"You girls be careful," Cassandra says as she heads out the door.

"I'll walk you out," Grace offers.

I turn to Gretchen. Her fingers fidget with a quarter, spinning it on the table surface and revealing uncharacteristic nerves. Gretchen doesn't show doubts or weakness. I reach my hand out and lay it on hers. "You will find him."

Grace returns a moment later. "Okay," she says. "I'm ready. Let's go find those boys."

As soon as my sisters and Sillus pull away in Gretchen's Mustang, I pull out my phone – ignoring the forty-seven unread text messages – and open the browser. I start searching for the details from my vision: the pond, the brick and glass buildings, the baby ducks.

One of the results directs me to part of the Presidio, in a corner that's become the campus for a division of Lucasfilm. I switch over to an image search, and the first picture is of the exact spot from my vision. Victory!

I switch over to my Muni app and find the bus route I'll need to take. I wish I had time to go get my car, but the next bus is only two minutes away. My Porsche is halfway across town. This will be faster.

I'm glad my sisters didn't fight me about going after Thane alone. He feels guilty – for something he didn't even do – and thinks he's not worthy of us. I want the chance to talk with him, to make him see the reality of the situation, without anyone else involved.

I owe him that.

Hurrying down the sidewalk, I hope the first part of my vision is right – the part where he's sitting on that bench at the Presidio, not when he's being beaten by the woman with flaming hair.

While I'm waiting for the bus, I pull out my phone to read through those texts. There really are forty-seven of them. I guess I have been kind of out of touch.

Quickly scrolling through the list, I don't see any from Mother or Dad. They must really be enjoying the tropical vacation I used my hypno powers to send them on.

Most of the rest are from my friends, wondering where I am, what happened at the tea, why I wasn't in school. They start off friendly and curious but quickly turn ugly. My friends got irritated because I wasn't texting back. I wouldn't even know where to begin an explanation. I could make up some fabulous holiday claim – pretend I went on that vacation with my parents – but, honestly, why bother? If my friends are more angry than concerned about my disappearance, they're not very good friends, are they?

There are a couple of texts from Kyle – decidedly my *ex*. I delete them without even reading them.

While I am checking, just as the bus pulls up to the stop, a new message pops up. This one is from an unknown number.

> Did you enjoy your trip to the underworld?
> You might have severed the connection to

> Apollo, but you and your sisters are always within my sights. See you on the battlefield.

Scowling, I climb on the bus, scan my pass and take a seat near the rear door. That message is unnervingly bizarre. I try calling the number back, but I get a recording that says, "The number you are trying to reach has been disconnected."

There is something extra creepy about the text message. Glancing around the half-full bus, I have the eerie feeling that whoever sent it is here, watching me.

No one on the bus seems to be paying me much attention.

"Really, Greer," I tell myself.

I'm overreacting. Whoever sent that text couldn't possibly know that I'm here, right now, on this bus, going to look for Thane. My supernatural tracking device has been decommissioned.

I lean back in my seat as the bus rolls down the street.

My phone dings with another text.

It's from the same unknown – and *disconnected* – number.

> Good luck with your search.

I freeze, not wanting to draw attention to myself by freaking out. I take a slow breath, paste a neutral smile on my face and force my shoulders to relax. I need to get out of here.

At the next stop, I walk casually off the bus. As I step onto the concrete, I have that feeling again. I'm being watched. Kneeling down, I pretend to retie the laces on my Keds while watching to see if anyone else gets off with me.

The bus pulls away, and I'm alone on the sidewalk.

I stand, sucking in a deep breath. Whoever is sending the texts must be toying with me.

Luckily, I'm not far from the Lombard Gate entrance to the Presidio. As I walk towards the lush, wooded park, I decide that as soon as I find Thane – and convince him not to be a self-punishing moron – I will call my sisters and tell them about the texts.

Suddenly, being all alone in the city is a very scary thing.

CHAPTER 26

Gretchen

From the peak of Buena Vista Park, I can see and smell the entire Bay Area. If I want to get in a good sniff test to pinpoint the boss's location in the city, I need the high elevation and the clear view. If he's still in the area, I'll be able to smell him from up here.

I only hope he is and that Nick is still with him.

I stand on the perch of the hill, close my eyes and draw a deep breath in through my nostrils. I can smell Grace next to me. I never really noticed, but we have a bit of a distinctive smell, too; it's not disgusting like the monsters – she doesn't smell like burning flesh or sulphur or mouldy bread – but something sweet, sugary, like the venom that runs through our fangs.

That fact might be useful in the future, in case I need to find my sisters. It's like a built-in compass.

I can smell Sillus, too. He doesn't smell nearly as sweet; more like sawdust and stale buttered popcorn.

Inhaling again, I smell beyond the immediate area. I seek out the boss's unique scent. Drawing on olfactory memory, I can remember his odour perfectly – maybe too well: a repulsive mix of wet dog and decaying fish. I've never smelled anything like it before, so it shouldn't be too hard to pick it out of the spectrum of smells that San Francisco has to offer.

Turning in a circle, I do a counter-clockwise three-sixty sniff, covering every sector of the city. Not in Fisherman's Wharf. Not in the Marina or the Presidio. Not in Golden Gate Park, Potrero Hill, or the Mission. I'm closing up the circle, sniffing over SoMa, heading for the financial district, when I catch the scent.

I open my eyes and find myself staring at the old harbour, a string of abandoned and abandoned-looking warehouse piers that used to manage most of the Bay Area imports before Oakland became the primary port.

"There," I say, pointing across the city. "The boss is in there."

Sillus claps.

"Okay," Grace says. "Let's go get him."

"You can't just burst inside," Grace insists, wrapping a hand around my forearm as I start for the door of the rusty old building that is the source of the boss's smell. "Trust me."

With a determined look, she pulls me around to the side of the warehouse.

I shake my head and let her. She's not usually this bossy, so I figure she must have a reason. When she starts up a stack of crates beneath a filthy window, I ask, "Grace, what are you—"

"Shhh!" She gives me a shut-the-heck-up look – I don't think Grace is capable of swearing – and then waves me up the crate mountain.

When I get to the top, she points at the window and whispers, "Look."

Why is she being so cryptic? I scowl at her before leaning forward to look inside.

"Bad," Sillus says. "Big bad."

"What the hell?"

The inside of the warehouse is wall-to-wall people and monsters and piles of stuff. The crates and boxes are covered with dust, and they look like they've been there for a decade or two. They're probably not stockpiles of weapons or anything, but anything is possible.

Besides the run-of-the-mill ranks of beasts – butt-ugly giants, dragons, hybrids and every other creature in the bestiary – there is an absolute army of humans. They stand stock-still, utterly frozen in the middle of space. There are so many of them that they have only a few inches of personal space in any direction. They are literally packed in like sardines.

"Greer and I came here when we were trying to capture a monster," she whispers after scowling at me for my outburst. "We think they're hypnotising humans."

"Obviously," I say as I stare at row after row of

zombie-like people. "There are so many."

She nods. "I know. And there are even more now than before."

"There must be hundreds."

I knew that monsterkind was hypnotising people in preparation for overrunning me and my sisters when we finally opened the door. I didn't imagine they had accumulated quite so many.

And who knows if this is their entire collection of hypno-drones? They might have more hiding in other warehouses, on other piers. This is bad.

"We don't have time for this right now," I mutter. "We need to get in, get Nick" – if he's here – "and get gone."

Not bothering to scan the crowd below – Nick's immune to my hypno powers, so I assume he's immune to monster control, too – I search the perimeter of the space. The damn place is so cluttered I wouldn't see a bright orange Hummer if it was parked down there.

"Look," Grace gasps, pointing inside at an elevated room at the top of a spiral staircase in the back of the warehouse. It looks like an office.

I squint to make out what's inside. Through the open door, I see Nick tied to a chair. His body looks slumped, like he's unconscious. My muscles tense and I feel the urge for a fight. It was one thing when *I* tied Nick to a chair and knocked him unconscious. But for anyone else – especially the monster freaks – to do the same? That just pisses me off.

I quickly evaluate the logistics of the interior. There are no entrances immediately around the office, which means gaining access will take me straight through the middle of the hypno-horde and the monsters guarding them.

"How am I going to get him?"

"Huntress no go," Sillus says. "Too many."

"I'll go," Grace volunteers.

Is she crazy? "Um, no."

"Not like that," she says, giving me a stern look. "I can autoport in, grab Nick and pop back out."

"Pop, pop," Sillus says.

I study Grace. She looks determined, like she's excited to be able to do this, to use her powers this way. "You're sure you can do this?"

"Yes."

"Fine." I glance inside at the ugly horde. "Get in, get out."

Closing her eyes, she scrunches up her face in concentration. I've seen her do this before, but it's still amazing to watch. One instant she's here, and the next... she's still here.

"Problem?" I ask.

Her eyes flash open. "I'm trying," she says, looking around helplessly. "I'm focusing on the room, but it's just not working."

"Big magic." Sillus presses his palm to the window,

sending a ripple of glowing green waves across the glass. "Keep huntress out."

Grace deflates. "Shoot."

"Looks like we're doing this the old-fashioned way."

If only I knew how. I can book it with the best of them, but here I need to make it through the crowd of creatures and back again – with a Nick-sized dead weight over my shoulder. Maybe there's another way in.

Dipping down, I look up at the ceiling: nope, no skylights. I won't be rappelling down into the warehouse. There goes that possibility.

"If I can distract them," Grace muses, her voice distant, "how fast can you get to him and get out?"

I don't question how she intends to distract them. After a quick mental calculation – seven seconds to run across the floor and three up the stairs, five to cut Nick loose and twenty-five to carry his limp body down the stairs and back across the floor – I say, "Forty seconds, give or take."

Grace nods. "If we can find the electrical panel, I can give them something else to think about for a minute or two."

"Good," I reply. "Let's find it, then."

Sillus climbs back to ground level ahead of us.

"Oh, one other thing," Grace says as she follows me down the stack of crates. "You might have to do it in the dark."

283

No problem. If Nick's life depends on it, I could do it blindfolded, with both hands tied behind my back and an Indos Worm wrapped around my ankles. I guess that sums up how I feel about him.

Now I just have to rescue him so I can tell him – in slightly more straightforward terms.

"Now, there might be a few sparks," Grace says as she pulls open the electrical panel near a side door to the warehouse. She smiles at me. "That'll be your cue to go."

I nod and, just because I feel the urge, give her a quick hug.

"Thanks," I say.

She squeezes me back. "You'd do the same for me."

She's right; I would. In a heartbeat.

"Go," she says. "Get ready."

I move into position next to the door. A twist of the handle confirms my suspicion that it would be locked. I give Grace the agreed-upon hand signal, and she nods, waiting for me to deal with the lock before proceeding with her distraction.

There might be more elegant ways to defeat a locked door, but I only know one.

Once this war is over, I definitely need to acquire some lock-picking skills.

Pulling a dagger out of my boot, I slide it between the door and the jamb, moving it down the crack until it connects with the shaft of the bolt. I hold the blade steady with one hand, angling down into the door, and then slam my palm into the end of the hilt.

The dagger jolts down halfway. One more palm to the hilt and the blade swings free, the deadbolt shaft severed in half. There are some definite advantages to super strength.

I smirk at the thought that this door will never lock again. The monsters will have to either repair or relocate.

Turning to Grace, I give her the thumbs-up.

She turns her attention to the electrical panel. I resheathe my dagger and then wait, hand on the doorknob, for her next signal. Seconds later, she squeals as the panel erupts in a spray of sparks.

Inside, the fire alarm roars to life, pounding out an ear-splitting siren.

"Okay, go!" she shouts.

But I'm already gone.

Inside, the main lights are out, but the faint glow of emergency backups is more than enough to illuminate my path. Enough to see the hypnotised human army staying utterly – and creepily – still while the monsters around them erupt in chaos.

No one notices me as I sprint from the broken door, through the field of human statues, to the spiral staircase. I climb three steps at a time, making it to the top winded, but in three seconds – right on my estimate.

Pulse pounding, I scan the office as I run through the door, finding it empty except for Nick.

"Nick," I bark as I spin his chair around and lift a dagger to the rope. "Wake up!"

He doesn't even groan.

Sawing through the ropes takes several seconds more than I guessed. My heart races faster the longer I take. I've just cut through the last rope when the alarm stops.

I curse. "Nick, Nick, come on."

I shove my dagger back into my boot as I haul him up out of the chair, ducking down so I can heft him onto my shoulder. Fine. I can do this.

I turn to leave.

"Going somewhere, huntress?" the boss asks, an ugly smirk on his ugly dog face.

The weapon in his flipper – what looks like a pistol that's been modified so he can fire it without fingers – stops me more than the two Cacus bodyguards at his back.

"Thought I'd take this off your hands," I say, nodding at Nick. "You have so much on your plate already, what with the plans for monster world takeover and everything. You should be thanking me."

His face contorts with what I think is rage.

Odds are not in my favour. With Nick over my shoulder, I'm not agile or nimble. I can't reach my daggers. I can't get the smoke bombs from my left pocket or the flash bombs from the right. All I have is my wit, and that only seems to make him angry.

"Oh, I *do* thank you, huntress," the dog boss says, "for walking right into my trap."

I shrug one shoulder. "I do what I can."

"Boys," the boss says, nodding at his bodyguards.

They step around him, reaching for—

An explosion rocks the entire building. The boss stumbles back, and his bodyguards, caught off-balance, tumble to the ground.

I can only hope this is the second wave of Grace's distraction plan.

I don't hesitate.

Securing my arm around Nick's waist, I leap over the guards and knock into the boss on my way to the staircase. I'm a third of the way down when I see the boss fall past me, landing on the concrete floor below with a sickening crunch.

Then I'm sprinting across the floor, towards the door that Grace is holding open. Sillus is sitting on her shoulders, waving at me to run faster.

"What *was* that?" I ask as I blow through.

"You were behind schedule," she says, panting but keeping pace next to me as we sprint down the pier. "Figured you could use some help, so I blew the transformer."

There's no time to manoeuvre Nick into a car seat.

As I pop Moira's trunk, I give Grace a grateful smile. "Thanks."

Before she can answer, Sillus is in the back, Nick is secured, and Grace and I are speeding away from the warehouse. I watch in the rearview mirror as the boss's bodyguards come chasing after us. I floor the gas and leave them breathing my exhaust.

With adrenaline filling my bloodstream, it's no wonder I'm driving a bit wild. Grace is gripping her seat belt with both hands, knuckles white, with a frightened look on her face. I take a quick survey of our surroundings and realise that we're on a direct path to the most tourist-dense part of town.

It's as good a place as any to get lost for a minute.

I cut left on Market and then merge right onto Geary. Barely stopping to snatch a parking ticket from the gate, I speed into the garage beneath Union Square Park.

When I cut the engine, I release a breath I think I've been holding since we squealed away from the pier. Grace releases the death grip on her seat belt.

Without waiting for her to make some comment about my driving, I jump out of the car and run around to the trunk, popping the release as I go. Nick is already waking when I pull the trunk lid up and out of the way.

"I thought we were past the locking-me-in-the-trunk phase," he grumbles as he pushes himself into a sitting position.

"We are." I grab him by the forearms and pull him out of the trunk – there are times when it's really useful to have super strength. "We are not, apparently, past the saving-your-butt-from-the-monster-horde phase."

"Oh yeah." He gives me a sheepish grin. "That."

"Yeah, that," I repeat.

He straightens to his full height – a few inches taller than me – and I have to resist the urge to wrap my arms around his waist and rest my cheek against his chest. I don't think my pulse has slowed to anything near normal since Grace first told me he'd been taken.

Now, finally, I can relax.

"Hey, Nick," Grace says as she finally forces herself out of the car. She walks up and punches him. Hard.

"Ow." He rubs the spot on his arm. "What was that for?"

"For throwing me in that elevator and getting yourself taken prisoner," she says without any venom. "Next time ask first if you're planning on sacrificing yourself. I would have said no."

His mouth curves up into an amused grin. "Note taken."

"Good." She flashes him a cheery smile. "Now, I'll be in the car with the monkey so you two can make out."

I pretend to kick her as she dances out of range.

When she closes the car door behind her, I give in to my urge. Wrapping both arms around Nick's waist, I lean into him and hug him tight.

"You weren't worried about me, were you, Sharpe?" he teases.

I can't answer. If I tell him the truth, he'll know how I feel about him. If I lie, he'll know I'm lying, which will tell him how I feel about him. Either way, I'm revealing more of those feelings that I try to keep locked up tight.

"You don't have to say it," he says, his voice soft and serious for once. "I was worried about you."

"Me?" I ask, pulling back to look at him. "I wasn't taken prisoner."

"But I was." His mouth quirks up to one side. "Who would protect you if I was dead?"

I narrow a scowl at him. "Who usually protects who in this relationship?"

"It's a relationship, then?" he counters.

Darn it. He is too good at these verbal games. I'm better at the physical. So rather than try to beat him with words, I use my mouth another way.

Our lips are just about to touch when the horn on my car blares. The sound echoes off the concrete of the parking structure, amplifying it to eardrum-damaging levels.

"Sorry," Grace shouts out her open window. "Sillus got a little handsy with the steering wheel."

I laugh and relax into Nick's chest.

"Can't we just stay here?" I ask.

"Forever?"

"Maybe," I reply. "Or even for a little while."

He rests his chin on my head. "Maybe a little while."

For a second, I close my eyes and pretend the rest of my life doesn't exist. I don't resent my legacy. I love my sisters, and I take pride in our destiny. But sometimes, in moments like this, with my arms around Nick and his heart beating against my ear, I want to be a normal girl with normal girl problems.

I know these moments never last for long, but I'm going to hold on to it for as long as I can, because by the time this one is over, I have a feeling that "normal" won't even be in my vocabulary any more.

I sigh and listen to the steady rhythm of his heartbeat. Normal. Just… normal.

CHAPTER 27

Greer

For the longest time, I just watch him.

He's sitting on a wrought iron bench in front of a small pond. There are ducks in the pond and blossoms on the tulip trees. Just like my vision. The setting is so peaceful, and so at odds with the emotions battling in him.

I almost don't want to add myself into the equation. I might tip the balance either way. But, in the end, I have to. We need him.

I move silently, my footsteps light on the path as I walk down to his bench. I half expect him to sense my presence, so I'm surprised when I make it all the way into his peripheral vision before he notices me.

"You lost the connection with Apollo."

It's a statement, not a question.

"I wouldn't call it a *loss*," I reply, moving around the bench to look down at him. "But, yes, I'm a beacon no more. How did you know?"

He glances up, his eyes dark with pain. "Didn't they tell you?"

"Tell me what?" I ask. "That you're secretly an assassin

sent to kill Grace and the rest of us so we can't open the door?"

His brow scrunches up in confusion. Clearly, he thought I would be a little more upset about his confession. He doesn't know me very well yet.

"What does that have to do with you reading my mind?"

He rests his elbows on his knees, clenching his hands together. "Artemis and Apollo are twins."

"I know that." I am well versed in classical mythology. "They are the children of Zeus and Leto, the goddess of motherhood."

"As twins," he explains, "they have a supernatural connection that links their thoughts. As a soldier of Artemis, I was branded with her mark."

He releases his hands and pulls up the right sleeve of his T-shirt. There, inked into the flesh where his arm meets his shoulder, is a dark green tattoo in the shape of a bow and arrow – the symbol of the goddess of the hunt.

"This connects me to her in the same way the pendant connected you to Apollo." He tugs his sleeve back down. "It connected me to you, until your death severed the bond."

"So you really could read my mind?"

He shifts uncomfortably. "Not exactly. It was more like some of your thoughts – mostly your visions – ended up in my mind too. I didn't go looking for them."

Well, that is a lot to process. Not only did I form

a magical connection to a god, but that connection also tied me to his twin sister and those who bear her mark.

The world of Greek mythology is exceptionally complicated.

Maybe things will begin to make more sense the longer I'm involved.

"We're not connected any more," I say, trying to weave the various threads together in my mind. "Does that worry you? I had already touched the pendant when we first met. Do you think it will change things? That I won't care for you any more?"

He looks up at me, his eyes full of emotion: fear, hope, uncertainty.

"Trust me when I say that a magical connection has nothing to do with what I feel for you." I reach down and cup his cheek with my hand. He closes his eyes and leans into my palm. "Is that why you left?"

He shakes his head. Pulling back, out of my touch, he says, "I'm a coward. I had to reveal my secrets, but I couldn't face your reaction. Or Grace's."

That's the heart of it. He was afraid we would reject him. He was afraid to see anything other than attraction in my eyes or admiration in Grace's. He should have trusted us more.

Gretchen has learned to trust, and, I am confident, so will Thane. And I'm just the girl to start his training.

I shrug. "We all have secrets." I cross my arms. "I, for

example, once bought a knock-off Dooney from a shop down by the wharf, because every department store in the city was out of stock."

"Not really the same," he argues with a disbelieving huff. "Not a betrayal."

I lift my brows. "You don't know my friends."

Hanging his head low, he rubs his hands over his short hair.

"I am pissed at you, though," I say. When he looks up, I explain, "If you don't ask me to sit down, I might never speak to you again."

He half rolls his eyes.

I drum my fingers against my arm.

"What about me makes you think I'm not serious?"

He shakes his head but scoots over to one side of the bench, making room for me. When I don't immediately sit, he looks up. I just stare at him.

"Great gods," he says, exasperated. "Greer, would you like to sit?"

Good. That nudged him a little further out of his funk.

I give him a sunny smile. "I'd love to."

Settling in next to him on the bench, I give him a moment before I start in. He stares out at the water, at the pond and the ripples caused by wind or fish or waddling ducklings. He's scared. He thinks he's committed an unforgivable betrayal against the people he cares about most – his sister and his parents.

From one perspective, he's right. He lied to them, or at least withheld the truth.

But, like I said, haven't we all?

From another perspective, he's a hero. He chose family over duty and training. He put himself at great risk by refusing to harm me and my sisters.

It's time for him to stop acting like a traitor, but I know that coming right out and saying that will be absolutely the wrong approach. I have to come at this sideways.

"My parents have never loved me," I say.

He looks up, startled. Clearly that was not what he expected me to say. To be honest, it's not quite what I expected to say, either. It just spilled out of me when I opened my mouth.

"I mean, not the way some parents love their children," I explain. "Not the way your parents love you and Grace."

"I'm sorry."

"If they found out about my lies," I continue, "if they learned the truth about my heritage, they would view that as a betrayal. They would never forgive me."

"Thanks," he half groans. "That makes me feel better."

"Did you think I came here to make you feel better?" I shake my head. "I'm here to tell you to pull your head out of your backside."

He jerks back, shocked by my directness.

"Your parents love you," I say, "unequivocally. So does Grace."

"Which makes this so much worse."

"No," I insist. "That makes it so much easier."

"How?" he asks, like he really wants to know, *needs* to know. "The stronger the love, the worse the betrayal, Greer. It's not like I betrayed an acquaintance or even someone I hate. They love me, and I…"

"You love them," I finish. I twist around to face him, tucking my ankle behind my knee, and place my palms on his cheeks. "Listen to me very closely, because I am only going to say this one time." I wait for him to nod before continuing. "You have betrayed no one. If anything, you proved your love by getting these scars."

I hold my breath as I lift the hem of his T-shirt to reveal the three scratches – only half healed and still an angry red – inscribed across his torso. It is only a partial relief to know the painful part of my vision is already behind him.

It also means he is still in pain.

He grabs my hand and yanks his shirt back down. "How did you know about that?"

I purse my lips and tap my temple. "Second sight, remember?"

He studies me. "You saw it?"

I nod. "Have you taken the antidote?"

"No," he says. "There isn't any."

"The woman with the flaming hair," I argue. "She said she would give it to you if you succeeded."

He looks up at me, his dark eyes shuttered. "She lied."

I scowl. "What aren't you telling me?"

Shaking his head, he says, "It's… Only the juice of a golden apple can counter her poison. They are fiercely guarded, their juice more valuable than ambrosia."

"We'll find some," I say with as much certainty as I can muster. "Whatever it takes."

"It's fine," he says, taking my hand in his. "It's not fatal. Just painful."

I squeeze his hand. He is so strong, but he believes himself to be so inadequate. Even if I can't heal his pain, maybe I can make his emotional hurt better.

"You have not betrayed your family. The only thing that could betray their love," I say, "is abandoning them in their time of need. And right now, until this thing is finished, Grace needs you."

He frowns and shakes his head, like he doesn't quite believe me.

"I need you."

I reach down and wrap both my hands around his. When he looks up, I can see the hope in his eyes. And I can see the emotions, the same feeling of belonging I experience when I look at him. Maybe it's not love – not the real thing, not yet – but it's not the mixed-up magic of some mythological connection. It's a beginning, and it's worth fighting for.

He squeezes my hand, and I know he feels the same way.

We're in this together. Both of us. *All* of us.

"I don't deserve you," he insists.

"No one does," I reply with a confident smile. "You'll get used to the feeling."

He laughs – actually laughs – and I feel it all the way in my toes.

"Good," I say, releasing a contented sigh. "Now that everything is settled, I vote we enjoy this peace and quiet for a few minutes before we return to the fray."

He tugs me closer to his side. "Sounds perfect."

I lean my head on Thane's shoulder, thread my fingers through his so our hands are palm to palm, and join him in staring out over the pond and the peaceful hillside below. It's quiet and restful – exactly what I need after the craziness of the last couple of days.

Exactly what we both need.

The world might be falling apart around us, but in this place, for these few moments, there is calm.

I can't believe I've never been here before. A lifetime in the city, and I thought the Presidio was nothing more than parkland and military buildings.

The new construction of the buildings, with shiny glass offices and airy coffee shops, is kind of inspiring. Imagine looking out your office each day, down over this beautiful hillside, over the trees and streets below. Cherry and magnolia trees dance among tiny periwinkles and late fall crocuses. I can imagine it looks beautiful in every season, with wave after wave of blooms and blossoms.

Just over the treetops, I can make out the roof of the Palace of Fine Arts.

Now *that* I know. It's one of my favourite places in the city. If I ever ran away to think for a while, I'd plant myself on a bench in front of the lagoon on the east side. Despite its beauty and fame, there never seem to be *too* many tourists crowding the green space. They all flock to the Exploratorium inside, if they're not zooming by on a bus to the Golden Gate Bridge. It's a place where I could let time stop for a while.

Where I could watch ducks and children play and enjoy the elegance of the classical architecture.

Where I could soak up some sun – beneath a shield of high-SPF sunscreen – and pretend the bustling city was miles away.

Where I could wonder once more why the Grecian women in flowing gowns who circle the top of the structure face inward, away from the world. I've always thought they look like they're crying.

Weeping, even.

Weeping...

"Oh my gods." I jerk upright.

"What?" Thane asks.

I stare at him. "Oh my *gods*."

"What?"

"I think I just found the door."

He looks at me like I'm either insane or a genius. "What? Here?"

"No." I point at the pale concrete dome peeking above the treetops. "There."

She whispers, *Finally.*

"Then Gretchen ran out with Nick over her shoulder," Grace says, nearly breathless, "and we took off down the pier. She was amazing."

I hold the phone away from my ear and glare at it.

She hasn't let me get a word in since I dialled her number. "That's great, but—"

"You should have seen the look on those charcoal guys' faces – what?" Gretchen says something to her in the background. "Oh, right – they're Cacuses."

"Grace, I—"

"It was priceless." She takes a breath. "Have you found Thane? Is he—"

"Grace!" I snap.

Her silence is deafening, and I immediately feel bad for shouting. But she'll understand once she hears my news.

"Look, I have something to tell you guys." I try to calm my tone. "Can you put me on speakerphone?"

"Sure," she says, sounding a little hurt, "hold on a sec." The sound from her end changes, and then she says, "Okay, you're on."

"What's up?" Gretchen asks.

"I seem to have a knack for finding things," I say, smiling, "because I've found something important we'd lost."

"Yay, you found Thane," Grace cheers.

"No," I say, annoyed. "I mean, yes, I found Thane."

"Is he there?" she asks. "Is he okay?"

"Yes, he's here," I explain. "And yes, he's fine."

"Can you put him on?" Grace asks.

Fighting an eye roll, I punch the speaker button on my phone. "You guys are on speaker now too." I glare at Thane. "Say hello."

"Hey, Grace-face," he says, his eyes on me. "I'm so sorry."

"Oh Thane," she says, and I can hear the emotion in her voice. "You have nothing to apologise for."

I give him a look that says, *Yes, I know exactly how right I am.*

"Is that all you found?" Gretchen's voice makes it clear she's not quite as forgiving as our sister.

"No, actually. I found one other thing," I say, not trying to hide my pride. "Well, kind of." I scan the area around the Palace lagoon. "I believe I've located the door."

Grace gasps.

"Where are you?" Gretchen demands. When I tell her, she says, "Stay put. We'll be right there."

The phone goes dead. As I put mine away, I give Thane a sunny smile.

"That went well," he says gruffly.

I smile bigger. "It did, didn't it?"

He gives me that insane-genius look again. I take him by the hand.

"Come on, we can go watch the ducks while we wait for the girls." As I tug him over to one of the benches, I ask, "Have you ever heard of a Coot?"

CHAPTER 28

Grace

I pull out my phone and find the note where I typed in the translation of the oracle's riddle; it feels like a million years ago that Greer and I captured that monster and forced it to interpret the ancient Greek. We were so desperate to get Gretchen back, we risked everything.

Just like Gretchen risked everything tonight to rescue Nick.

He's still a bit groggy from whatever the boss used to knock him out – judging from the giant knot at the base of his skull, I'd say a baseball bat. Gretchen hasn't left his side since she got him out of the trunk of her car.

Gretchen also called Euryale to let her know we might have located the door. She and Sthenno are on their way here to meet us. From what she said, it's going to take them a while to get here. Who knows where they ended up on their search for the oracle. Guess we didn't need her to find the door after all. She left us the riddle instead. I have a feeling that's not all we'll need from her before this is over – she's too important to the whole thing.

I can't help grinning at Thane, who is practically glued

to Greer's side. He's never been a particularly happy person – the burden of that dark secret he's been carrying his whole life, I guess – but standing with Greer, he looks as close to content as I've ever seen. And now that his secret is in the open, maybe things will start to get better for him.

Sillus looks exhausted, leaning up against Gretchen's legs with his eyes drifting shut. I can't believe we're friends with a monkey monster. Who would have imagined?

All in all, the whole world around me feels completely different from the one I inhabited just a few weeks ago. And I feel like an entirely different person.

"Were you going to read that?" Gretchen demands, nodding at my phone.

Oops; caught daydreaming. My cheeks burn as I start to read the riddle out loud again. "In the space beneath the sky—"

"That must mean it's outdoors," Greer says, clearly excited by her find.

"Right," Gretchen agrees. "That makes sense."

Greer gestures at the park space around us. "And this is most definitely outdoors."

"Definitely." I smile at her before continuing. "Between harbour and haunted ground…"

That line is a little more specific.

"There is a giant cemetery in the Presidio," Greer says. "The Palace is between the Presidio and the water – the harbour at the marina."

"Between harbour and haunted ground," Nick says. "Check."

"Where graces and muses weep at gentle water's shore," I read.

Greer points up at the statues surrounding the roof of the building. "See how the women – the Graces and Muses – look like they're weeping?"

"I see the weeping muses," Gretchen concedes.

Thane nods.

"And the pond is definitely gentle water," Greer says smugly. "It fits all the criteria."

"What about the rest of it?" Gretchen asks.

If the first half of the riddle is meant to help us locate the door, I think the second half tells us what to do when we find it.

"Be three within three, join life with death in thee," I finish. "To find the lost and take up destiny."

My heart races a little faster. We are so close to the end game, to opening the door and beginning our guardianship. It's terrifying, but also thrilling.

"Last line seems obvious," Nick says. "'Find the lost' means find the door."

"And 'take up destiny,'" Greer adds, "must mean embracing our legacy. Guarding the door."

I put my phone away and look around the grounds of the Palace of Fine Arts. I haven't visited here yet. I've been too busy chasing and being chased by monsters to do much sightseeing at all since we moved to the city a few weeks ago. But this looks like a nice place to spend an afternoon. Plus Greer says the science museum inside is amazing. I wish we had time to go explore.

Probably should take care of saving the world first, though.

"The part about joining life with death," I say, glancing at Greer. "What if that means joining our blood? Like when we open a portal."

"That makes sense," Greer says. "Merging the healing blood of one side with the deadly blood of the other."

"That leaves one part to figure out," I say.

Gretchen kicks a rock out of the path. "Three within three."

"That part is tougher," I say, surveying the area.

Nick adds, "There are a lot of threes around here."

"It's neoclassical," Greer says. "It's practically all threes."

Thane squints into the sun as he looks around at all the threes.

Gretchen frowns, like she's still not one hundred percent convinced this is the right spot. I am.

"You have to admit," I say, "a lot of the criteria make sense. There can't be many places in the city that fit all of those things."

"Especially the weeping muses." Greer points to the carved women on the structures across the pond. "That feature is unique."

Gretchen clenches and unclenches her jaw.

"They're right," Nick says. "This has to be the spot."

"If that's even what the riddle is talking about." She considers it for a moment and then shrugs. "It can't hurt to look. Let's split up."

We agree to separate, to split up so we can search the area more thoroughly and quickly. Hopefully by the time the gorgons arrive from wherever they are, we'll be ready to open the door. Greer stops us.

"One thing," she says, leaning in close to whisper. "If you find it – or think you have – don't draw attention to the location. Let's meet back here when we're done searching."

Her voice is strained, like she's worried about something.

"What's wrong?" I ask.

"Nothing, I—" Greer looks over her shoulder, like she's expecting someone to be eavesdropping on us. Considering how many people are trying to control the outcome of this war, it wouldn't be a surprise. "I got a couple of weird texts earlier, and I think maybe…"

"We're being watched?" Gretchen suggests.

"Yes."

"I've been feeling it, too," Gretchen says.

"I—" I want to say that I've noticed something, but I haven't really. Maybe I'm just not as observant as my sisters. I whisper, "Then we'll be extra careful."

Gretchen volunteers to check out the parking-lot side of the Palace, the entire far side of the building that's full of locked doors and service entrances, in case the door turns out to be an actual door, I guess. Nick goes with her.

Greer and Thane head off to the pond side of the building, the exterior rotunda and open-air porticos with lots of columns and great photo ops. It's swarming with tourists trying – and mostly failing – to get pictures without anyone else in the frame.

Gretchen orders Sillus to go take a nap so he won't slow us down; she sounds harsh, but I think she feels bad for him. He scrambles to the nearest empty bench and curls up in a tiny ball.

I get the lucky job of checking out the grassy areas and the open space around the eastern side of the pond. It's a beautiful day, and I'm glad to be out in the sun. It almost makes me feel like I'm back in Orangevale. Not back *home* in Orangevale, because San Francisco is finally starting to feel like home. I wish Milo was here to enjoy the day with me.

There's not very much to inspect on my side of the pond – a few trees, some benches, a tree-dense minipeninsula at one end. Lots of ducks and a pair of pristine white swans. Nothing that looks like a door, or even a door that's not a door. It only takes me a few minutes to walk the entire length and back again.

I don't notice any standout threes – I'm not counting

the trio of seagulls that tried to chase me up a small hill. Nothing exceptional. Now what?

I sit down on the bench next to Sillus and stare out over the water.

The door is probably somewhere near the building anyway, right? The building has doors and archways and other door-like things.

Then what Sthenno said echoes in my mind: the door doesn't *look* like a door. It's a location – a certain place where, if my sisters and I open a portal, the door will appear.

Maybe I need to reorient my thinking. If we're looking for a door that's not a door, then the things that look like doors – the arches and actual doors – are less likely to be right.

As I survey the world around me, I run the third line of the riddle through my mind over and over again.

"Be three within three," I mutter.

Three columns? Three benches? Three... I-don't-know-whats.

Three within three, three within—

I gasp. "Three trees."

It's right there, right in front of me. As in *directly* in front of me.

Three gnarled and ancient-looking trees arranged in a triangular shape on a little piece of land that juts out into the pond just a tiny bit. They are tall, and their bark is almost black. Three within three. Three sisters within the triangle of three trees.

I quickly compare them to the other trees in the park. The rest look completely ordinary. There are none like them.

This has to be it.

Part of me wants to jump up and down, run over to the three trees – maybe hug them – and shout for my sisters to hurry up and join me. But I remember what Greer said about the weird texts, and what Gretchen said about feeling like we're being watched. The last thing I want to do is draw attention to the door.

If anyone from the Olympic faction – Zeus, Apollo, or one of their many allies – finds out we've located the door before we're ready, they won't think twice about killing us to keep us from breaking the seal.

For all I know, one of their agents is somewhere here among the tourists, just waiting for a reason to strike.

Or someone from the monster side is hiding out nearby so they're ready to attack the moment we open the door.

If we thought things were dangerous before, when we were just beginning to figure things out, then it's going to be all-out war when the factions involved find out we've found the door.

There is no place more dangerous for me and my sisters to be.

So, without sparing the three trees another glance,

I lean back on the bench, drape my arms over the back above Sillus's snoring body, and wait for my sisters to return.

"Nothing," Gretchen says with a huff when she and Nick return. "All normal doors and architectural details. This is a waste of time."

She flops down on the bench next to me while Nick stays standing in front of us. Sillus sits up at the sound of her voice and climbs over my lap to cuddle into hers.

I can barely contain my excitement. Her hand moves to pet Sillus's furry head.

"Um, Gretchen?" I ask offhandedly.

She turns her head to look at me.

"Don't look," I say, moving my lips as little as possible, "but the door is right in front of us."

She immediately looks. "Where?"

"Gretchen," I growl.

She quickly turns back to me. "Right. Where?"

"There—"

"I found several likely candidates," Greer says, stepping in between me and Gretchen and the three trees. "We will have to test them to be certain. Though I'm not really sure how to do that."

I glance up and give her a try-to-be-subtle look, but she's not paying attention.

"We should narrow it down before we attempt anything.

The rotunda would be a prime candidate," she explains, "but there weren't any noticeable threes. They could be hidden, of course, so we might as well start there."

When Thane nudges her, she looks at him. Then, following his gaze, she finally looks at me.

Gretchen cuts to the chase. "Sit down, shut up and act like nothing's happening."

Sillus lifts his head. "Huntress quiet."

Greer purses her lips like she's irritated, but then Gretchen gives her a fierce glare and her eyes widen as she sits down on my other side. I lean back and stare off to the south. Nick stands casually in front of Gretchen, while Thane – more relaxed than usual, but still way more tense than Nick – stands practically at attention between me and Greer.

"Directly in front of us," I whisper, "is a triangle of trees. *Three* trees."

From the corner of my eye, I see Gretchen subtly scan her gaze over the trees, checking it out. She returns her attention to me.

"You think that's it?"

I shrug and shake my head. "I can't be one hundred percent sure until we try."

"Of course. It makes perfect sense," Greer whispers. "It's outdoors, under the sky."

"And it would be easy enough to be three within three," I explain.

313

Gretchen scowls, like she's thinking it through. "And trees could be here forever and no one would notice."

"Three tree," Sillus whispers reverently.

"They look like they could have been here since the time of the gorgons," I say.

Greer nods. "This must be it."

"Agreed," Gretchen says.

"So…" I look from one sister to the other. "Now what?"

CHAPTER 29

Greer

All my years of service in student government, mock United Nations, and various leadership roles in clubs and activities have trained me to step up and take charge. So that's what I do.

"First," I say, standing and stepping away from the bench, "we need to go somewhere else."

The last thing we need to do is have a brainstorming session right here in front of the door, where anyone and everyone can see. We need to plan and strategise without worrying that one of the factions is going to burst in on the scene.

Gretchen and Grace stand with me while Nick and Thane flank us on either side, like bodyguards.

"The marina is two blocks that way," I say, pointing to the northeast. I smile tightly. "It's a lovely day to watch the boats sail by."

And figure out how to save the world without getting ourselves killed in the process. Dying again would be so anticlimactic.

We walk in silence, lost in our thoughts. I don't know

about my sisters, but my heart is racing. I feel like all of a sudden this is all too real. Certainly I've seen monsters before. I have been in the abyss and the dungeons of Mount Olympus and fought creatures most humans have never even imagined. But *this*? It's the gold ring. It's what we've been talking about, what we've been trying to do. What we've been risking everything to make happen. What we were born to do, literally.

It's fairly overwhelming.

If it weren't so important or so immediate, I might stop to wonder if we can really do it. There is fear and doubt, no matter how much I tell myself I don't believe in either. The truth is, it doesn't matter if I think we can. We don't have a choice. A lot of lives are depending on us, on our success. We *have* to do it.

We reach the corner of the marina, the spot where sailboats sleep and waves from the Bay gently slap against their hulls. It's quiet, peaceful. And we've come here to talk about war.

I'm not certain whether that's ironic or simply sad.

"Before we do anything else," Gretchen says as soon as we're settled, "we have a decision to make. Are we opening the door?"

"What?" Grace gasps.

I meet Gretchen's gaze. "I didn't think that was up for debate."

Gretchen doesn't blink as she speaks. "Maybe it's not,"

316

she says, "but we are in this together. The responsibility will be ours together. We need to decide this *together*."

"There's nothing to discuss." Nick looks like he wants to be sick.

"I'm sorry, Nick," Gretchen replies, "but you don't get a vote. We're the Key Generation. There are other alternatives and I don't want there to be any regrets."

Alternatives? Gretchen is right. Even if we believe we are decided, we need to at least consider the other options. This decision will affect the rest of our lives. We need to think this through. What if we don't open the door? What if we seal it forever or just let it seal itself through our inaction?

A picture of my life before – before I met my sisters, before I started seeing monsters again, before I knew that I had an ancient legacy to fulfill – flashes through my mind. At first, I'd thought that life was worth holding on to at all costs. Do I still want that? The success and the pressure and the twenty-year career plan?

The very thought makes me want to yawn.

"Well, I vote yes," Grace says after the slightest hesitation. "It's our destiny. We can't just let all those creatures *die*."

Those creatures – some of them – are our friends.

I think back to our time in the abyss. Sealing the door forever – and we do mean *forever* – would mean the death of every living thing inside. The Nemean lions and skorpios hybrids I'm not terribly compassionate about – I wouldn't mind fewer run-ins with them – but the golden maiden? The oceanid? The onyx guards? Sillus?

How could I live with myself if I sacrificed countless innocent creatures for the selfish purpose of preserving my social life? I couldn't.

Grace is right; we can't condemn them to death for the evils of others. They are pawns in this game of the gods.

Besides, the image of the picture-perfect life I once thought I wanted doesn't seem all that appealing any more. New student socials and mid-term study groups have lost their allure. They're downright boring. I've become kind of used to danger and adventure. I'm not about to give that up now.

"I agree," I finally say. "We open the door."

Gretchen nods, smiling like I passed a test. "Then it's unanimous."

Nick visibly relaxes. Did he really think Gretchen – any of us – would say no? Maybe he did. Maybe the old Gretchen would have. The Gretchen I first met, only a few weeks ago, would not have thought twice about the innocent creatures. Monsters were monsters were monsters; her only job was to send them home, by any means necessary. She's changed a lot in a short time. We all have.

Wise choice, the woman says.

"Oh for the love of Gucci," I shout. "Who are you and what are you doing in my brain?"

"Um, Greer?" Grace asks.

"What?" I snap.

My sisters exchange a look. Gretchen asks, "Who were you talking to?"

Oh, just the voices in my head – yeah, that confession would go over real well. They're still freaked out that I'm going to rekindle my connection to Apollo. I don't need to make them worry, not when we are at such a critical point in the prophecy.

"Then" – Grace looks at each of us – "what next?"

"Well, if we've interpreted the riddle correctly," I reply, "we stand within the triangle of trees, join our blood and the door opens."

"Just like that?" Grace asks, sceptical.

"No," Gretchen says, "not just like that. First, we have to battle the Olympic faction that wants to prevent us from opening the door. They will try to kill us before we have a chance to pull out the dagger."

"They'll have numbers on you," Nick says. "They've been planning this for millennia."

"They might not find us," Grace suggests. "We might be able to open the door without them ever finding out."

"Only if our luck changes," Gretchen says.

Thane shakes his head. "They'll find you. With Apollo on their side, it's only a matter of time."

Grace looks at me. "At least he isn't magically connected to you any more."

Yeah, thankfully. Thankfully I died and severed that—

"Oh!" I say, remembering the message the Fates – another important trio – gave me on my visit to Hades. "There is something else we need to do before we open the door."

"What's that?" Gretchen asks.

"Fight not alone," I say, repeating the words of advice.

"What?" Gretchen frowns.

Grace asks, "What does that mean?"

"It's the advice from the Fates," I say. "I think it means we need to call for help."

"From who?" Gretchen asks.

"The gorgons are on their way," Grace offers.

"We'll need more than the gorgons," I reply. "We'll need as much help as we can get."

"From *who*?" Gretchen repeats.

I resist the urge to correct Gretchen's grammar. "From everyone. From the monster realm, from our friends." I look each of my sisters in the eye. "Right now, I have to believe that the more people we have on our side, the better."

Grace nods like she agrees. "Before *and* after we open the door."

Gretchen scowls, thinking.

"Both factions will have armies working against us," Thane says.

"The more numbers we have, the better," Nick adds.

"You're right," Gretchen finally says. "We need to have an army of our own."

We agree to meet back here in an hour, with our makeshift troops gathered to our sides. We're going to do everything we can to balance the odds.

School is in session.

When I push through the front doors of Immaculate Heart, I'm stunned to realise I don't even know what day it is. I have no idea how many school days have passed since I last attended classes. Two? Ten? Twenty-seven? How many truancies have I accrued?

My parents are going to hear about it when they get home. Mother is adamant about a perfect attendance record – of course, Mother is adamant about many things. That used to matter to me. I used to exhaust myself trying to please her, even though I never could. Now I don't have time to worry about something as trivial as a few unexplained absences.

The first place I check is the maintenance office on the first floor, at the end of the first hall near the front door. The door is locked, and my knocks go unanswered.

He could be anywhere in the school.

After I discovered who – *what* – I am and started seeing monsters again, I suddenly saw through the friendly school janitor's human glamour to the furry spider inside. He knew I was a descendant of Medusa, a member of the Key Generation, and he promised to help when the time came.

Well, the time has come. And where is Harold?

As I walk past the front office, the secretary calls out my name.

"Greer," she shouts into the hallway. "Miss Morgenthal?"

I suck in a deep breath as I stop. I don't have time for this discussion, but the school secretary is a battle-axe. I can spare a few seconds, if only long enough to use my hypno powers to make her forget she saw me. If I don't at least listen to her reprimand, things will only be worse later. Of course, if I die in the upcoming battle – or, rather, die *again* – I won't be around to care. Still, this will make things easier in the long run.

I turn back to face the secretary.

"Miss Tregary," I say, pasting a huge smile on my face. "How are you this lovely morning?"

"Fine, dear, fine," she says, waddling out from behind her desk.

I never noticed before, but she does walk rather awkwardly. Perhaps that's why she wears long Gypsy skirts. I always thought it was to hide really hideous legs.

"I apologise for my recent absences," I say, trying to deflect the confrontation by confessing my wrongdoing before she can accuse me. "I've had some pressing outside responsibilities that I could not ignore."

I've mastered nothing if not the ability to be vaguely evasive.

"I'm not worried about that, dear," she says, waddling closer. "I'm sure ye have yer reasons."

She reaches into her bosom and pulls out a piece of paper.

"Harold asked me to pass this along if I saw you."

I take the note. "Um, thank you."

"You're welcome," she says. "Now ye'd best get going."

She turns to walk back to her desk. I'm about to leave the room when I catch a glimpse of something beneath her skirt. It looks like... well, the tip of a lizard's tail.

"Miss Tregary?"

She looks up as she settles back into her desk. "Yes, dear?"

For a moment, I consider asking her about it – asking her to help – but I quickly dismiss the idea. The older woman can barely walk; how could she ever help us fight?

Besides, she's worked here for ages – longer even than Harold. She couldn't be a monster in hiding.

I must be seeing things. I'm already hearing things – the madness is just progressing. The pressure is finally getting to me.

"Never mind," I say, and I turn to leave.

Out in the hall, I unfold the note from Harold, written in surprisingly elegant handwriting – I would have imagined it hard for a spider monster to grip a pen.

Miss Greer,
I had to return home unexpectedly. If
the time comes while I'm gone, please ask
Miss Tregary for assistance. She can get
you the help I promised.
Sincerely,
Harold

I fold the note back up and press my palms against my stomach. All right, maybe I *hadn't* been seeing things. I guess I'll have to confront Miss Tregary about her lizard tail after all. Pushing away from the wall, I turn and walk back into the office.

"Oh, Miss Tregary," I say, with a more genuine smile on my face, "there is something I need to ask you."

CHAPTER 30
Gretchen

The moment Greer leaves to rally her troops, Sillus tugs on my trouser leg.

"Sillus have friend," the little monkey dude says, looking up at me with wide eyes. "Family. Lots. Go get, they help huntress."

Nick and I exchange a questioning look. It's not like either of us has a broad circle of friends or family to call on. If Greer is right and we need every last bit of help we can get, we don't want to overlook his friends. Sillus has help, so we should take advantage.

Sillus directs me to the Bay Bridge underpass where I first found him and sent him home. I pull Moira up onto the sidewalk and put her in park.

There, in that abandoned lot, is a huge group of cercopes – at least two dozen little furry monkeys who look just like Sillus.

They rush us as we climb out of the car.

"Huntress!" they shout, jumping up and down to get my attention.

"Dude," I say to Sillus, "there are so many of you."

"Family," he says, looking over the monkeys with pride. "Is mom" – he points to one who jumps up and waves – "dad" – another monkey bounces above the crowd – "brother, sister, niece, nephew, aunt, uncle, cousin." The group erupts in high-pitched cheers. Turning back to me, Sillus grins. "Family."

I almost don't believe it. Little Sillus has a *huge* family. It seems so… human.

In a flash, I'm taken back to when I first met him. That moment – my conversation with the little freak – seemed so ordinary at the time. He was just another beastie, living in the wrong realm.

"All right, monkeys," I say to the excited group. "If you want to help—"

"Yes, help."

"Help huntress."

"Help, help, help."

My words drown in the sea of shouts. Nick coughs to cover up a laugh. I hold up my hand, and eventually they calm down.

"If you want to help," I try again, giving them a glare when they look like they want to riot again, "then get in my car."

Without hesitation, the entire group races for my Mustang. While they are climbing over each other to get inside, I look down at Sillus to find him beaming with pride.

Finding him was a turning point. He seemed so…

innocent. Every creature I had encountered up until then had been a monster in the worst sense, intent on killing or controlling humans. Sillus just wanted to live in the city, to make his home in this empty lot and get by like any one of the city's millions of residents.

From that moment, I looked at monsters differently. Instead of grouping them into a single black or white category, I started seeing shades of grey.

Since then, everything has changed. I'm proud to call some monsters my friends. And Sillus is first among them – which makes what I'm about to ask him even harder.

"Sillus," I say, kneeling down on the ground in front of him, "I need a favour."

I slip my arms around his tiny body and hug him. The look Nick gives me over the furry head is full of pride and understanding.

"Anything, huntress," he says with a serious look. "Sillus do anything for huntress."

That's what I'm afraid of. That's where the guilt comes in.

I sigh. "You might not want to do this."

He scowls but says, "Anything. Swear."

Taking in a deep breath, I say, "I need to send you back."

I see his earnestness flicker. "Back?"

"I need you to go back," I explain, "to let everyone know."

"The war is coming," Nick says. "They need to be ready."

I nod. "We will need their help from the inside."

Sillus jumps to his feet. "Sillus understand. Sillus help."

I smile. It's weird, but I've grown to really like the little guy. I like having him around. When my sisters and I open the door and defeat the factions on either side – because I *know* we will – maybe he'll be able to live here full time, without fear of being sent back again.

The risk, if we don't succeed, is too great to even consider. I won't let the potential for defeat enter the realm of possibility. If he is trapped inside and we fail to open the door, he and every other creature in the abyss will die instantly.

The pressure only drives me harder.

"Thank you," I tell him as I push aside my guilt.

We all have to take risks in this situation. We're all in danger until it's over, one way or another.

With a brave smile, he lifts up his foot. As I sink my fangs into him, I hope he gets there in time and that we all get through this alive.

When Sillus is gone, I sit back on my heels and sigh. There's an uncomfortable tightness in my chest. I stare up at the underside of the bridge, taking a moment to get my emotions under control. They're not going to help me win this war; if anything, they'll distract me. So many people are counting on me – my sisters, our friends, our families, thousands upon thousands of people who don't even know I exist. It's overwhelming if I think about it too much.

Nick kneels down in front of me.

"I need to go, too."

"What?" I ask, too shocked to hide it. "What do you mean?"

He can't leave. He can't abandon me. I need him. I don't want to do this alone.

After four years of going it solo – a whole lifetime, really, if I consider my adoptive guardians – it's amazing how much I've come to rely on others – Nick, my sisters, everyone fighting on our side in this war. Guess loner Gretchen is a thing of the past.

"It's time for me to rally the third faction," Nick says, "to spread the word that the prophesied time has come."

He stands, takes my hand and pulls me back to my feet.

"You need as many allies as you can find," he says. "The door will not open quietly."

As much as I know he's right, I still don't want him to go. But what I want has never mattered very much. Duty and destiny come first.

"Fine," I say, nodding. I know this is what he needs to do, even though I want him at my side, where I can protect him. Then, daring to reveal some of my feelings for him, I add, "Be careful."

He grins. Cocky bastard knows exactly how I feel.

"I will be faster than you can imagine," he says. He reaches into the neckline of his T-shirt and pulls out a necklace. It's very old-looking – ancient, even – a heavy gold chain with a pendant at the end: a single feathered wing. He holds it up to catch the sun. "A gift from Hermes."

I reach out to touch it, but then I pull back. Last time one of us touched a godly pendant, her brain almost exploded and she became telepathically connected to a god. No thanks.

"Protect yourself," I say, echoing back the words he said to me when he left the abyss, "until you're back at my side and I can do it myself."

There I go, exposing those feelings again.

"I will," he answers.

I look into his midnight blue eyes. "Promise?"

Instead of responding, he cups the back of my neck and presses his mouth to mine. My eyes fall shut and I focus on the sensation – warm, firm and full of promise. If I could freeze myself in one moment in time, it would be this one. My sisters and I have accomplished so much already, and we're about to risk our lives to save countless others. But right now, in this moment between pride and fear, held by the boy I'm pretty sure I'm growing to love, I'm tempted to pull him closer and forget the rest of the world. I have to force myself back to reality.

I push against his shoulders.

His eyes glow with the same fire running through my veins.

"I will meet you back at the marina before you leave to open the door."

Then he grabs the wing pendant in his fist, whispers something in a language I don't understand and vanishes into the ether. He was right – that was fast.

I stand there for a few moments, just breathing in and out, while the tingle in my lips fades. When it's gone, I finally turn and walk back to my car full of monkeys – I'll have to give her an extra-special bath once this is all over. The time for romance and fantasy is over. I have to earn the right to bring it back.

The war is about to begin – my sisters and I are going to start it. And if we want to finish it, we're going to have to be heavily armed when we do.

"Come on monkeys," I say. "Time to find some weapons."

CHAPTER 31

Grace

While Greer goes to her school and Gretchen goes off with Nick and Sillus, Thane and I stay at the marina. He gives me a little distance, moving off under a nearby tree as I pull out my phone. My hand shakes as I start to dial Milo's number.

Sure, he's been very understanding about all of this – he didn't run screaming from the room, never to be seen again – but this might cross a line. Knowing this world exists and participating in it are two different things.

But my sisters are right. We need as many people helping us, fighting on our side, as possible. And the results of the war, whether we win or lose, affect the humans who live in this world, too.

He picks up on the third ring.

"Grace?" he asks, his voice a hushed whisper.

Shoot; I forgot it was a school day. He's probably in class right now. I can't remember the last time I was in class. Time has just slipped away from me.

"Sorry," I say. "I shouldn't have—"

"Hold on," he whispers. His voice is muffled as he says,

"Mr Johnson? I need to use the restroom." Moments later, he's back at full volume. "What's up? Everything okay?"

I smile at how easily he got out of class. He is such a charmer.

Then I remember why I called.

"Actually..." How do I say this? I'm about to be involved in a mythological battle for my life, and I'd like you at my side? Well, maybe that. "It's time," I say quietly. "We've found the door, and we're about to—"

"Where are you?" he asks.

"I'm at the marina," I say. "We're trying to gather some forces to our side before all Hades breaks loose."

"I'll be right there," he says.

Then the phone goes dead, and I'm left silent and stunned. He's coming. He's really coming. Just like that. I need him, and he'll be right here. How did I get so lucky?

Thane walks back over to me. "Okay?"

I look up at him. "Yeah," I say, confused. "I didn't even have to ask. He's... he's on his way."

Thane winks at me. "I pick good friends."

He does. Milo might not have any godly blood in him, no personal reasons to get involved with this war, but his friendship with Thane and his feelings for me are enough. He's in.

Next, I scroll to Cassandra's contact info.

"Grace?" she asks when she answers two rings later. "Is it time?"

"Yes. We've found it," I whisper; even though we're not near the door, I don't want to risk being overheard – not if we really are being watched. "We're ready."

I tell her where the door is and where we're meeting.

"I'll be there soon," she says. "And I'll bring the reinforcements."

Before I can ask what that means, she's gone.

I walk over to Thane and sit down next to him on a bench. I place my hand over his.

"You know I love you, right?" I ask him.

He twists to look at me, surprised by my question.

"I know you're worried that I'll hold your past against you." I squeeze his hand. "But nothing can change the fact that you're my brother in every way that matters."

"I—" He tries to pull his hand away, but I hold on tight. "I lied to you, Grace-face. Since day one."

I turn to face him and make sure he's looking at me when I ask, "Were you lying when you told me that Sherwood Pierce was a moron if he didn't see how great I was?"

Thane laughs and shakes his head. "No."

"Were you lying when you crawled into my bed and told me you were scared of thunderstorms?"

Again, "No."

"Were you lying when you told me you would protect me with your life?"

"Of course not," he says, trying to look away.

I tug him back to face me. "Then nothing else matters. You're my brother," I say again, "and I love you. End of story."

The emotions battling inside him show on his handsome face, the hope and the guilt fighting for prominence. But I know Thane – the core of him, not the pesky details – and I know that hope will win in the end.

I don't say this out loud, but I'm relieved to finally have the secrets of his past out in the open. They have been eating at him for so long, he could never truly be his whole self with us, with his family. No matter how much he loved us and wanted to belong, he always kept himself at a bit of a distance.

Now, he'll be able to shed all that armour.

The first step, I think, is whatever is growing between him and Greer. He's never dated before, never seemed interested in forming relationships outside the family. Probably because he thought he wouldn't live long enough for them to matter when his bosses found out he was defying them.

I'm glad he's finally taking that step.

"You and Greer are a good match," I say, turning to look back out over the water.

He doesn't say anything; he doesn't have to.

As we both stare out at the boats, we fall into a peaceful silence as we wait for everyone to return – for my sisters and the support they're bringing with them.

I'm shocked when the first car that pulls up is our station wagon. Mom jumps out of the passenger side and runs over to me.

She wraps me in a big bear hug. "Oh good," she cries. "We're not too late."

"Not too – ?" I pull back and look at her. "Mom, what's going on? What are you doing here?"

"When Thane called," she says, her eyes damp, "I was afraid we wouldn't get here in time."

I give my brother a questioning look as Dad gets out of the car and walks over.

"I told them. Everything." Thane shrugs. "I thought they should know."

"We want to help," Dad says, walking up to Thane and proudly wrapping an arm around his shoulder. For once, Thane doesn't pull away.

"No," I say, glaring at Thane. "It's too dangerous."

Thane looks at me. "I got some good advice recently," he says. "When you love someone, you don't abandon them in their time of need." His mouth lifts into a half smile, telling me exactly who gave him this advice. "You're in need. They love you and want to help."

"You're both in need," Mom says. "And we love you both."

Thane won't admit it, but he needed to hear her say that more than almost anything.

"We'll do whatever we can," Dad adds. "Even if you

tell us to stay out of the way. Whatever we can."

I feel so loved. My heart feels like it might burst. Between Thane, Mom and Dad, and Milo, I can't believe I'm so lucky – to have people willing to risk everything, to take a stand side by side with me and my sisters. I pull my family into a group hug.

"Thanks," I say with an emotional sniff. "It means... a lot."

"That's what family is for," Mom says.

And it only makes me cry harder.

Greer returns first, leading an alarmingly large crowd of monsters across the parking lot. Her eyes are wide, like she can't quite believe she's at the head of this parade.

"Hi," she says, sounding kind of shocked. Waving over her back, she says, "These are, um, some of the monsters who have, um, been living in our fair city."

Greer is not an *um* kind of girl. I can tell she's uncomfortable with the swarm of beasties following her. There are a *lot* of them. It's hard to imagine all of these creatures living in San Francisco without anyone – Gretchen especially – noticing. Gretchen *before* things started changing. Then again, I suppose they kept pretty low under the radar.

Well, at least we'll have some good backup.

I wave at the crowd.

Then Milo arrives – with half the soccer team. I hurry

up to him. "What are they doing here?"

He gives me an uncertain shrug. "Davidoff saw me skipping out of class and decided to join me."

A tall, lanky boy with straight hair that falls to his shoulders waves at me.

I turn back to Milo. "So?"

"So…" He looks over his shoulder. "Then the rest of the guys caught us leaving and followed us out."

"You couldn't have told them not to come?"

He gives me a helpless look. "I tried." He leans forward and whispers. "They want to help. Once a team, always a team."

I breathe in and out, trying to decide what to do. Well, I guess it can't hurt to have their help. We can always hypno their memories away later.

"Okay," I tell Milo, lifting up to press a kiss to his cheek. "It'll be fine. Just keep them away from the most dangerous fighting."

He nods.

"And keep yourself there, too," I add. "Stay safe."

He grins, tracing an X on his chest. "Not a scratch."

Next comes Gretchen, without Nick. What happened to him? She squeals into the parking lot, pops her trunk and starts hauling duffel bags out of her car. A furry monkey jumps out after her, and at first I think it's Sillus. But then another monkey climbs out, and another, and even more – at least twenty little Silluses pile out of

338

the Mustang. They run around to the trunk and try to help Gretchen.

She already has all four duffel bags out and on the ground. They're totally stuffed to the brim.

She says something to the monkeys and then hefts a bag onto each shoulder, walks over to the rendezvous spot and drops them to the ground with a clatter.

"Weapons," she says, glancing around at the gathered crowd, not acting at all surprised by the sheer number of monsters in our group. "Lots of them."

Thane crosses to her car and grabs the other two duffel bags away from the monkeys who are trying – and failing – to drag them across the concrete. My brother brings them over and adds them to the pile.

"Who are your friends?" I ask Gretchen, hiding a smile.

"Apparently," she says with a wary look at the monkeys, "this is Sillus's extended family."

Two of the little guys have climbed onto Gretchen's roof and are trying to shove the trunk door down from above without success. A few are *in* the trunk, jumping up and down to make the car bounce as they giggle and laugh. Another pair sit in the driver's seat – one standing behind the steering wheel pretending to drive, the other on the floor playing with the pedals.

I hope Gretchen has her keys secured.

"They're adorable," I say.

"They smell," she replies, but there is no venom in her tone. She likes them.

"So," I ask, "where's Nick?"

She shakes her head. "He had to—"

"Right here," Nick says.

We all turn as he appears out of nowhere – literally out of nowhere. That must be what my autoporting looks like. Nick brings with him a couple dozen of his closest friends. Most of them look… more than human: women with leaves and flowers in their hair, men with tree trunks for legs, and various beings of both sexes who look like they're made out of soil, rock and water.

"I brought more troops," he says with a wink.

"What are they?" Gretchen asks in a suspicious whisper.

"Nature creatures," he replies. "Dryads, naiads and all the other 'ads. These are the nymphs."

"Did you just autoport?" I ask. I thought that was my special gift – mine and Euryale's, anyway.

"No," a woman's voice says. "But we did."

Speaking of Euryale, she and Sthenno appear right in front of us.

"I did not find the oracle," Sthenno confesses. "She has truly gone to ground."

"That's all right," Greer replies. "We found the door without her."

"That is most impressive." Euryale grants me a brilliant smile.

340

I can understand why Gretchen is always so determined to make her proud. She has a way of making you feel like a superstar.

"I had success as well," Euryale says. "Our Olympic allies will be ready when the battle begins."

"That's great news," I cheer. "Right?"

"Yes, it's stupendous," Gretchen says, handing me a dagger. "Now let's get back to business. Start coating the weapons with venom."

I stare at the knife for a few seconds before asking, "With venom? How do we do that?"

Gretchen grabs another dagger, drops her fangs and then traces them over the blade. When she holds it out for me to inspect, I can see the glisten of clear purple liquid on the edge.

"Only our venom can send the monsters home," she says. "Once the door is open, they'll be pouring out into our realm, so we're going to give as many people as possible the power of our venom."

That's assuming we get the door open.

I nod and let my fangs drop.

Gretchen hands a knife to Greer, who does the same. We each take a duffel bag of weapons, coating every dagger, sword and arrow, along with weapons I can't even name, with our sweet purple venom. Gretchen coats two duffel bags full in the time it takes me and Greer to each do one.

When all the weapons have been envenomed, we hand them out to our growing crew of volunteers.

"We'll need to be armed too."

I look up and see Cassandra leading a crowd of women into the group.

"Who are all of these women?" I ask.

"Your family," she replies.

"I thought there were only three daughters born to every generation," Greer says. "There must be almost fifty women here."

"Not all are blood relatives," Cassandra explains. "This is the Sisterhood of the Serpent. There are aunts and sisters-in-law and adopted cousins and stepdaughters and other women who married into the Medusa clan. Since the time of prophecy, the Sisterhood has gathered the women in our family to prepare them for this very moment. We have known for generations that you would need help."

Without stopping to think, I pull her into a tight hug. "That's amazing."

Sthenno clears her throat. Loudly.

"Oh, right!" I step back and perform the introductions. "Cassandra, this is Sthenno, she's—"

"An immortal gorgon," Cassandra finishes. "Our ancient aunt."

Before I can confirm, she pulls Sthenno into a tight hug. To my amazement, Sthenno hugs her back.

"It has been too long, niece."

"And I am Euryale," our other aunt says.

When Cassandra releases Sthenno, she turns and hugs Euryale, too. It is as much a family reunion for the gorgons as it is for me and my sisters. Our mother is the descendant of their sister, too.

As I look around at our gathered numbers, I'm in awe. For the first time, I think maybe we won't be quite so ridiculously outnumbered. Maybe we'll stand a chance of coming out of this alive.

"Do we have a plan?" Euryale asks.

"Don't lose?" Greer suggests.

Gretchen and Sthenno spear her with identical unamused looks.

"The plan is simple," Gretchen explains. "We make for the door, while everyone else here holds off anyone who tries to stop us."

Euryale traces the hem of her flowing top. "The envenomed weapons will do no good against the gods and their army."

"Our forces will just have to stand their ground," Gretchen replies. "If we can't make it to the door, then none of this matters."

We need to get to the door in order to break the seal. That is the only way we can fulfill the prophecy and take up our legacy.

"Then we open the door," I offer. "Right?"

Gretchen nods.

"When that happens, the tides will shift," Sthenno says. "Most of the gods will change sides. A flood of monsters will enter this realm."

"We'll send them home," Gretchen says, spinning one of her daggers on her fingers, "but they will come back just as fast."

Greer stretches to her full height. "We will win," she insists. "No matter how many monsters come out, no matter how many gods try to kill us. We will win, because we are right. And that makes us strong."

Sthenno claps her on the back.

Euryale smiles. "It is time."

"We need to brief the troops," Gretchen says. She climbs onto a bench and faces the crowd. They must sense her leadership role, because they fall silent. "First priority will be the three of us getting to the door and getting it open."

The crowd of humans and monsters murmurs in agreement.

Nick shouts, "We protect the sisters at any cost. *All costs.*"

I bite my lips. That is a lot of pressure, a lot of responsibility. Others will be protecting us, putting our safety before theirs. I'm humbled.

And I'm all the more driven to succeed. I won't let their risks – and potential sacrifices – be in vain.

"Once the door is open," Gretchen continues, "the battle will change."

"The Olympic faction will no longer wish you dead," Sthenno says. Then she hastily adds, "We hope that, with the door open, their focus will shift to fighting the monsters. They should be on our side at that point."

"They will fight with us," Euryale adds, "not against us."

"Monsters will pour out of the abyss, trying to overrun us – kill us – so they can have absolute freedom to take over this world," Gretchen says. "This is when you will use the venom-dipped weapons. Send them back to the abyss." Under her breath she adds, "Even if they keep coming right back out."

The crowd boos, clearly not any more thrilled with the idea of a monster takeover than we are. They have no idea.

"With the door open, there will be other forces working against us from this side of the door," Gretchen says. "Some monsters, as well as an army of hypnotised humans, being forced to fight."

More boos.

"Do *not*," Gretchen shouts over them, "kill the humans. Immobilise them if you have to, or knock them unconscious. They are innocent in this, and will be acting against their will. Is that understood?"

The crowd murmurs.

"Is that *understood*?" she repeats.

"Yes."

"Okay."

"No kill."

Gretchen nods and then jumps down from her perch.

"So, girls," she says, giving me and Greer serious looks as the crowd around us applauds, "are we ready?"

"Yes," I reply, even though I feel like throwing up.

Greer nods and looks like she feels the same.

Gretchen pats each of us on the back. "Let's do this."

CHAPTER 32
Gretchen

We approach from the north end of the pond. Everything looks calm. Nothing out of the ordinary about the tourists and families milling around, snapping pictures and chasing ducks. The path is clear. The air smells like salt and sea – monster-free. An ordinary day in an ordinary place.

For a split second I think opening the door might turn out to be a nonissue. Maybe no one on either side will notice, and we'll be able to open it without having to fight for our lives against the Olympus faction.

I'm about to suggest we speed it up, get down there and get the door open before anything changes, when something changes.

It's minor, just a shift in the atmosphere, and then—

"Run!" I shout as the sky above transforms into a sea of flying creatures.

Silver birds and winged dragons and countless other airborne beasties swarm overhead. The fear in the crowd behind us is palpable. Those with mythological blood see exactly what they are. To the humans in our army, it might look like nothing more than a sky full of ordinary birds, but even a flock of seagulls would be alarming in these numbers. They sense trouble.

I grab a sister in each hand and sprint for the door. That has to be our only concern: opening the door.

Something swoops down in front of us. I keep running.

I don't know how they knew what was coming. It doesn't matter how they knew we'd found the door. They knew. And they're ready for the battle.

The world explodes around us into a chaos of fights and combat among humans, monsters, nymphs and gods. The uninvolved humans – just out to enjoy the day – flee, frightened by the outbreak of random violence. If they only knew what they were really running from.

I duck and dodge, keeping my sisters moving and my eye on the prize – the door.

Greer screams.

My arm jerks back. I release Grace and spin around to see a catoblepa grabbing Greer by the shoulders. I swing my arm down, grab a dagger from my boot and reverse the momentum, striking up into the hoofed creature's chest.

Thane comes out of nowhere, launches himself onto the catoblepa's back and knocks it to the side. As he struggles to pin it to the ground, he turns and shouts, "Keep moving!"

I grab Greer by the hand and take off.

We're only about fifty feet closer to the door when a

trio of hippocampi jump out of the pond and position themselves between us and our destination. I hesitate, holding my sisters back as I decide on a tactic.

"Go left," I shout, shoving my sisters to the side as I run the opposite way.

The hippocampi look confused, unsure of which way to go. Their uncertainty gives me time to get in position. In the end, they decide to go after the easier target, the single girl. Me.

Big mistake.

"Come on," I say, taunting them, trying to draw them closer as I back towards the water.

"Coming my way?" a sickening voice says behind me.

I spare a glance and see a man – tall, broad-shouldered, with grey hair and a long grey beard – rise out of the water. "What…?"

He raises his hands, and the water shoots out of the pond.

Poseidon?

"We cannot allow you to open the door," he bellows as water rains down on me.

"Not your call, big guy," I reply.

I *really* don't like being told what I can and can't do.

First things first. I turn back to face the hippocampi, only to find my sisters tackling them to the ground. I trained them well. Fine, I'll deal with Poseidon now.

A blonde woman with hair flowing down to her waist

and swirls of pink fabric wrapped around her body rises out of the water in front of the sea god.

"You have lost the path of right, uncle," the woman says.

Poseidon scoffs. "Love cannot protect the human world from monsters, Aphrodite."

She spreads her hands wide and a bright glow surrounds her. "You would be surprised by the power of love."

The bright glow expands in a quick burst. Aphrodite turns her head. "Run, Gretchen," she shouts. "Get to the door."

My mind is reeling at the idea that a god – an honest-to-goodness god – is here to fight me. To fight us. To *kill* us. And a goddess is just as determined to protect us.

I glance around the battlefield and am amazed to see more gods battling. A goddess with wheat in her hair – Demeter, maybe – is grappling with another who has a regal bearing – the queen goddess, Hera. A god with dark looks and an air of evil flings bolts of flame at a goddess who returns fire with golden arrows. Hades and Artemis are battling over whether or not we'll die now… or later. I'm voting for neither.

I'm ready to end this phase of the war.

"Come on," I yell to my sisters. "We need to get the door open. Now!"

I sprint for the spot, with my sisters right behind me.

When we finally reach the location, there is a giant

serpent winding its way around the three trees. The thing is huge, with muscles that bulge and ripple as it circles. At first I hesitate – it could crush the air out of all three of us without much effort – but then it winds itself around so tightly that it's practically in a knot.

It's stuck, and I see our chance.

I leap over its coils, into the space between the trees. Into the door.

My skin feels like I walked into a ball of static electricity – sparks and tingles everywhere.

"Hurry." I hold my hands out to my sisters.

Grace jumps over as I help Greer climb the slimy serpent.

Once we're all together, the three sisters of the Key Generation standing in the heart of the ancient door to the monster abyss, the weight of what we're about to do hits me. What we do next will change everything. Forever.

With one action, we will set our futures in stone.

My hand tightens around the hilt of my dagger.

I almost wish we had time to absorb this moment, to take in every detail. But it's probably better that we don't. Too much thinking would just muddy a decision that we already made. There's no thinking left to do.

Time to fulfill that prophecy.

"Let's open this sucker," I say, drawing the blade over my palms. "Quickly."

I trace the same lines in Greer and Gretchen's outstretched palms.

We stand in a circle, inside the circle of trees.

Three within three.

I look first at Grace – the first sister I found – and then at Greer. I'm a sister. I love them and I can't imagine going back to the way things were before. Who would have thought I would be so comfortable relying on others? So *happy* to not be alone any more?

Life truly has come full circle.

As I take Grace's palm in one hand and Greer's in the other, I smile and brace myself for whatever comes, knowing that together we can take it on.

Greer and Grace exchange a look. Then Grace takes Greer's hand, closing the circle, and the world explodes around us.

I don't know what I expected to follow the opening of the door, but the blinding light and hurricane-force wind seem reasonable. Those last for only a split second, just long enough for me to shut my eyes against the glare and get thrown back against one of the trees.

Quickly regaining my footing, I turn back to fight, ready to face Athena or the hippocampi or whatever other creature is coming after us.

But it's like we hit the pause button. Now everything is rewinding. The beasts in the sky stop attacking. The serpent around the door slithers away. The epic battle raging beyond quits full stop. It's as if everyone decided, right in the middle of battle, that they didn't want to fight after all.

"What's happening?" Grace asks.

I shake my head. "I don't know."

"The door is open," a deep voice says.

I turn and look up to find Zeus standing next to us – over us – imposing, intimidating and about the size of a garbage truck. He is the leader of the faction that has been trying to kill us. Instinctively, I step in front of my sisters and raise my dagger.

"Put that aside," he says, brushing my arm away. "You have initiated the prophecy. We are no longer enemies."

I blink several times. "What?"

"Now," he says, gesturing at the swirling vortex that is the door, "we face the same foe."

Almost as soon as he says that, monsters start climbing out of the abyss, two, four, even six at a time. If we don't act fast, we'll be outnumbered before we can get our first bites in. My sisters and I dive forward as the rest of our friends and supporters come to our aid. Fangs bared, we start venoming beasties, not bothering to care about pulse points or bite placement. We send them back as fast as we can, while our support army slashes venom-dipped weapons into the ones that get through our line of defence. Creatures are coming out in greater numbers than we can stop, even with the extra help.

This is a losing battle.

"Oh no," Grace says. "Look!"

I turn to see where she's pointing. Through the battlefield, between the clash of blades, teeth and fur, I see a legion of hypnotised humans approaching from the other side. There must be hundreds of them.

All of this to defeat three teenage girls.

How will we ever fight them? How can we defeat them without killing them? We're trapped between innocent humans and a sea of monsters flooding through the door.

For the first time, I have real doubts that we will succeed.

"Perhaps I can help."

Spinning to my left, I find myself face-to-face with the oracle, here, now, after we've been looking for her for so long. My first instinct is to hug her. My second is to punch her. She has been missing for how long? And *now* is the time she decides to make her grand reappearance.

Better late than never.

"Please," I say as a monster grabs me from behind. I pull its arm towards my mouth. "Do whatever you can."

As I sink my fangs into to the beastie's wrist, the oracle walks off into the crowd. Magically, no one touches her. It's like she's invisible – or wearing an invisible force field.

Then I'm too busy fighting monsters to watch her progress.

CHAPTER 33

Greer

When the woman in billowing robes shows up, Gretchen looks like she wants to throttle her – and I'm relieved that, for once, I'm not the one on the receiving end of that look. But then Gretchen goes back to fighting and the woman walks off into the crowd.

I'm busy trying to get my bite in on an onocentaur, but I keep my eye on the woman. There is something mystical about her, magical. I'm drawn to her, wanting to follow her when I know I should be fighting at my sisters' sides.

We share a gift, the woman's voice says in my mind, *something we shall discuss when this battle is over and my pendant has been returned.*

I gasp. The voice in my head – the woman gliding through the battle – is the oracle.

I should have guessed. Who else would be able to maintain that connection? Who else would know so much about the situation, about me and my sisters, and be able to help us figure out what we had to do?

Who else would have remained so mysteriously anonymous?

I watch as she reaches the edge, the line between our people and the hypnotised human army they are trying to hold back without causing any harm. Lifting her hands out to her sides, she shouts something at them, and then, in a flash, all the humans stop.

For a second, I'm afraid she killed them all, they're so still – Gretchen will be furious. But then, gradually, they start moving, shaking their heads and looking around, confused.

Coming out of their hypnosis.

The ordinary humans breaking free of the monster-induced trance don't see the beasts in their true form; they see them as other humans, fighting and clawing at each other like alley cats. They must think they've landed in the middle of the biggest brawl San Francisco's ever seen. Suddenly realising that there's an epic fistfight going on around them – one they don't know how they wound up trapped in the middle of – most of them turn and run. A few scream. The rest back slowly away.

Then the humans are gone, and it's just us against gods and monsters.

Though we have more gods on our side, the monsters outnumber us by a factor of ten, with more emerging – and reemerging – from the abyss every second. Unless something changes, we might be fighting a losing battle.

I don't like to lose.

I turn back to the door, determined to find a way to

turn the tide, just in time to see Gretchen's little monkey friend leaping through.

"Sillus here!" he shouts as he lands on the ground near her feet. "Bring help."

Behind him, our friends from the abyss follow – the golden maiden, the oceanid who led us to Mount Olympus, the big onyx guards, the unicorn and dozens more.

Behind them, a ragged group steps through the door. At the lead is the gaunt man from the dungeons of Olympus, that prisoner Gretchen spoke with when we were looking for the gorgons.

He and Gretchen exchange nods, and I think I understand. We freed them, and that has earned us their loyalty. They will fight by our sides.

Most of the newcomers are immediately drawn into the battle, turning to face the continual stream of monsters pouring through the open door. I'm shocked to see my friendly school janitor – the big fuzzy spider – stand side by side with the golden maiden.

"Harold?"

"Miss Greer," he replies with a smile before turning to wrap four of his legs around the neck of a one-eyed giant.

"We have others still inside," the golden maiden says. "They are holding back the horde within."

Gretchen pats her on the back.

Now I notice that the continual stream of monsters flowing through the open door has slowed to a trickle.

My sisters and I are biting as many as we can, sending them home, while our family and friends use our envenomed weapons to do the same. The numbers are nearly balanced now, and we are holding our ground. But we are not gaining on them.

If things continue as they are, the battle will be a draw.

"Ssstop!"

A woman's voice echoes over the crowd.

Everyone turns to stare at her – and I mean *everyone*.

Though she is dark haired and unexceptional, I recognise her. She's the woman who led the hypnotised humans into the gym at my tea the other day – the same woman who confronted me on the street before that.

"Mrs Knightly," Gretchen spits.

"You may call me that, Missss Sharpe," she hisses, a knowing smirk on her face. "But the time for falsssities has passed. I prefer my true name."

"What's that?" Gretchen asks.

The woman's mouth spreads in a dark smile. "I am Nyx."

The goddess of night?

She flicks a bored glance at me. In a graceful movement, she rolls her shoulders and her entire body shimmers. Like fog burning off in the afternoon sun, her ordinary-looking appearance fades away, leaving a shadowy woman with inky black hair cloaked in a shroud of equally black smoke. Her ivory-pale skin gleams like moonlight.

There is an aura of malice around her.

"You're behind this, aren't you?" I ask, stepping to Gretchen's side.

Nyx turns to me. "I told you I would sssee you on the battlefield."

She did? When? Oh my sugar, the creepy text messages. She sent them.

Shivers race down my spine. "Why?" I demand. "Why have you done all this?"

Nyx shrugs as if it's no big deal. "My children," she says, "deserve to walk in the sssun, more than the humans who claim this realm."

Grace moves to Gretchen's other side, and we three face our primary foe.

"Your children?" Grace asks.

"Creatures you call monster," Nyx replies. "Cursed by Olympusss, sentenced to a life in the dark. What kind of mother would I be if I allowed that injustice to ssstand?"

As we confront Nyx, the battle continues to rage around us. Our friends and family are sending the monsters back into the abyss, using the weapons dipped in our venom. Though some creatures are still managing to break through the defence on the abyss side of the door, we are reducing their numbers. Even a casual glance tells me that our side is gaining.

"Your children will have to pass through us," I say, straightening my spine, "just like everyone else."

"Look around," Gretchen says. "We are winning the battle."

"Stand down, cousin," a deep male voice says from behind us. "Retreat, before your children are destroyed."

The look of pure fury on Nyx's face could melt hardened steel. I glance over my shoulder to see a man – tall, strong and more than human. Everything about him screams *power*.

"The blame is yours, Zeus," Nyx spits. "You divided the realms and banished my children to the absssss."

Oooh, I would not push him like that.

The king of the gods does not react. "What is done cannot be undone."

From the corner of my eye, I see Sthenno sprint towards our foe. "Murderer!"

The pain and anger in her voice slice at my heart. She has just realised that this woman, this goddess, is the one ultimately responsible for Medusa's death. Her reaction is understandable.

With barely any effort, Nyx swings her hand and knocks Sthenno aside, sending the supernaturally strong gorgon soaring into the lagoon. That is tremendous power.

Zeus takes a step towards Nyx, but she casts a swirl of black around her that sweeps out in an ever-widening circle, pushing away every creature in its path. Every creature… except us.

My sisters and I stand alone in the middle of the black

circle, facing down our enemy, the ancient enemy of our family.

She seems invincible.

The only way to defeat the night, the oracle's voice says in my mind, *is to raise the sun.*

Raise the sun? What on earth does that mean?

How do we do that? I ask.

She replies, *The pendant.*

An image appears in my mind: the oracle's pendant lifted high above my head. It catches the sun and spreads brilliant beams of light in all directions.

"The pendant," I shout, getting my sisters' attention.

"What?" Gretchen demands.

"No, Greer!" Grace shakes her head. "You can't."

I clench my jaw and my mouth thins to a tight line. "Trust me."

Gretchen studies me for a second, then bends down and reaches into one of the pockets on her cargo trousers. She pulls out the oracle's pendant. Holding it by the chain, she thrusts it towards me.

I'm not that foolish.

Closing the distance between us in two strides, I grab Gretchen's wrist and shove her hand high into the air.

The gem at the centre catches the rays of the late afternoon sun. Just like in my vision, brilliant streaks of sunshine radiate out from the pendant, bathing everything around us in warm, golden light.

Where the light touches the circle of black, Nyx's dark cloud crackles and disappears.

I turn to watch as the rays reach Nyx herself. The look on her face could boil the entire San Francisco Bay. I almost step back, trying to escape her gaze. But Grace steps up to my side, taking my free hand in hers and squeezing me tight.

We will not back down.

"You think the light of Apollo can defeat me?" she shouts, sounding equal parts desperate and crazy.

"The sun always chases away the shadows," a male voice says.

I glance over my shoulder and see Apollo standing a few feet away. We exchange a look – I hope mine says clearly that I have not forgotten our last meeting. But Apollo is no longer our enemy.

Turning back to face Nyx, I take a step forward, closer to our foe, pulling Gretchen and Grace with me. Apollo is right: sunlight defeats shadows. Good defeats evil. And we will defeat the goddess who has spent so many lifetimes trying to destroy our family.

"Go!" I shout. "You have already lost!"

Then there is a flash of light and Nyx is gone, pulled back though the door into the abyss. Her cloud disappears, and the pendant's light spreads further than the laws of physics should allow, touching every last creature involved in the battle. Around us, the monsters scream, sensing their leader's absence. Our forces take advantage of the shift and push harder. The monster side turns and runs, rushing the door in retreat. Within a matter of moments, our enemies are gone and the fight is over.

The air around us stills, heavy with dragon smoke and the lingering stench of a monster army. My sisters and I look at each other warily.

It's over, just like that?

I release Gretchen's wrist and let her lower her arm.

"Did we just win?" Grace asks.

I look around. There is no fighting, no one trying to kill us. The battle is finished.

"I think so," I say.

Grace and I exchange a cautiously hopeful look.

Gretchen spins slowly in a circle, as if she can't believe it's finally done. The seal is broken, the battle is over, and we're alive to talk about it. After completing three complete turns, Gretchen finally releases a long breath.

"We did it," she says, though not too loud, as if she's afraid of jinxing things. "This may not be the end of the war, but I think this battle is over."

"After this," I say, "the rest should seem easy by comparison."

"Well, maybe not *easy*..." Grace says.

No, not easy. But after this hard-won success, at least we know what we can accomplish. Some of my secret doubts vanished with our retreating enemy.

Zeus faces the gorgons. "Your daughters have proven themselves." He gestures at us, and I fight the urge to duck. "They have proven your cause. It is right that balance is restored."

Another flash of light, and Zeus and the rest of the Olympic faction are gone, leaving me, my sisters, and our family and friends alone on the battlefield. No gods, no monsters; just me and my sisters and our exhausted human – and not quite human – friends. I look around, surprised to see no signs of violence or destruction.

How can there be no signs of the epic battle that raged just moments ago?

The gods may act childish at times, the oracle says in my mind, *but they do know how to clean up after messes.*

I spin around, trying to spot her, but she is nowhere to be seen. And I thought *I* was the queen of aloof and mysterious.

Gretchen throws her arms up in the air as she shouts, "We did it!"

Our crowd of supporters cheers.

Overcome by emotion, I step closer to my sisters, wrap an arm around each one and pull them into a hug. We share a moment, just for us. The battle we fought, and won, was about far more than three girls who look – mostly – alike. It was about balance and justice and protecting countless humans from bloodthirsty monsters. But it came down to the three of us. It all rested on our shoulders, and we held strong.

"We are amazing," I whisper so only my sisters can hear.

"Of course we are," Gretchen says. "We're the Key Generation."

"But more than that," Grace says, her voice tight with emotion, "we're sisters. And we *are* amazing."

When we break up our hug, all three of us have unshed tears in our eyes. I smile, knowing that Grace is right. It's not just our legacy or our gorgon blood that makes us great. It's our strength as sisters. And no god or monster can take that away from us.

Nick walks up to Gretchen, wraps a hand behind her neck and pulls her into a very meaningful kiss.

Grace plunges into the crowd, no doubt looking for Milo.

I turn and find Thane standing right behind me.

He is covered with sweat, the sleeve of his T-shirt is torn and he's bleeding from a slash above his left eye.

We share a private smile, and then I step into his arms without hesitation. I don't even care that he is sweating and bleeding all over my Marc Jacobs tank. Well, I don't care *much*.

"We really did it?" I whisper.

He nods. "Would you accept anything less?"

"Of course not." I smile. "You're learning."

Even without our supernatural connection, I feel the

bond between us. It's only growing stronger with time. With Thane, unlike with anyone else in my life – except maybe my sisters – I can be absolutely, unequivocally, unreservedly myself. No image to maintain, no facade of perfection. No striving to be better, smarter, stronger, faster. Just… me. For the first time in my life, I am content.

Not that I'm going to sit back on my heels and drift along. That's just not my way. But when Mother and Dad return, they are going to find a different Greer than they're used to.

And she is going to be so much happier.

"I believe you have something that belongs to me."

I turn at the sound of the oracle's voice – her real voice, not the echo inside my head.

She looks untouched by the battle. No bruises or scratches mar her smiling, wrinkled face. Even her voluminous robes look as if she's just pulled them out of her closet.

Her eyes study me, knowing. They sparkle with the power to see everything in everyone. She has powers I can only imagine.

It's a good thing she's on our side.

She lifts her brows.

Right. Her pendant.

I reach into my jeans pocket, pulling out the bundle

wrapped in a piece of my tank that was about to fall off anyway. I carefully hand it over to the oracle. She peels off the layer of fabric. Grabbing the heavy gold chain, she places the pendant back where it belongs – around her neck.

"It suits you better," I say with a half smile. "Gold isn't really my metal."

"No," she replies, giving me a wry look. "You are more of a platinum girl."

"Yes." I sigh, and my smile fades. We have more serious things to talk about – like how I am supposed to deal with my gift. "Does it get easier?"

She shakes her head slowly. "No, I'm afraid it does not."

Great. That is precisely what I wanted to hear.

"Possession of the second sight," she says, "is both powerful and dangerous. You must always retain your awe and respect for the power."

"It's overwhelming." I force myself to hold on to tight control of my emotions. "How do I know if what I'm seeing has happened or will happen? How do I know what to do about it?"

"You will not always know. You must trust that the gift does not give what you do not need." She pats me on the arm. "When you sought me, you found Thane. Though you did not see clearly at the time, that led you to the door."

Wow. Now that all makes sense.

"What about my vision of Grace's death?" I whisper. "That didn't come true."

No; I died instead.

"Any vision of the future," she explains with a cryptic smile, "is of but one of many possible futures. The mere act of seeing a path can alter the course. You saw your sister's death so that you could prevent it, and so that you could receive my message from the Fates."

"*Your* message?"

All at once the pieces of the puzzle fall into place, and I realise that the oracle must have had this planned from the very beginning. Everything leading up to my trip to Hades – my connection with Apollo, Gretchen diving into the abyss, all the way back to Grace moving to the city – had to go exactly according to schedule in order for me to wind up dead and have that chat with the Fates.

I gape. I never gape.

"You left the pendant on purpose," I assert. "You knew I would become a beacon. You knew *everything.*"

Her smile remains unreadable, but she does nothing more than shrug.

I narrow my gaze. "Did everything go according to your plan?"

"My plan?" She shakes her head. "I make no plans. Events pass as I see them to be."

Then, without another word, she turns and walks away.

A sound to my left draws my attention, but I see nothing there. When I look back, the oracle is gone.

But I will never be far, she echoes in my mind. *All you have to do is think my name.*

Oracle? I ask.

No, she replies with a snort. *Metrodora.*

Metrodora?

Do not judge, she says. *You should see how odd your name will seem in two thousand years.*

The feeling in my brain changes – it's hard to describe, but it's almost like a breeze – and I know she's gone. For now.

"Such a mystery," I mutter.

"What's that?" Thane asks, walking up behind me and slipping his arms around my waist.

"Oh, nothing," I say, turning in the circle of his embrace. I lift up to whisper against his mouth, "Now, about those golden apples…"

CHAPTER 34

Grace

I want to jump up and down for joy. My sisters and I just fought a battle that had been brewing for millennia – and we *won*. Even if it's only the first of many to come, it's definitely worth celebrating.

Pushing through the crowd, I'm looking for Milo, but I run into my parents first.

Dad looks a bit overwhelmed, like he's still in shock about everything that happened. I'm not surprised. Engineers don't usually have to face anything more daunting than a set of technical drawings and a deadline.

Mom, on the other hand, looks exhilarated.

"Gracie!" she shouts, waving at me and then hurrying over.

"Hi Mom." I check her and Dad over real quick. "You guys are okay?"

"We're great," she gasps. "That was amazing."

Dad looks like he wants to be sick.

"Do you do this all the time?" he asks, his voice weak and distant.

"No," I promise, "not... *quite* like this."

I'm not delusional. I know that things aren't going to be easy breezy Medusa girl from here on out. We will still be battling monsters, and I'm sure some of the gods – not just Nyx – will want to change things somewhere down the line.

But I have to believe that this was the hardest fight we'll ever face. Now that we've faced it and won, we'll be more confident about whatever comes next.

"Hi Grace, have you seen—" Cassandra freezes when she sees that I'm talking with my parents. "Oh. Hello."

This is kind of awkward – my parents meeting my biological mother on the battlefield between the world of monsters and the world of man. I almost laugh. If this isn't a perfect reflection of what my life has become, I don't know what is.

"Mom, Dad," I say, giving them a wide-eyed look, "this is Cassandra. Our biological mother."

There is a long pause. I'm not sure how they're going to react. My parents are good, loving people, but this is a very unusual situation. And I barely know Cassandra at all.

When Mom steps up in front of her, I suck in a breath.

"Thank you," Mom says, with tears in her eyes, "for bringing her into this world. And for letting us love her."

Cassandra pulls Mom into a tight hug. "You have raised her to become a remarkable young woman. You have done well by your daughter."

Your daughter. I don't miss Cassandra's pointed use of the word *your*. She wants Mom to understand that she isn't claiming me. Not that the decision is hers; I like Cassandra well enough, but Mom and Dad are my parents. I would choose them over anyone.

Mom finally pulls out of the weepy hug and moves back to Dad's side. "We had better get going," she says. "I'm sure you girls have some things to, um" – she gestures at the battlefield around us – "take care of."

"For a second," Dad says, sounding completely confused, "I thought one of the soldiers we were fighting was a—" He shakes his head. "No. No, I must have been seeing things."

Cassandra and I exchange a look, and I burst out laughing.

"You need some rest, Dad," I advise.

"Is it safe to go home now?" Mom asks.

I nod. "Definitely safe."

"We'll see you there?"

I give them each a quick hug and a kiss on the cheek. "I'll be home by curfew."

After a quick goodbye, they head back towards the parking lot where they left the station wagon. I have a feeling that things at home will never be the same – in a good way.

"You were amazing, Grace," Cassandra says.

I feel my cheeks blush. "Thanks."

"I should get going too," she says.

It's weird, saying goodbye to my biological mother. She hasn't been a part of my life before, but she is integral to everything that's happened – to everything that I am and have become.

"We'll still see you, right?" I ask. I mean, it's not like we won't be needing her or the Sisterhood any more just because the door has been opened and the prophecy fulfilled.

"Of course!" She grins, and I feel her joy in my heart. "You'll have a hard time keeping me away, now that your identity doesn't need to be protected any more."

"I'm glad," I say.

"You know, it was the hardest thing I ever did," she says, her eyes growing sad, "giving you and your sisters up for adoption. It broke my heart."

"I know why you did it. You saved us." I gesture at the friends and family around us. "You made this possible."

"I'm glad you are happy," she says. "Your parents and your brother love you as much as I hoped they would." She glances over at Gretchen. "I wish I had known how terrible some parents could be."

She's right. Gretchen's adopted parents were awful. Cassandra couldn't have known, and she couldn't have done anything about it if she had. Gretchen is tough, and her family situation only made her tougher. It made her strong enough to bring us together, to lead us into war,

373

and to make sure we came out on top. She became exactly who she needed to be.

Maybe Gretchen and Cassandra need to spend some time together to see that things turned out okay in the end. Maybe we all need to.

"The four of us should have lunch sometime," I suggest. "You and me and Gretchen and Greer."

"Lunch?" she replies.

I shrug. "Or something. We have sixteen years to catch up on."

Cassandra wraps her arms around me and squeezes tight. "I would love that."

"Me too," I whisper as I hug her back.

"There you are," a familiar boy voice calls out. Milo appears out of the crowd, looking sweaty and scratched, but otherwise okay.

Cassandra pulls away. "You have my number."

"I do." I give her a sunny smile. "I'll call it."

Then she's turning and walking away, disappearing into the crowd. I watch until I can't see her any more.

"That was," Milo exclaims, "completely insane."

"Yeah," I reply, facing him, "it totally was."

I take a step towards him; at the same time, he steps closer to me. We wind up an inch apart, staring into each other's eyes, my silver-grey ones gazing up into his pale green ones. His soft mouth spreads into a wide smile as he lifts his palms to cup my jaw.

"My life isn't normal, you know," I say before he starts to lower his head.

"I know," he replies, his smile growing. "Normal is boring."

"Good. I just wanted to get that out of the way."

I drape my arms around his neck, running my fingers through his dark curls. It's hard to believe we only met a few weeks ago. Then again, it's hard to believe what a different girl I was when we met.

Some things have stayed the same, though. I still love my family more than anything – there are just more of them to love now. I'm still a computer genius, straight-A student and all-around good girl. I still have slightly less confidence than I would like, but I'm getting more every day. And Milo's smile still makes my stomach do little flip-flops of joy.

As Milo's lips find mine, I tug him even closer.

I hope none of those things ever change.

CHAPTER 35

Gretchen

When everyone else is gone – all the friendly monsters, Grace's folks and the women of the Sisterhood of the Serpent – the gorgons ask to speak with us privately in front of the door. The boys wait for us in the parking lot to give us time to talk. Sillus races after them and tugs on Nick's hand, and Nick lifts the furry freak onto his shoulders for a ride. I watch with a smile.

"What's up?" I ask, turning back to our immortal aunts.

Ursula and Sthenno glance at each other and nod, which makes me nervous.

"You girls did a marvellous job today," Ursula says. "Far better than we ever dreamed."

Sthenno smiles. "You made us proud."

When she says that, I feel myself stand up straighter. It is amazing how powerful and proud that makes me feel. There is more behind her statement than a simple acknowledgment of success. There are thousands of years of expectation and anticipation.

"We have awaited this moment for millennia," Ursula

continues, "to see, if not our sister's death avenged, then at least proper order restored."

I can't imagine what it's been like. Their sister was murdered, and the killer has been running free, living guiltless while raising troops to kill even more of their family. If something happened to Grace or Greer, I don't think I would have the patience to wait until some prophesied future date.

They have more patience than I could ever hope – or want – to have.

That makes our victory all the sweeter.

"Us too," Grace says. "I mean, we haven't been waiting that long, but…"

"We are glad to take over the legacy," Greer finishes.

Grace gives her a grateful smile.

"Yes," Ursula says, "taking over. That is what we wish to speak with you about."

Things will change now. In the short time since I learned about the entire scope of our destiny, about opening the door and becoming the guardians, I've never had much chance to think about what would happen after. I was too busy trying to keep my sisters alive, trying to get to this point.

"Now that the battle is over," Sthenno explains, "you must close the door."

"Close the door?" Greer tilts her head.

I ask, "How do we do that?"

"It is the same to close the door," Ursula says, "as it is to open the door."

Sthenno gestures at the portal. "Now that the seal has been broken, it will only require one sister to perform the ritual."

Pulling out one of my daggers, I quickly slice the blade over my palms, drawing out thin stripes of blood. I tuck the dagger under my arm and slap my palms together. Just as quickly as it opened, the door swirls shut, contracting like a whirlpool.

"You must always remember," Ursula says, "to open the door at least once each day. Otherwise it will seal, with all the consequences that accompany a permanent closure."

Always remember? Why does this sound like some kind of last lecture?

"What do we do when we open it?" Greer asks.

"I have the scanned versions of the monster ring binders," Grace says. "Will they help us figure out which ones to let through?"

"Yes, they will help," Ursula answers. "But you should know by now that the world in which we exist is not black and white. You cannot look in a book to know a creature's heart."

I have listened to enough of her lessons over the years to understand her meaning. "We have to trust our judgement."

"Yes," she says.

I can feel her pride.

"We won't be perfect," I argue.

"Of course not," she replies. "You are human."

"Besides," I say, flashing my fangs. "That's what these babies are for."

"Now that the seal is broken," Sthenno explains, "things will change in the abyss. Access to the door from that side will be more orderly. All creatures within will have an equal opportunity."

"But how many do we let through?" Grace asks. "How long do they get to stay? How far are they allowed to go?"

Ursula shrugs.

"I think that's up to us," I say, finally getting the message. "We're the head girls in charge, and we sail this ship however we see fit."

"Your sole charge is to ensure the balance in this realm." Sthenno looks at each of us in turn. "Interpretation of that charge is yours to determine."

"That is the true responsibility of the legacy," Euryale finishes. "To balance the freedom of the monster realm with the safety of the human one." She beams at me. "I am certain you will be fair and generous guardians."

"But you'll be here to advise us, right?" Grace asks. "You can help us figure things out."

My gut clenches. I'm afraid I know the answer to Grace's question. The gorgons are passing us the torch – preparing us to carry on… without them.

My fears are confirmed when Ursula shakes her head.

"We have trespassed in this world too long," she states. "It is time for us to move on."

"Move on?" Grace chirps.

"It is time for us to leave this realm," Ursula says. "To go to Mount Olympus."

"The Olympians have extended us an invitation we cannot refuse," Sthenno explains. "In an attempt to make amends for… all that has passed, they will elevate us to the rank of goddesses."

"We shall sit on the council of justice." Ursula presses her palms to her stomach, and I can tell she's excited. "We will be able to prevent wars like this from happening in the future."

"Besides," Sthenno says, "this world is rightfully yours now. You have earned it."

I don't understand why they're doing it, why they're leaving just when we've made everything right. I want to argue, to tell them we will still need them, maybe more than ever.

But I know how stubborn Ursula is. She's made up her mind and there is no changing it.

Grace does the arguing for me.

"You can't leave," she insists. "We need you."

Ursula smiles in that way she has that says there is no point in arguing. Goodness knows she's given me that look enough over the years.

"You have all that you need right here." She gestures at me and my sisters. "As long as you have each other, you will not fail."

"And as this afternoon has proved," Sthenno adds, "you have abundant help should you need more."

My emotions break free. I rush forward and hug Ursula.

"Thank you," I whisper so only she can hear. "For… saving me."

"It is you who saved me." She leans back, presses her palms against my cheek. "You are the daughter I could never have."

My chest tightens, because that's how I feel too. She is the only mother I've ever known. The thought of losing her… it hurts. But if she's taught me anything, it's how to push past the pain.

When she pulls away, taking her sister by the hand, I let her go.

"With our departure," she says, "we give you not only the legacy of guardianship…"

"We give you our immortality," Sthenno finishes.

"Immortality?" Grace echoes.

Greer stands utterly still.

"There is a catch," Sthenno says. "We have but two immortalities to give."

"The balance must remain as before," Euryale explains. "Two immortal sisters…"

"One mortal," I fill in.

She nods. "We shall leave it to you three to decide. When you are ready, speak the decision and it will be done."

Grace, Greer and I exchange a glance. Grace looks confused. Greer looks terrified. I'm sure I look determined. My sisters can have the immortality. I refuse to watch either of them die.

"Time to go, sister," Sthenno says, tugging at Euryale's hand. "Olympus awaits."

"Goodbye, Gretchen, Grace and Greer," Euryale says. "The world is safe in your hands."

Then, as I watch, they disappear into mist. I can't stop the tears from streaming. Except in those moments before we brought Greer back to life, I have never felt so much emotional pain. I have to physically squeeze myself to keep from sobbing.

Next thing I know, I'm wrapped in a big hug with one sister on either side.

"I love you both," Grace says. "So much."

I suck in a deep breath. "Me too."

There is such a long pause that Grace and I pull back. Greer is scowling as tears stream down her cheeks. She looks like she's struggling to keep it all together.

"Oh, all right," she finally blurts. "I love you too."

I smile at my sisters. I'm amazed by how far we've come – how much we've grown and changed and accomplished

– in such a short time. We are amazing, and the monster world had better behave, because the Key Generation can kick some serious beastie butt.

We found and opened the door between the realms without even a single casualty on our side. We're taking up the legacy that began with our ancient ancestor, Medusa, and has been passed down through countless generations. We have each other, we have boys and friends and family who care about us, and we have definitely earned the right to enjoy the moment.

"That's it, enough blubbering." I start towards the parking lot, one sister under each arm. "Let's go celebrate."

CHAPTER 36

Grace

Around us, the coffee shop bustles with late afternoon activity. I'm amazed to watch these ordinary humans go about their daily lives, unaware of just how close they came to a monster apocalypse earlier today.

It's better this way, I suppose. Better my sisters and I keep them from ever finding out.

Milo and Thane return to the table, each with an armful of drinks.

"One strawberries-and-cream frappé," Milo says, handing me my drink as he takes the seat next to me, "and a double espresso for you, man."

Nick accepts the drink with a nod of thanks. He looks pretty comfortable, sitting there with his arm around Gretchen's chair – around her. And she looks pretty comfortable too.

Thane hands her a red eye – more caffeine than a person should be legally allowed to consume in a single cup – and she relaxes back against Nick's arm. Then Thane takes a sip of Greer's non-fat, half-caff vanilla latte before setting it down at her empty spot.

"Not bad," he says with a shrug, but then he goes back to his hot apple cider.

When Greer gets back from the restroom, I raise my cup.

"A toast," I say. "To a battle hard won."

"And more to come," Gretchen adds.

That's a fair toast. We might have succeeded today, but there will be more challenges to come. Not as big, I hope, and not as terrifying. We all cheer and are about to take sips of our drinks when we are interrupted.

"Isn't this sweet," a sickly female voice says. "Three pretty huntresses and three pretty boys."

I turn, appalled to find Nyx standing at our table, all dark and cloudy looking, though now she's more of a charcoal grey than the inky black that surrounded her earlier.

I knew we hadn't go rid of her permanently, but I thought we might at least have a little break before she returned. Clearly not.

My hands start to shake, so I shove them into my lap.

"Oh, worry not," she says when Gretchen starts to her feet, "my powers are weakened. I am not here to rekindle the fight."

"Then why *are* you here?" Gretchen spits.

"To give warning," Nyx says. "You might have won today's clash, but this war is far from over. My forces might have suffered losses today, but we will rise again."

To my utter shock, Gretchen laughs. "You can try."

Greer sits up a little straighter. "Rise again," she says, "and we will defeat you again."

My sisters are right. We have nothing to be afraid of. We beat them today, we will beat them tomorrow. It's our destiny. Our legacy.

Nyx glares at each of us for a moment. Then there's a swirl of grey smoke, and she's gone.

"Nice exit," Greer says with a shaky laugh.

Gretchen lifts her cup again. "To battles, past and future."

"Past and future," I say.

Everyone echoes the toast, and we drink. I'm happy to have this battle behind us, and I'm ready for whatever battles are coming. Everything is so very different now. And different is definitely good.

ABOUT THE AUTHOR

Photograph by Amy K. Smith

Tera Lynn Childs is the award-winning author of many books for teens, including the mermaid romances *Forgive My Fins* and *Fins are Forever*, published by Templar. She spends her time writing and blogging wherever she can find a comfy chair and a steady stream of caffeinated beverages.

Although Tera always dreamed of discovering a secret twin (or triplet), she's sad to report she's still an only child.

For more about Tera and her books, visit www.teralynnchilds.com

OUT NOW!

GRACE is new in town. It's scary, starting over, but it gets scarier when she runs into a minotaur. And scarier still when a girl who looks just like her rocks up to fight it.

GRETCHEN is fed up of fighting monsters, especially on school nights. Getting rid of a minotaur is easy, but she never expected to run into her double in the process.

GREER is perfection personified. But her world is knocked off its immaculate axis when two identical girls appear on her doorstep and claim they're all demon-hunting sisters.

Meet the teenage descendants of Medusa – three sisters who must embrace their fates in a world where mythological monsters lurk in plain sight.

 **templar** publishing

Also available as an ebook

ISBN 978-1-84877-932-7

£6.99

OUT NOW!

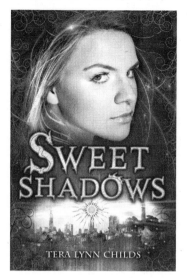

The sisters are now reunited, but their battle against the vile beasties of the abyss rages on.

And as if training to become fully-fledged huntresses weren't enough, the boys in their lives are causing them problems. Is Nick all he seems? And where's Thane? He's gone missing, and Grace is sure he's hiding something from her.

As the girls discover more about their heritage, they find themselves in greater danger than ever. Can they face up to the sacrifices they must make in order to fulfil their destiny?

templar publishing

Also available as an ebook

ISBN 978-1-84877-940-2

£6.99

Fins are forever

Lily Sanderson's life was never going to be plain sailing. Just when things seem to be going swimmingly, her human-hating cousin Dosinia is exiled from the mer kingdom of Thalassinia and sent to land. But why was Doe exiled in the first place? And why, why, why is she batting her eyelashes at Brody, Lily's former crush?

As if her bratty cousin weren't enough to handle, the reappearance of a merboy from Lily's past makes her question her decision to renounce her kingdom and stay on land with Quince.

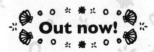